The
VIRAGO BOOK
of FAIRY TALES

The
VIRAGO BOOK
of FAIRY TALES

edited by
ANGELA CARTER
illustrated by CORINNA SARGOOD

PUBLISHED by VIRAGO PRESS Limited 1990
20–23 Mandela Street, Camden Town, London NW1 0HQ

Collection, Introduction and Notes copyright © Angela Carter 1990
Illustrations copyright © Corinna Sargood 1990

A CIP catalogue record for this book is available from the British Library

Typeset by Goodfellow & Egan
Printed and bound in Great Britain by Billings & Sons Ltd.

Designed by Lore Morton

Contents

4. GOOD GIRLS AND WHERE IT GETS THEM

5. WITCHES

6. UNHAPPY FAMILIES

7. MORAL TALES

Acknowledgements

Permission to reproduce these fairy tales is gratefully acknowledged to the following: Capra Press, Santa Barbara, CA, USA, for 'Sermessuaq', 'Kakuarshuk', 'Blubber Boy', 'The Woman Who Married Her Son's Wife', 'Tuglik and Her Granddaughter', 'Old Age' and 'The Two Women Who Found Freedom' from *A Kayak Full of Ghosts: Eskimo Tales 'Gathered and Retold'* by Lawrence Millman, copyright © 1987; Angela Carter, translator of *The Fairy Tales of Charles Perrault*, for 'Little Red Riding Hood', copyright © 1977, published by Victor Gollancz Ltd.; Columbia University Press for 'Mr Fox', 'Aunt Kate's Goomer-Dust' and 'The Good Girl and the Ornery Girl' from *The Devil's Pretty Daughter and Other Ozark Folk Tales*, collected by Vance Randolph, copyright © 1955; Constable Publishers for 'Mrs Number Three' from *Chinese Ghouls and Goblins* by G. Willoughby-Meade, copyright © 1924; Harvard University Press, Cambridge, Mass., for 'Young Man in the Morning', 'The Boy Who Had Never Seen Women' and 'The Cat-Witch' from *Negro Folktales in Michigan*, collected and edited by Richard M. Dorson, copyright © 1956 by the President and Fellows of Harvard College, 1980 by Richard M. Dorson; Indiana University Press for 'The Furburger' from *Jokelore: Humorous Folktales from Indiana*, edited by Ronald L. Baker, copyright © 1986; the International African Institute for 'Keep Your Secrets' and 'The Wicked Stepmother' from *Tales Told in Togoland*, edited by A. W. Cardinall, copyright © 1931, published by Oxford University Press for the International African Institute; Jan Knappert, translator and collector of *Myths and Legends of the Swahili*, for 'The Hare', 'The Pupil' and 'Tongue Meat', copyright © 1970, published by William Heinemann Ltd.; The Mercier Press for 'Feet Water' from *Folktales from the Irish Countryside* by Kevin Danaber, copyright © 1967; Oxford University Press for: 'The Search for Luck' and 'The Three Measures of Salt' from *Modern Greek Folktales*, chosen and translated by R. M. Dawkins, copyright © 1953, 'The Promise' from *Burmese Law Tales* by Maung Htin Aung, copyright © 1962, and 'The Fisher-Girl and the Crab' and

Introduction

LTHOUGH this book is called 'The Virago Book of Fairy Tales', you will find very few actual fairies within the following pages. Talking beasts, yes; beings that are, to a greater or lesser extent, supernatural; and many sequences of events that bend, somewhat, the laws of physics. But fairies, as such, are thin on the ground, for the term 'fairy tale' is a figure of speech and we use it loosely, to describe the great mass of infinitely various narrative that was, once upon a time and still is, sometimes, passed on and disseminated through the world by word of mouth – stories without known originators that can be remade again and again by every person who tells them, the perennially refreshed entertainment of the poor.

Until the middle of the nineteenth century, most poor Europeans were illiterate or semi-literate and most Europeans were poor. As recently as 1931, 20 per cent of Italian adults could neither read nor write; in the South, as many as 40 per cent. The affluence of the West has only recently been acquired. Much of Africa, Latin America and Asia remains poorer than ever, and there are still languages that do not yet exist in any written form or, like Somali, have acquired a written form only in the immediate past. Yet Somali possesses a literature no less glorious for having existed in the memory and the mouth for the greater part of its history, and its translation into written forms will inevitably change the whole nature of that literature, because speaking is public activity and reading is private activity. For most of human history, 'literature', both fiction and poetry, has been narrated, not written – heard, not read. So fairy tales, folk tales, stories from the oral tradition, are all of them the most vital connection we have with the imaginations of the ordinary men and women whose labour created our world.

For the last two or three hundred years, fairy stories and folk tales have been recorded for their own sakes, cherished for a wide variety of reasons, from antiquarianism to ideology. Writing them down – and especially printing them – both preserves, and also inexorably changes, these stories. I've gathered together sixty or seventy stories from published sources for this book. They are part of a continuity with a past that is in many respects now alien to us, and becoming more so day by day. 'Drive a horse and plough over the bones of the dead,' said William Blake. When I was a girl, I thought that everything Blake said was holy, but now I am older and have seen more of life, I treat his aphorisms with the affectionate scepticism appropriate to the exhortations of a man who claimed to have seen a fairy's funeral. The dead know something we don't, although they keep it to themselves. As the past becomes more and more unlike the present, and as it recedes even more quickly in developing countries than it does in the advanced, industrialized ones, more and more we need to know who we were in greater and greater detail in order to be able to surmise what we might be.

The history, sociology and psychology transmitted to us by fairy tales is unofficial – they pay even less attention to national and international affairs than do the novels of Jane Austen. They are also anonymous and genderless. We may know the name and gender of the particular individual who tells a particular story, just because the collector noted the name down, but we can never know the name of the person who invented that story in the first place. Ours is a highly individualized culture, with a great faith in the work of art as a unique one-off, and the artist as an original, a godlike and inspired creator of unique one-offs. But fairy tales are not like that, nor are their makers. Who first invented meatballs? In what country? Is there a definitive recipe for potato soup? Think in terms of the domestic arts. 'This is how *I* make potato soup.'

The chances are, the story was put together in the form we have it, more or less, out of all sorts of bits of other stories long ago and far away, and has been tinkered with, had bits added to it, lost other bits, got mixed up with other stories, until our informant herself has tailored the story personally, to suit an audience of, say, children, or drunks at a wedding, or bawdy old ladies, or mourners at a wake – or, simply, to suit herself.

I say 'she', because there exists a European convention of an archetypal female storyteller, 'Mother Goose' in English, 'Ma Mère l'Oie' in French, an old woman sitting by the fireside, spinning – literally 'spinning a yarn' as she is pictured in one of the first self-conscious collections of European fairy tales, that assembled by Charles Perrault and published in Paris in 1697 under the title *Histoires ou contes du temps passé*, translated into English in 1729 as *Histories or Tales of Past Times*. (Even in those days there was already a sense among the educated classes that popular culture belonged to the past – even, perhaps, that it *ought* to belong to the past, where it posed no threat, and I am saddened to discover that I subscribe to this feeling, too; but this time, it just might be true.)

Obviously, it was Mother Goose who invented all the 'old wives' tales', even if old wives of any sex can participate in this endless recycling process, when anyone can pick up a tale and make it over. Old wives' tales – that is, worthless stories, untruths, trivial gossip, a derisive label that allots the art of storytelling to women at the exact same time as it takes all value from it.

Nevertheless, it is certainly a characteristic of the fairy tale that it does not strive officiously after the willing suspension of disbelief in the manner of the nineteenth-century novel. 'In most languages, the word "tale" is a synonym for "lie" or "falsehood",' according to Vladimir Propp. '"The tale is over; I can't lie any more" – thus do Russian narrators conclude their stories.'

Other storytellers are less emphatic. The English gypsy who narrated 'Mossycoat' said he'd played the fiddle at Mossycoat's son's twenty-first birthday party. But this is not the creation of verisimilitude in the same way that George Eliot does it; it is a verbal flourish, a formula. Every person who tells that story probably added exactly the same little touch. At the end of 'The Armless Maiden' the narrator says: 'I was there and drank mead and wine; it ran down my mustache, but did not go into my mouth.' Very likely.

Although the content of the fairy tale may record the real lives of the anonymous poor with sometimes uncomfortable fidelity – the poverty, the hunger, the shaky family relationships, the all-pervasive cruelty and also, sometimes, the good humour, the vigour, the straightforward consolations of a warm fire and a full belly – the form of the fairy tale is not usually constructed so as to invite the audience to share a sense of lived experience. The 'old wives' tale' positively parades its lack of verisimilitude. 'There was and there was not, there was a boy,' is one of the formulaic beginnings favoured by Armenian storytellers. The Armenian variant of the enigmatic 'Once upon a time' of the English and French fairy tale is both utterly precise and absolutely mysterious: 'There was a time and no time . . .'.

When we hear the formula 'Once upon a time', or any of its variants, we know in advance that what we are about to hear isn't going to pretend to be true. Mother Goose may tell lies, but she isn't going to deceive you in *that* way. She is going to entertain you, to help you pass the time pleasurably, one of the most ancient and honourable functions of art. At the end of the story, the Armenian storyteller says: 'From the sky fell three apples, one to me, one to the storyteller, and one to the person who entertained you.' Fairy tales are dedicated to the pleasure principle, although since there is no such thing as pure pleasure, there is always more going on than meets the eye.

We say to fibbing children: 'Don't tell fairy tales!' Yet children's fibs, like old wives' tales, tend to be over-generous with the truth rather than economical with it. Often, as with the untruths of children, we are invited to admire invention for its own sake. 'Chance is the mother of invention,' observed Lawrence Millman in the Arctic, surveying a roistering narrative inventiveness. 'Invention', he adds, 'is also the mother of invention.'

These stories are continually surprising:

So one woman after another straightway brought forth her child.
Soon there was a whole row of them.
Then the whole band departed, making a confused noise.
When the girl saw that, she said: 'There is no joke about it now.
There comes a red army with the umbilical cords still hanging on.'

Like that.

'"Little lady, little lady," said the boys, "little Alexandra, listen to the watch, tick tick tick: mother in the room all decked in gold."'

And that.

'The wind blew high, my heart did ache,
To see the hole the fox did make.'

And that.

This is a collection of old wives' tales, put together with the intention of giving pleasure, and with a good deal of pleasure on my own part. These stories have only one thing in common – they all centre around a female protagonist; be she clever, or brave, or good, or silly, or cruel, or sinister, or awesomely unfortunate, she is centre stage, as large as life – sometimes, like Sermerssuaq, larger.

Considering that, numerically, women have always existed in this world in at least as great numbers as men and bear at least an equal part in the transmission of oral culture, they occupy centre stage less often than you might think. Questions of the class and gender of the collector occur here; expecta-tions, embarrassment, the desire to please. Even so, when women tell stories they do not always feel impelled to make themselves heroines and are also perfectly capable of telling tales that are downright unsisterly in their attitudes – for example, the little story about the old lady and the indifferent young man. The conspicuously vigorous heroines Lawrence Millman discovered in the Arctic are described by men as often as they are by women and their aggression, authority and sexual assertiveness probably have societal origins rather than the desire of an Arctic Mother Goose to give assertive role models.

Susie Hoogasian-Villa noted with surprise how her women informants among the Armenian community in Detroit, Michigan, USA, told stories about themselves that 'poke fun at women as being ridiculous and second-best'. These women originally came from resolutely patriarchal village communi-ties and inevitably absorbed and recapitulated the values of those communities, where a new bride 'could speak to no one except the children in the absence of the men and elder women. She could speak to her husband in privacy.' Only the most profound social changes could alter the relations in these communities, and the stories women told could not in any way materially alter their conditions.

But the final story in this book, 'How a Husband Weaned His Wife from Fairy Tales', shows just how much fairy stories could change a woman's desires, and how much a man might fear that change, would go to any lengths to keep her from pleasure, as if pleasure itself threatened his authority.

Which, of course, it did.

It still does.

The stories here come from Europe, the USA, the Arctic, Africa, the Middle East and Asia; the collection has been consciously modelled on those anthologies compiled by Andrew Lang at the turn of the century that once gave me so much joy – the Red, Blue, Violet, Green, Olive Fairy Books, and so on, through the spectrum, collections of tales from many lands.

I haven't put this collection together from such heterogeneous sources to show that we are all sisters under the skin, part of the same human family in spite of a few superficial differences. I don't believe that, anyway. Sisters under the skin we might be, but that doesn't mean we've got much in common. (See Part Six, 'Unhappy Families'.) Rather, I wanted to demonstrate the extraordinary richness and diversity of responses to the same common predicament – being alive – and the richness and diversity with which femininity, in practice, is represented in 'unofficial' culture: its strategies, its plots, its hard work.

Most of the stories here do not exist in only the one form but in many different versions, and different societies procure different meanings for what is essentially the same narrative. The fairy-tale wedding has a different significance in a polygamous society than it does in a monogamous one. Even a change of narrator can effect a transformation of meaning. The story 'The Furburger' was originally told by a twenty-nine-year-old Boy Scout executive to another young man; I haven't changed one single word, but its whole meaning is altered now that *I* am telling it to *you*.

The stories have seeded themselves all round the world, not because we all share the same imagination and experience but because stories are portable, part of the invisible luggage people take with them when they leave home. The Armenian story 'Nourie Hadig', with its resemblance to the 'Snow White' made famous via the Brothers Grimm and Walt Disney, was collected in Detroit, not far from the townships where Richard M. Dorson took down stories from African Americans that fuse African and European elements to make something new. Yet one of these stories, 'The Cat-Witch', has been current in Europe at least since the werewolf trials in France in the sixteenth century. But context changes everything; 'The Cat-Witch' acquires a whole new set of resonances in the context of slavery.

Village girls took stories to the city, to swap during endless kitchen chores or to entertain other people's children. Invading armies took storytellers home with them. Since the introduction of cheap printing processes in the seventeenth century, stories have moved in and out of the printed word. My grandmother told me the version of 'Red Riding Hood' she had from her own mother, and it followed almost word for word the text first printed in this country in 1729. The informants of the Brothers Grimm in Germany in the early nineteenth century often quoted Perrault's stories to them – to the irritation of the Grimms, since they were in pursuit of the authentic German *Geist*.

But there is a very specific selectivity at work. Some stories – ghost stories, funny stories, stories that already exist as folk tales – move through print into memory and speech. But although the novels of Dickens and other nineteenth-century bourgeois writers might be read aloud, as the novels of Gabriel Garcia Marquez are read aloud in Latin American villages today, stories about David Copperfield and Oliver Twist did not take on an independent life and survive as fairy tales – unless, as Mao Zedong said about the effects of the French Revolution, it is too soon to tell.

Although it is impossible to ascribe an original home for any individual story and the basic plot elements of the story we know as 'Cinderella' occur everywhere from China to Northern England (look at 'Beauty and Pock Face', then at 'Mossycoat'), the great impulse towards collecting oral material in the nineteenth century came out of the growth of nationalism and the concept of the nation-state with its own, exclusive culture; with its exclusive affinity to the people who dwelt therein. The word 'folklore' itself was not coined until 1846, when William J. Thomas invented the 'good Saxon compound' to replace imprecise and vague terms such as 'popular literature' and 'popular antiquities', and to do so without benefit of alien Greek or Latin roots. (Throughout the nineteenth century, the English believed themselves to be closer in spirit and racial identity to the Teutonic tribes of the North than to the swarthy Mediterranean types that started at Dunkirk; this conveniently left the Scots, the Welsh and the Irish out of the picture, too.)

Jacob Ludwig Grimm and his brother, Wilhelm Carl, philologists, antiquarians, medievalists, sought to establish the cultural unity of the German people via its common traditions and language; their 'Household Tales' became the second most popular and widely circulated book in Germany for over a century, dominated only by the Bible. Their work in collecting fairy tales was part of the nineteenth-century struggle for German unification, which didn't happen until 1871. Their project, which involved a certain degree of editorial censorship, envisaged popular culture as an untapped source of imaginative energy for the bourgeoisie; 'they [the Grimms] wanted the rich cultural tradition of the common people to be used and accepted by the rising middle class,' says Jack Zipes.

At roughly the same time, and inspired by the Grimms, Peter Christen Asbjornsen and Jorgen Moe were collecting stories in Norway, publishing in 1841 a collection that 'helped free the Norwegian language from its Danish bondage, while forming and popularizing in literature the speech of the common people,' according to John Gade. In the mid nineteenth century, J.F. Campbell went to the Highlands of Scotland to note down and preserve ancient stories in Scots Gaelic before the encroaching tide of the English language swept them away.

The events leading up to the Irish Revolution in 1916 precipitated a surge of passionate enthusiasm for native Irish poetry, music and story, leading eventually to the official adoption of Irish as the national language. (W.B. Yeats compiled a famous anthology of Irish fairy tales.) This process continues; there is at present a lively folklore department at the University of Bir Zeit: 'Interest in preserving the local culture is particularly strong on the West Bank as the status of Palestine continues to be the subject of international deliberation and the identity of a separate Palestinian Arab people is called into question,' says Inea Bushnaq.

That I and many other women should go looking through the books for fairy-tale heroines is a version of the same process – a wish to validate my claim to a fair share of the future by staking my claim to my share of the past.

Yet the tales themselves, evidence of the native genius of the people though they be, are not evidence of the genius of any one particular people over any other, nor of any one particular person; and though the stories in this book were, almost all of them, noted down from living mouths, collectors themselves can rarely refrain from tinkering with them, editing, collating, putting two texts together to make a better one. J.F. Campbell noted down in Scots Gaelic and translated verbatim; he believed that to tinker with the stories was, as he said, like putting tinsel on a dinosaur. But since the material is in the common domain, most collectors – and especially editors – cannot keep their hands off it.

Removing 'coarse' expressions was a common nineteenth-century pastime, part of the project of turning the universal entertainment of the poor into the refined pastime of the middle classes, and especially of the middle-class nursery. The excision of references to sexual and excremental functions, the toning down of sexual situations and the reluctance to include 'indelicate' material – that is, dirty jokes – helped to denaturize the fairy tale and, indeed, helped to denaturize its vision of everyday life.

Of course, questions not only of class, gender, but of personality entered into this from the start of the whole business of collecting. The ebullient and egalitarian Vance Randolph was abundantly entertained with 'indelicate' material in the heart of the Bible Belt of Arkansas and Missouri, often by women. It is difficult to imagine the scholarly and austere Grimm brothers establishing a similar rapport with their informants – or, indeed, wishing to do so.

Nevertheless, it is ironic that the fairy tale, if defined as orally transmitted narrative with a relaxed attitude to the reality principle and plots constantly refurbished in the retelling, has survived into the twentieth century in its most vigorous form as the dirty joke and, as such, shows every sign of continuing to flourish in an unofficial capacity on the margins of the twenty-first-century world of mass, universal communication and twenty-four-hour public entertainment.

I've tried, as far as possible, to avoid stories that have been conspicuously 'improved' by collectors, or rendered 'literary', and I haven't rewritten any myself, however great the temptation, or collated two versions, or even cut anything, because I wanted to keep a sense of many different voices. Of course, the personality of the collector, or of the translator, is bound to obtrude itself, often in unconscious ways; and the personality of the editor, too. The question of forgery also raises its head; a cuckoo in the nest, a story an editor, collector, or japester has made up from scratch according to folkloric formulae and inserted in a collection of traditional stories, perhaps in the pious hope that the story will escape from the cage of the text and live out an independent life of its own amongst the people. Or perhaps for some other reason. If I have inadvertently picked up any authored stories of this kind, may they fly away as freely as the bird at the end of 'The Wise Little Girl'.

This selection has also been mainly confined to material available in English, due to my shortcomings as a linguist. This exercises its own form of cultural imperialism upon the collection.

On the surface, these stories tend to perform a normative function – to reinforce the ties that bind people together, rather than to question them. Life on the economic edge is sufficiently precarious without continual existential struggle. But the qualities these stories recommend for the survival and prosperity of women are never those of passive subordination. Women are required to do the thinking in a family (see 'A Pottle o' Brains') and to undertake epic journeys ('East o' the Sun and West o' the Moon'). Please refer to the entire section titled: 'Clever Women, Resourceful Girls and Desperate Stratagems' to see how women contrived to get their own way.

Nevertheless, the solution adopted in 'The Two Women Who Found Freedom' is rare; most fairy tales and folk tales are structured around the relations between men and women, whether in terms of magical romance or of coarse domestic realism. The common, unspoken goal is fertility and continuance. In the context of societies from which most of these stories spring, their goal is not a conservative one but a Utopian one, indeed a form of heroic optimism – as if to say, one day, we might be happy, even if it won't last.

But if many stories end with a wedding, don't forget how many of them start with a death – of a father, or a mother, or both; events that plunge the survivors directly into catastrophe. The stories in Part Six, 'Unhappy Families', strike directly at the heart of human experience. Family life, in the traditional tale, no matter whence its provenance, is never more than one step away from disaster.

Fairy-tale families are, in the main, dysfunctional units in which parents and step-parents are neglectful to the point of murder and sibling rivalry to the point of murder is the norm. A profile of the typical European fairy-tale family reads like that of a 'family at risk' in a present-day inner-city social worker's casebook, and the African and Asian families represented here offer evidence that even widely different types of family structures still create unforgivable crimes between human beings too close together. And death causes more distress in a family than divorce.

The ever-recurring figure of the stepmother indicates how the households depicted in these stories are likely to be subject to enormous internal changes and reversals of role. Yet however ubiquitous the stepmother in times when the maternal mortality rates were high and a child might live with two, three or even more stepmothers before she herself embarked on the perilous career of motherhood, the 'cruelty' and indifference almost universally ascribed to her may also reflect our own ambivalences towards our natural mothers. Note that in 'Nourie Hadig' it is the child's real mother who desires her death.

For women, the ritual marriage at the story's ending may be no more than the prelude to the haunting dilemma in which the mother of the Grimms' Snow White found herself – she longed with all her heart for a child 'as white as snow, as red as blood, as black as ebony', and died when that child was born, as if the price of the daughter were the life of the mother. When we hear a story, we bring all our own experience to that story: 'They all lived happy and died happy, and never drank out of a dry cappy', says the ending of 'Kate Crackernuts' Cross fingers, touch wood. The Arabian stories from Inea Bushnaq's anthology conclude with a stately dignity that undercuts the whole notion of a happy ending: ' . . . they lived in happiness and contentment until death, the parter of the truest lovers, divided them' ('The Princess in the Suit of Leather').

'They' in the above story were a princess and a prince. Why does royalty feature so prominently in the recreational fiction of the ordinary people? For the same reason that the British royal family features so prominently in the pages of the tabloid press, I suppose – glamour. Kings and queens are always rich beyond imagining, princes handsome beyond belief, princesses lovely beyond words – yet they may live in a semi-detached palace, all the same, suggesting that the storyteller was not over-familiar with the lifestyle of real royalty. 'The palace had many rooms and one king occupied one half of it and the other the other half,' according to a Greek story not printed here. In 'The Three Measures of Salt', the narrator states grandly: 'in those days everyone was a king'.

Susie Hoogasian-Villa, whose stories came from Armenian immigrants in a heavily industrialized part of the (republican) USA, puts fairy-tale royalty into perspective: 'Frequently kings are only head men of their villages; princesses do the menial work.' Juleidah, the princess in the suit of leather, can bake a cake and clean a kitchen with democratic skill, yet when she dresses up she makes Princess Di look plain: 'Tall as a cypress, with a face like a rose and the silks and jewels of a king's bride, she seemed to fill the room with light.' We are dealing with imaginary royalty and an imaginary style, with creations of fantasy and wish-fulfilment, which is why the loose symbolic structure of fairy tales leaves them so open to psychoanalytic interpretation, as if they were not formal inventions but informal dreams dreamed in public.

This quality of the public dream is a characteristic of popular art, even when as mediated by commercial interests as it is today in its manifestations of horror movie, pulp novel, soap opera. The fairy tale, as narrative, has far less in common with the modern bourgeois forms of the novel and the feature film than it does with contemporary demotic forms, especially those 'female' forms of romance. Indeed, the elevated rank and excessive wealth of some of the characters, the absolute poverty of others, the excessive extremes of good luck and ugliness, of cleverness and stupidity, of vice and virtue, beauty, glamour and guile, the tumultuous plethora of events, the violent action, the intense and inharmonious personal relationships, the love of a row for its own sake, the invention of a mystery for its own sake – all these are characteristics of the fairy tale that link it directly to the contemporary television soap opera.

The now defunct US soap opera 'Dynasty', whose success was such a phenomenon of the early 1980s, utilized a cast list derived with almost contemptuous transparency from that of the Brothers Grimm – the wicked stepmother, the put-upon bride, the ever-obtuse husband and father. 'Dynasty's proliferating subplots featured abandoned children, arbitrary voyages, random misadventure – all characteristics of the genre. ('The Three Measures of Salt' is a story of this kind; R.M. Dawkins's marvellous collection of stories from Greece, most from as recently as the 1950s, frequently demonstrate Mother Goose at her most melodramatic.

See also 'The Battle of the Birds' for the way in which one story can effortlessly segue into another, if there is time to spare and an enthusiastic audience, just as the narrative in soap opera surges ceaselessly back and forth like a tide – now striving towards some sort of satisfactory consummation, now reversing itself smartly as if it has been reminded that there are no endings, happy or otherwise, in real life: that 'The End' is only a formal device of high art.

The narrative drive is powered by the question: 'What happened then?' The fairy tale is user-friendly; it always comes up with an answer to that question. The fairy tale has needed to be user-friendly in order to survive. It survives today because it has transformed itself into a medium for gossip, anecdote, rumour; it remains hand-crafted, even in a period when television disseminates the mythologies of advanced industrialized countries throughout the world, wherever there are TV sets and the juice to make them flicker.

'The people of the North are losing their stories along with their identities,' says Lawrence Millman, echoing what J.F. Campbell said in the West Highlands a century and a half ago. But this time, Millman may be right: 'Near Gjoa Haven, Northwest Territories, I stayed in an Eskimo tent which was unheated, but equipped with the latest in stereo and video gadgetry.'

Now we have machines to do our dreaming for us. But within that 'video gadgetry' might lie the source of a continuation, even a transformation, of storytelling and story-performance. The human imagination is infinitely resilient, surviving colonization, transportation, involuntary servitude, imprisonment, bans on language, the oppression of women. Nevertheless, this last century has seen the most fundamental change in human culture since the Iron Age – the final divorce from the land. (John Berger describes this in fictional terms, with visionary splendour, in his trilogy *Into Their Labours*.)

It is a characteristic of every age to believe that it is unique, that our experience will obliterate everything that has gone before. Sometimes that belief is correct. When Thomas Hardy wrote *Tess of the d'Urbervilles* a century and a half ago, he described a country woman, Tess's mother, whose sensibility, sense of the world, aesthetic, had scarcely changed in two hundred years. In doing so, he – perfectly consciously – described a way of life at the very moment when profound change was about to begin. Tess and her sisters are themselves whirled away from that rural life deeply rooted in the past into an urban world of ceaseless and giddily accelerating change and innovation, where everything – including, or even especially, our notions of the nature of women and men – was in the melting pot, because the very idea of what constitutes 'human nature' was in the melting pot.

The stories in this book, with scarcely an exception, have their roots in the pre-industrialized past, and unreconstructed theories of human nature. In this world, milk comes from the cow, water from the well, and only the intervention of the supernatural can change the relations of women to men and, above all, of women to their own fertility. I don't offer these stories in a spirit of nostalgia; that past was hard, cruel and especially inimical to women, whatever desperate stratagems we employed to get a little bit of our own way. But I *do* offer them in a valedictory spirit, as a reminder of how wise, clever, perceptive, occasionally lyrical, eccentric, sometimes downright crazy our great-grandmothers were, and their great-grandmothers; and of the contributions to literature of Mother Goose and her goslings.

Years ago, the late A.L. Lloyd, ethnomusicologist, folklorist and singer, taught me that I needn't know an artist's name to recognize that one had been at work. This book is dedicated to that proposition and, therefore, to his memory.

Angela Carter, London, 1990

Sermerssuaq
(Eskimo)

SERMERSSUAQ was so powerful that she could lift a kayak on the tips of three fingers. She could kill a seal merely by drumming on its head with her fists. She could rip asunder a fox or hare. Once she arm-wrestled with Qasordlanguaq, another powerful woman, and beat her so easily that she said: 'Poor Qasordlanguaq could not even beat one of her own lice at arm-wrestling.' Most men she could beat and then she would tell them: 'Where were you when the testicles were given out?' Sometimes this Sermerssuaq would show off her clitoris. It was so big that the skin of a fox would not fully cover it. *Aja*, and she was the mother of nine children, too!

Part One

BRAVE, BOLD AND WILFUL

The Search for Luck
(Greek)

O go on and on with the story: there was an old woman and she had a hen. Like her the hen was well on in years and a good worker: every day she laid an egg. The old woman had a neighbour, an old man, a plague-stricken old fellow, and whenever the old woman went off anywhere he used to steal the egg. The poor old woman kept a lookout to catch the thief, but she could never succeed, nor did she want to make accusations against anyone, so she had the idea of going to ask the Undying Sun.

As she was on the way she met three sisters: all three of them were old maids. When they saw her they ran after her to find out where she was going. She told them what her trouble had been. 'And now,' said she, 'I am on my way to ask the Undying Sun and find out what son of a bitch this can be who steals my eggs and does such cruelty to a poor tired old woman.' When the girls heard this they threw themselves upon her shoulders:

'O Auntie, I beg you, ask him about us; what is the matter with us that we can't get married.' 'Very well,' said the old woman. 'I will ask him, and perhaps he may attend to what I say.'

So she went on and on and she met an old woman shivering with cold. When the old woman saw her and heard where she was going, she began to entreat her: 'I beg you, old woman, to question him about me too; what is the matter with me that I can never be warm although I wear three fur coats, all one on top of the other.' 'Very well,' said the old woman, 'I will ask him, but how can I help you?'

So she went on and on and she came to a river; it ran turbid and dark as blood. From a long way off she heard its rushing sound and her knees shook with fear. When the river saw her he too asked her in a savage and angry voice where she was going. She said to him what she had to say. The river said to her: 'If this is so, ask him about me too: what plague is this upon me that I can never flow at ease.' 'Very well, my dear river; very well,' said the old woman in such terror that she hardly knew how to go on.

So she went on and on, and came to a monstrous great rock; it had for very many years been hanging suspended and could neither fall nor not fall. The rock begged the old woman to ask what was oppressing it so that it could not fall and be at rest and passers-by be free from fear. 'Very well,' said the old woman, 'I will ask him; it is not much to ask and I will take it upon me.'

Talking in this way the old woman found it was very late and so she lifted up her feet and how she did run! When she came up to the crest of the mountain, there she saw the Undying Sun combing his beard with his golden comb. As soon as he saw her he bade her welcome and gave her a stool and then asked her why she had come. The old woman told him what she had suffered about the eggs laid by her hen: 'And I throw myself at your feet,' said she: 'tell me who the thief is. I wish I knew, for then I should not be cursing him so madly and laying a burden on my soul. Also, please see here: I have brought you a kerchief full of pears from my garden and a basket full of baked rolls.' Then the Undying Sun said to her: 'The man who steals your eggs is that neighbour of yours. Yet

see that you say nothing to him; leave him to God and the man will come by his deserts.'

'As I was on my way,' said the old woman to the Undying Sun, 'I came upon three girls, unmarried, and how they did entreat me! "Ask about us; what is the matter with us that we get no husbands."' 'I know who you mean. They are not girls anyone will marry. They are like to be idle; they have no mother to guide them nor father either, and so it happens that every day they start and sweep the house out without sprinkling water and then use the broom and fill my eyes with dust and how sick I am of them! I can't bear them. Tell them that from henceforth they must rise before dawn and sprinkle the house and then sweep, and very soon they will get husbands. You need have no more thought about them as you go your way.'

'Then an old woman made a request of me: "Ask him on my behalf what is the matter with me that I cannot keep warm although I wear three fur coats one on top of the other."' 'You must tell her to give away two in charity for the sake of her soul and then she will keep warm.'

'Also I saw a river turbid and dark as blood; its flow entangled with eddies. The river requested me: "Ask him about me; what can I do to flow at ease?"' 'The river must drown a man and so it will be at ease. When you get there, first cross over the stream and then say what I have said to you; otherwise the river will take you as its prey.'

'Also I saw a rock: years and years have passed and all the time it has hung like this suspended and cannot fall.' 'This rock too must bring a man to death and thus it will be at ease. When you go there pass by the rock, and not till then, say what I have said to you.'

The old woman arose and kissed his hand and said Farewell and went down from the mountain. On her way she came to the rock, and the rock was waiting for her coming as it were with five eyes. She made haste and passed beyond and then she said what she had been told to say to the rock. When the rock heard how he must fall and that to the death of a man, he grew angry; what to do he knew not. 'Ah,' said he to the old woman: 'If you had told me that before, then I would have made you my prey.' 'May all my troubles be yours,' said the old woman and she – pray excuse me – slapped her behind.

On her way she came close to the river and from the roar it was making she saw how troubled it was and that it was just waiting for her to hear what the Undying Sun had said to her. She made haste and crossed over the stream, and then she said what he had told her. When the river heard this, it was enraged, and such was its evil mood that the water was more turbid than ever. 'Ah,' said the river, 'why did I not know this? Then I would have had your life, you who are an old woman whom nobody wants.' The old woman was so much frightened that she never turned round to look at the river.

Before she had gone much farther she could see the reek coming up from the roofs of the village and the savour of cooking came across to her. She made no delay but went to the old woman, she who could never keep warm, and said to her what she had been told to say. The table was set all fresh and she sat down and ate with them: they had fine lenten fare and you would have eaten and licked your fingers, so good it was.

Then she went to find the old maids. From the time the old woman had left them their minds had been on her; they were neither lighting the fire in their house nor putting it out: all the time they had their eyes on the road to see the old woman when she came by. As soon as the old woman saw them, she went and sat down and explained to them that they must do what the Undying Sun had told her to tell them. After this they rose up always when it was still night and sprinkled the floor and swept it, and then suitors began to come again, some from one place and some from another; all to ask them in marriage. So they got husbands and lived and were happy.

As for the old woman who could never keep warm, she gave away two of her fur coats for the good of her soul and at once found herself warm. The river and the rock each took a man's life and so they were at rest.

When the old woman came back home she found the old man at the very gate of death. When she had gone off to find the Undying Sun he was so much frightened that a terrible thing happened to him: the hen's feathers grew out of his face. No long time passed before he went off to that big village whence no man ever returns. After that the eggs were never missing and the old woman ate them until she died, and when she died the hen died too.

Mr Fox
(English)

ADY Mary was young, and Lady Mary was fair. She had two brothers, and more lovers than she could count. But of them all, the bravest and most gallant, was a Mr Fox, whom she met when she was down at her father's country-house. No one knew who Mr Fox was; but he was certainly brave, and surely rich, and of all her lovers, Lady Mary cared for him alone. At last it was agreed upon between them that they should be married. Lady Mary asked Mr Fox where they should live, and he described to her his castle, and where it was; but, strange to say, did not ask her, or her brothers, to come and see it.

So one day, near the wedding-day, when her brothers were out, and Mr Fox was away for a day or two on business, as he said, Lady Mary set out for Mr Fox's castle. And after many searchings, she came at last to it, and a fine strong house it was, with high walls and a deep moat. And when she came up to the gateway she saw written on it:

Be bold, be bold.

But as the gate was open, she went through it, and found no one there. So she went up to the doorway, and over it she found written:

Be bold, be bold, but not too bold.

Still she went on, till she came into the hall, and went up the broad stairs till she came to a door in the gallery, over which was written:

Be bold, be bold, but not too bold,
Lest that your heart's blood should run cold.

But Lady Mary was a brave one, she was, and she opened the door, and what do you think she saw? Why, bodies and skeletons of beautiful young ladies all stained with blood. So Lady Mary thought it was high time to get out of that horrid place, and she closed the door, went through the gallery, and was just going down the stairs, and out of the hall, when who should she see through the window, but Mr Fox dragging a beautiful young lady along from the gateway to the door. Lady Mary rushed downstairs, and hid herself behind a cask, just in time, as Mr Fox came in with the poor young lady who seemed to have fainted. Just as he got near Lady Mary, Mr Fox saw a diamond ring glittering on the finger of the young lady he was dragging, and he tried to pull it off. But it was tightly fixed, and would not come off, so Mr Fox cursed and swore, and drew his sword, raised it, and brought it down upon the hand of the poor lady. The sword cut off the hand, which jumped up into the air, and fell of all places in the world into Lady Mary's lap. Mr Fox looked about a bit, but did not think of looking behind the cask, so at last he went on dragging the young lady up the stairs into the Bloody Chamber.

As soon as she heard him pass through the gallery, Lady Mary crept out of the door, down through the gateway, and ran home as fast as she could.

Now it happened that the very next day the marriage contract of Lady Mary and Mr Fox was to be signed, and there was a splendid breakfast before that. And when Mr Fox was seated at table opposite Lady Mary, he looked at her. 'How pale you are this morning, my dear.' 'Yes,' said she, 'I had a bad night's rest last night. I had horrible dreams.' 'Dreams go by contraries,' said Mr Fox; 'but tell us your dream, and your sweet voice will make the time pass till the happy hour comes.'

'I dreamed,' said Lady Mary, 'that I went yestermorn to your castle, and I found it in the woods, with high walls, and a deep moat, and over the gateway was written:

Be bold, be bold.'

'But it is not so, nor it was not so,' said Mr Fox.

'And when I came to the doorway over it was written:

Be bold, be bold, but not too bold.'

'It is not so, nor it was not so,' said Mr Fox.

'And then I went upstairs, and came to a gallery, at the end of which was a door, on which was written:

Be bold, be bold, but not too bold,
Lest that your heart's blood should run cold.'

'It is not so, nor it was not so,' said Mr Fox.

'And then – and then I opened the door, and the room was

filled with bodies and skeletons of poor dead women, all stained with their blood.'

'It is not so, nor it was not so. And God forbid it should be so,' said Mr Fox.

'I then dreamed that I rushed down the gallery, and just as I was going down the stairs, I saw you, Mr Fox, coming up to the hall door, dragging after you a poor young lady, rich and beautiful.'

'It is not so, nor it was not so. And God forbid it should be so,' said Mr Fox.

'I rushed downstairs, just in time to hide myself behind a cask, when you, Mr Fox, came in dragging the young lady by the arm. And, as you passed me, Mr Fox, I thought I saw you try and get off her diamond ring, and when you could not, Mr Fox, it seemed to me in my dream, that you out with your sword and hacked off the poor lady's hand to get the ring.'

'It is not so, nor it was not so. And God forbid it should be so,' said Mr Fox, and was going to say something else as he rose from his seat, when Lady Mary cried out:

'But it is so, and it was so. Here's hand and ring I have to show,' and pulled out the lady's hand from her dress, and pointed it straight at Mr Fox.

At once her brothers and her friends drew their swords and cut Mr Fox into a thousand pieces.

Kakuarshuk
(Eskimo)

LONG ago women got their children by digging around in the earth. They would pry the children loose from the very ground itself. They would not have to travel far to find little girls, but boys were more difficult to locate – often they would have to dig extremely deep in the earth to get at the boys. Thus it was that strong women had many children and lazy women very few children or no children at all. Of course, there were barren women as well. And Kakuarshuk was one of these barren women. She would spend nearly all of her time digging up the ground. Half the earth she seemed to overturn, but still she could find no children. At last she went to an *angakok*, who told her, 'Go to such-and-such a place, dig there, and you will find a child . . .' Well, Kakuarshuk went to this place, which was quite a distance from her home, and there she dug. Deeper and deeper she dug, until she came out on the other side of the earth. On this other side, everything seemed to be in reverse. There was neither snow or ice and babies were much bigger than adults. Kakuarshuk was adopted by two of these babies, a girl-baby and a boy-baby. They took her around in an *amaut* sack and the girl-baby lent her her breast to suck. They seemed to be very fond of Kakuarshuk. Never was she without food or attention. One day her baby-mother said: 'Is there anything you want, Dear Little One?' 'Yes,' Kakuarshuk replied, 'I would like to have a baby of my own.' 'In that case,' her baby-mother replied, 'You must go to such-and-such a place high in the mountains and there you must start digging.' And so Kakuarshuk travelled to this place in the mountains. She dug. Deeper and deeper the hole went, until it joined many other holes. None of these holes appeared to have an exit anywhere. Nor did Kakuarshuk find any babies along the way. But still she walked on. At night she was visited by Claw-Trolls who tore at her flesh. Then there was a Scourge-Troll who slapped a live seal across her chest and groin. At last she could walk no further and now she lay down to die. Suddenly a little fox came up to her and said: 'I will save you, mother. Just follow me.' And the fox took her by the hand and led her through this network of holes to the daylight on the other side. Kakuarshuk could not remember a thing. *Aja*, not a thing. But when she woke up, she was resting in her own house and there was a little boy-child in her arms.

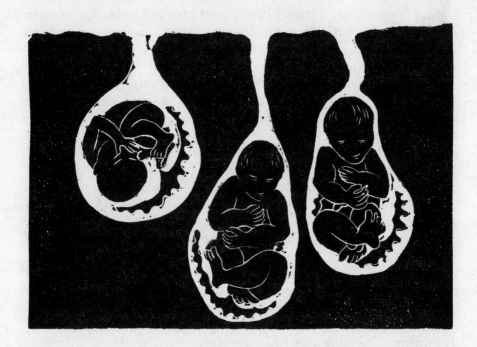

The Promise
(Burmese)

NCE upon a time the beautiful daughter of a Rich Man was studying at a University. She was a most assiduous scholar and one day as she sat by the window of the classroom inscribing on a palm leaf with a stylus a valuable formula which the learned Teacher was reciting to the class, the stylus slipped through her tired fingers and fell through the window on to the ground. She thought that it would be disrespectful to the Teacher to ask him to pause, but if she left her seat to pick up the stylus, she would have missed the formula. While she was in that dilemma, a fellow-student passed by her window and she begged him in a whisper to pick up the stylus for her. Now the passer-by was a King's Son and a mischievous youth. In fun he replied, 'Promise me that you will offer me your First Flower on the First Night.' The Girl, engrossed in the Teacher's formula, comprehended at that moment only the word 'flower' and nodded. He forgot his joke in a short time, but thinking over the incident, the Girl comprehended later the full meaning of the Prince's words but thought no more of them and hoped that the words were said in fun.

At the end of their respective studies in the University, the Prince returned to his kingdom and soon after succeeded to his father's throne, and the Girl returned to her home in a neighbouring kingdom and soon after she married a Rich Man's Son. On the night of the wedding, her memory flew back to the incident of the stylus, and troubled by her conscience she confessed to her husband of her promise but expressed the belief that the young man was only joking. 'My dear,' replied the Husband, 'it is for him to say whether it was a joke or not. A promise made in honour must never be broken.' The Girl, after making obeisance to her husband, started at once on a journey to the neighbouring kingdom to fulfil her promise to the King if he should exact such fulfilment.

As she walked alone in the darkness, a Robber seized hold of her and said, 'What woman is this that walks in the night, bedecked with gold and jewels? Surrender me your jewels, and

13

your silken dress.' 'Oh, Robber,' replied the Girl, 'take my jewels, but leave me my silken dress, as I cannot enter the King's palace, naked and ashamed.' 'No,' said the Robber, 'your silken dress is as precious as your jewels. Give me the dress also.' The Girl then explained to the Robber the reason why she was travelling all alone in the dark. 'I am impressed with your sense of honour,' said the Robber, 'and if you will but promise to return here after giving the First Flower to the King, I shall let you go.' The Girl made the promise, and was· allowed to continue her journey. She walked on until she passed under a banyan tree. 'What woman is this, that is so fresh and tender and yet walks alone at night?' said the Ogre of the tree. 'I will eat you up, as all those who pass under my tree during the hours of darkness belong to me.' 'Oh, Ogre,' pleaded the Girl, 'please spare me, for if you eat me now, my promise to the Prince will ever remain unkept.' After she had explained the purpose of her journey by night, the Ogre said, 'I am impressed by your sense of honour and if you will but promise to return here after you have met the King, I will let you go.' The Girl made the promise and she was allowed to continue her journey.

At last, without further adventure, she arrived at the city and was soon knocking at the gates of the King's palace. 'What manner of woman are you?' asked the palace guards. 'What mean you by coming to the palace and demanding entry at this hour of midnight?' 'It is a matter of honour,' replied the Girl. 'Please go and tell my lord the King that his fellow-student at the University has come to keep her promise.' The King, hearing the commotion, looked out of his bedroom window, and saw the Girl standing in the light of the torches of the guards, in the full bloom of her beauty. He recognized her and desired her, but when he had heard her tale he admired her for her loyalty to her oath, and her courage in facing all dangers and difficulties to keep her promise. 'My friend,' he said, 'you are a marvellous woman, for you prize your honour even above maidenly modesty. Your promise was demanded by me as a jest and I had forgotten it. So return you to your Husband.' So the Girl went back to the Ogre of the banyan tree, and said, 'Oh, Ogre, eat my body, but after eating, take my silken dress and my jewels, and give them to the Robber who is waiting for me only a few yards from here.' The Ogre said, 'Friend, you are a marvellous woman, for you prize your honour even above your life. You are free to go, as I absolve you from your promise.' The Girl went back to the Robber, and said, 'Oh, Robber, take my jewels and my silken dress. Although I shall have to go back to my Husband naked and ashamed, the servants will let me in, for they will recognize me.' The Robber replied, 'Friend, you are a marvellous woman, for you prize your promise above jewels and fine dresses. You are free to go, as I absolve you from your promise.' So the Girl returned to her Husband, who received her with affection and regard, and they lived happily ever after.

Kate Crackernuts
(English)

NCE upon a time there was a king and a queen, as in many lands have been. The king had a daughter, Anne, and the queen had one named Kate, but Anne was far bonnier than the queen's daughter, though they loved one another like real sisters. The queen was jealous of the king's daughter being bonnier than her own, and cast about to spoil her beauty. So she took counsel of the henwife, who told her to send the lassie to her next morning fasting.

So next morning early, the queen said to Anne, 'Go, my dear, to the henwife in the glen, and ask her for some eggs.' So Anne set out, but as she passed through the kitchen she saw a crust, and she took and munched it as she went along.

When she came to the henwife's she asked for eggs, as she had been told to do; the henwife said to her, 'Lift the lid off that pot there and see.' The lassie did so, but nothing happened. 'Go home to your minnie and tell her to keep her larder door better locked,' said the henwife. So she went home to the queen and told her what the henwife had said. The queen knew from this that the lassie had had something to eat, so watched the next morning and sent her away fasting; but the princess saw some country-folk picking peas by the road-side, and being very kind she spoke to them and took a handful of the peas, which she ate by the way.

When she came to the henwife's, she said, 'Lift the lid off the pot and you'll see.' So Anne lifted the lid, but nothing happened. Then the henwife was rare angry and said to Anne, 'Tell your minnie the pot won't boil if the fire's away.' So Anne went home and told the queen.

The third day the queen goes along with the girl herself to the henwife. Now, this time, when Anne lifted the lid off the pot, off falls her own pretty head, and on jumps a sheep's head.

So the queen was now quite satisfied, and went back home.

Her own daughter, Kate, however, took a fine linen cloth and wrapped it round her sister's head and took her by the

16

hand and they both went out to seek their fortune. They went on, and they went on, and they went on, until they came to a castle. Kate knocked at the door and asked for a night's lodging for herself and a sick sister. They went in and found it was a king's castle, who had two sons, and one of them was sickening away to death and no one could find out what ailed him. And the curious thing was, that whoever watched him at night was never seen any more. So the king had offered a peck of silver to anyone who would stop up with him. Now Katie was a very brave girl, so she offered to sit up with him.

Till midnight all went well. As twelve o'clock rang, however, the sick prince rose, dressed himself, and slipped downstairs. Kate followed, but he didn't seem to notice her. The prince went to the stable, saddled his horse, called his hound, jumped into the saddle and Kate leapt lightly up behind him. Away rode the prince and Kate through the greenwood, Kate, as they passed, plucking nuts from the trees and filling her apron with them. They rode on and on till they came to a green hill. The prince here drew bridle and spoke: 'Open, open, green hill, and let the young prince in with his horse and his hound,' and Kate added, 'and his lady him behind.'

Immediately the green hill opened and they passed in. The prince entered a magnificent hall, brightly lighted up, and many beautiful fairies surrounded the prince and led him off to the dance. Meanwhile, Kate, without being noticed, hid herself behind the door. There she saw the prince dancing, and dancing, and dancing, till he could dance no longer and fell upon a couch. Then the fairies would fan him till he could rise again and go on dancing.

At last the cock crew, and the prince made all haste to get on horseback; Kate jumped up behind, and home they rode. When the morning sun rose they came in and found Kate sitting down by the fire and cracking her nuts. Kate said the prince had a good night; but she would not sit up another night unless she was to get a peck of gold. The second night passed as the first had done. The prince got up at midnight and rode away to the green hill and the fairy ball, and Kate went with him, gathering nuts as they rode through the forest. This time she did not watch the prince, for she knew he would dance, and dance, and dance. But she saw a fairy baby playing with a wand and overheard one of the fairies say: 'Three strokes of that wand would make Kate's sick sister as bonny as ever she was.'

So Kate rolled nuts to the fairy baby, and rolled nuts till the baby toddled after the nuts and let fall the wand, and Kate took it up and put it in her apron. And at cockcrow they rode home as before, and the moment Kate got home to her room she rushed and touched Anne three times with her wand, and the nasty sheep's head fell off and she was her own pretty self again.

The third night Kate consented to watch, only if she should marry the sick prince. All went on as the first two nights. This time the fairy baby was playing with a birdie; Kate heard one of the fairies say: 'Three bites of that birdie would make the sick prince as well as ever he was.' Kate rolled all the nuts she had to the fairy baby until the birdie was dropped, and Kate put it in her apron.

At cockcrow they set off again, but instead of cracking her nuts as she used to do, this time Kate plucked the feathers off and cooked the birdie. Soon there arose a very savoury smell. 'Oh!' said the sick prince, 'I wish I had a bite of that birdie,' so Kate gave him a bite of the birdie, and he rose up on his elbow. By-and-by he cried out again: 'Oh, if I had another bite of that birdie!' so Kate gave him another bite, and he sat up on his bed. Then he said again: 'Oh! if I but had a third bite of that birdie!' So Kate gave him a third bite, and he rose hale and strong, dressed himself, and sat down by the fire, and when the folk came in next morning they found Kate and the young prince cracking nuts together. Meanwhile his brother had seen Annie and had fallen in love with her, as everybody did who saw her sweet pretty face. So the sick son married the well sister, and the well son married the sick sister, and they all lived happy and died happy, and never drank out of a dry cappy.

The Fisher-Girl and the Crab
(Indian Tribal)

N old Kuruk and his wife had no children. The old man sowed rice in his field and, when after some days the rice had sprouted, he took his wife to the field to see it. On one side of the field was a gourd, and they took it home for food. But when the old man was about to cut it up, the gourd said, 'Cut me gently, gently, grandfather!' The old man was so frightened that he dropped it. He ran to his wife and said, 'This is a talking gourd.' 'Nonsense,' said the old woman and took the knife herself. But the gourd said, 'Cut me, gently, gently, old mother!'

So the old woman cut the gourd up carefully and slowly, and from inside there came out a crab. They got a new pot and put the crab inside. The woman tied a basket to her belly and

covered it with cloth. Then she went to the bazaar and told the neighbours, 'Look, in my old age Mahapurub has given me a son.'

After some time, she removed the basket and took the crab out of the pot and told everyone, 'Look, I have given birth to this crab.'

When the crab was grown up, they went to find him a wife. They got him a nice girl, but when she came to the house she was angry at finding herself married to such a creature. Every night she waited for him, but what could a crab do? Then the girl thought, 'I must find another man.' Whenever the crab spoke to the girl, she used to kick it away.

One day, the girl wanted to go to visit a man in another village. She let her parents-in-law and the crab go to sleep, and then crept out of the house. But the crab saw her go and he got out by another way and went ahead of her along the road. By the roadside there was a banyan tree; to this the crab said, 'Are you my tree, or whose tree are you?' The tree said, 'I am yours.' Then said the crab, 'Fall down.' The tree fell down. Now inside that tree there lived the shape of a youth. The crab took this on itself, and put its crab-shape into the tree instead. It went along the road a little and then told the tree to stand up again.

After a time, along came the girl. When she saw the beautiful youth under the tree, she was very pleased, and said, 'Where are you going?' He said, 'Nowhere, I am going home.' She said, 'Come and lie with me.' He said, 'No, I'm afraid. Your husband will beat me. But I'll come another day.'

Disappointed, the girl went on. She met a Chamar girl and two pretty Mahara girls. They too were looking for men. The Kuruk girl told them her story, and they took her with them to a dance, promising her a fine gallant. When they got there, they found that the crab-youth was there already. When they saw him, each girl longed to have him as a lover. He went to the Kuruk girl and she drew him aside. But he did nothing. She gave him her ornaments, and he went away.

When he reached the tree, he bade it fall down, and took his own crab-shape again, returning the shape of the youth to the tree. 'Stand up again,' he told the tree, and went home. After a little while the girl also came home. The crab asked her where she had been, but she was in a temper and kicked him out of bed. Then the crab gave her back her ornaments. The girl was frightened and declared that they were not hers.

The next day, the girl again gave everyone food and put them to sleep. This time she hid by the roadside, and watched to see what the crab would do. The crab came to the banyan tree and said, 'Are you my tree, or whose are you?' The tree said, 'I am your tree.' Then the crab said, 'If you are mine, then fall down.' The tree fell down, and the crab took the shape of the handsome youth, and let the tree stand up again.

The girl was watching all that happened. When the boy had gone on his way, she went to the tree and said, 'Are you my tree or whose are you?' The tree said, 'I am yours.' She said, 'If you are mine, then fall down.' The tree fell down, and the girl pulled out the crab-shape and killed it and threw it on a fire. Then she hid behind the tree and waited.

The youth went to the dance, but he could not find his girl, so he came back to the tree. The girl jumped out from behind the tree and caught him and took him home. After that they lived happily together.

Part Two

CLEVER WOMEN,
RESOURCEFUL GIRLS
& DESPERATE STRATAGEMS

Maol a Chliobain
(Scots Gaelic)

NCE upon a time there was a widow, and she had three daughters; and they said to her that they would go to seek their fortune. She baked three bannocks. She said to the big one, 'Whether dost thou like best the little half and my blessing, or the big half and my curse?' 'I like best,' said she, 'the big half and thy curse.' She said to the middle one, 'Whether dost thou like best the big half and my curse, or the little half and my blessing?' 'I like best,' said she, 'the big half and thy curse.' She said to the little one, 'Whether dost thou like best the big half and my curse, or the little half and my blessing?' 'I like best the little half and thy blessing.' This pleased her mother, and she gave her the two other halves also. They went away, but the two eldest did not want the youngest to be with them, and they tied her to a rock of stone. They went on; but her mother's blessing came and freed her. And when they looked behind them, whom did they see but her with the rock on top of her. They let her alone a turn of a while, till they reached a peat stack, and they tied her to the peat stack. They went on a bit but her mother's blessing came and freed her, and they looked behind them, and whom did they see but her coming, and the peat stack on the top of her. They let her alone a turn of a while, till they reached a tree, and they tied her to the tree. They went on a bit but her mother's blessing came and freed her, and when they looked behind them, whom did they see but her, and the tree on top of her.

They saw it was no good to be at her; they loosed her, and let her come with them. They were going till night came on them. They saw a light a long way from them; and though a long way from them, it was not long that they were in reaching it. They went in. What was this but a giant's house! They asked to stop the night. They got that, and they were put to bed with the three daughters of the giant. The giant came home, and he said, 'The smell of the foreign girls is within.' There were twists of amber knobs about the necks of the giant's daughters, and strings of horse hair about their own necks. They all slept, but Maol a Chliobain did not sleep. Through the night a thirst came on the giant. He called to his bald, rough-skinned gillie to bring him water. The rough-skinned gillie said that there was not a drop within. 'Kill,' said he, 'one of the strange girls, and bring to me her blood.' 'How will I know them?' said the bald, rough-skinned gillie. 'There are twists of knobs of amber about the necks of my daughters, and twists of horse hair about the necks of the rest.'

Maol a Chliobain heard the giant, and as quick as she could she put the strings of horse hair that were about her own neck and about the necks of her sisters about the necks of the giant's daughters; and the knobs that were about the necks of the giant's daughters about her own neck and about the necks of her sisters; and she laid down *so* quietly. The bald, rough-skinned gillie came, and he killed one of the daughters of the giant, and he took the blood to him. He asked for MORE to be brought him. He killed the next. He asked for MORE; and he killed the third one.

Maol a Chliobain awoke her sisters, and she took them with her on top of her, and she took to going. She took with her a golden cloth that was on the bed, and it called out.

The giant perceived her, and he followed her. The sparks of fire that she was putting out of the stones with her heels, they were striking the giant on the chin; and the sparks of fire that the giant was bringing out of the stones with the points of his feet, they were striking Maol a Chliobain in the back of the head. It is this was their going till they reached a river. She plucked a hair out of her head and made a bridge of it, and she run over the river, and the giant could not follow her. Maol a Chliobain leaped the river, but the river the giant could not leap.

'Thou art over there, Maol a Chliobain.' 'I am, though it is hard for thee.' 'Thou killedst my three bald brown daughters.' 'I killed them, though it is hard for thee.' 'And when wilt though come again?' 'I will come when my business brings me.'

They went on forward till they reached the house of a farmer. The farmer had three sons. They told how it happened to them. Said the farmer to Maol a Chliobain, 'I will give my eldest son to they eldest sister, and get for me the fine comb of gold, and the coarse comb of silver that the giant has.' 'It will cost thee no more,' said Maol a Chliobain.

She went away; she reached the house of the giant; she got in unknown; she took with her the combs, and out she went. The giant perceived her, and after her he was till they reached the river. She leaped the river, but the river the giant could not leap. 'Thou art over there, Maol a Chliobain.' 'I am, though it is hard for thee.' 'Thou killedst my three bald brown daughters.' 'I killed them, though it is hard for thee.' 'Thou stolest my fine comb of gold, and my coarse comb of silver.' 'I stole them, though it is hard for thee.' 'When wilt though come again?' 'I will come when my business brings me.'

She gave the combs to the farmer, and her big sister and the farmer's big son married. 'I will give my middle son to thy middle sister, and get me the giant's sword of light.' 'It will cost thee no more,' said Maol a Chliobain. She went away, and she reached the giant's house; she went up to the top of a tree that was above the giant's well. In the night came the bald rough-skinned gillie with the sword of light to fetch water. When he bent to raise the water, Maol a Chliobain came down and she pushed him down in the well and she drowned him, and she took with her the sword of light.

The giant followed her till she reached the river; she leaped the river, and the giant could not follow her. 'Thou art over there, Maol a Chliobain.' 'I am, if it is hard for thee.' 'Thou killedst my three bald brown daughters.' 'I killed, though it is hard for thee.' 'Thou stolest my fine comb of gold, and my coarse comb of silver.' 'I stole, though it is hard for thee.' 'Thou killedst my bald rough-skinned gillie.' 'I killed, though it is hard for thee.' 'Thou stolest my sword of light.' 'I stole, though it is hard for thee.' 'When wilt though come again?' 'I will come when my business brings me.' She reached the house of the farmer with the sword of light; and her middle sister and the middle son of the farmer married. 'I will give thyself my youngest son,' said the farmer, 'and bring me a buck that the giant has.' 'It will cost thee no more,' said Maol a Chliobain. She went away, and she reached the house of the giant; but when she had hold of the buck, the giant caught her. 'What,' said the giant, 'wouldst thou do to me: if I had done as much harm to thee as thou hast done to me, I would make thee burst thyself with milk porridge; I would then put thee in a pock! I would hang thee to the roof-tree; I would set fire under thee; and I would set on thee with clubs till thou shouldst fall as a faggot of withered sticks on the floor.' The giant made milk porridge, and he made her drink it. She put the milk porridge about her mouth and face, and she laid over as if she were dead. The giant put her in a pock, and he hung her to the roof-tree; and he went away, himself and his men, to get wood to the forest. The giant's mother was within. When the giant was gone, Maol a Chliobain began – "Tis I am in the light! 'Tis I am in the city of gold!' 'Wilt thou let me in?' said the carlin. 'I will not let thee in.' At last she let down the pock. She put in the carlin, cat, and calf, and cream-dish. She took with her the buck and she went away. When the giant came with his men, himself and his men began at the bag with the clubs. The carlin was calling, "Tis myself that's in it.' 'I know that thyself is in it,' would the giant say, as he laid on to the pock. The pock came down as a faggot of sticks, and what was in it but his mother. When the giant saw how it was, he took after Maol a Chliobain; he followed her till she reached the river. Maol a Chliobain leaped the river, and the giant could not leap it. 'Thou art over there, Maol a Chliobain.' 'I am, though it is hard for thee.' 'Thou killedst my three bald brown daughters.' 'I killed, though it is hard for thee.' 'Thou stolest my golden comb, and my silver comb.' 'I stole, though it is hard for thee.' 'Thou killedst my bald rough-skinned gillie.' 'I killed, though it is hard for thee.' 'Thou stolest my sword of light.' 'I stole, though it is hard for thee.' 'Thou killedst my mother.' 'I killed, though it is hard for thee.' 'Thou stolest my buck.' 'I stole, though it is hard for thee.' 'When wilt thou come again?' 'I will come when my business brings me.' 'If thou wert over here, and I yonder,' said the giant, 'what wouldst thou do to follow me?' 'I would stick myself down, and I would drink till I should dry the river.' The giant stuck himself down, and he drank till he burst. Maol a Chliobain and the farmer's youngest son married.

The Wise Little Girl
(Russian)

TWO brothers were traveling together: one was poor and the other was rich, and each had a horse, the poor one a mare, and the rich one a gelding. They stopped for the night, one beside the other. The poor man's mare bore a foal during the night, and the foal rolled under the rich man's cart. In the morning the rich man roused his poor brother, saying: 'Get up, brother. During the night my cart bore a foal.' The brother rose and said: 'How is it possible for a cart to give birth to a foal? It was my mare who bore the foal!' The rich brother said: 'If your mare were his mother, he would have been found lying beside her.' To settle their quarrel they went to the authorities. The rich man gave the judges money and the poor man presented his case in words.

Finally word of this affair reached the tsar himself. He summoned both brothers before him and proposed to them four riddles: 'What is the strongest and swiftest thing in the world? What is the fattest thing in the world? What is the softest thing? And what is the loveliest thing?' He gave them three days' time and said: 'On the fourth day come back with your answers.'

The rich man thought and thought, remembered his god-mother, and went to ask her advice. She bade him sit down to table, treated him to food and drink, and then asked: 'Why are you so sad, my godson?' 'The sovereign has proposed four riddles to me, and given me only three days to solve them.' 'What are the riddles? Tell me.' 'Well, godmother, this is the first riddle: "What is the strongest and swiftest thing in the world?"' 'That's not difficult! My husband has a bay mare; nothing in the world is swifter than she is; if you lash her with a whip she will overtake a hare.' 'The second riddle is: "What is the fattest thing in the world?"' 'We have been feeding a spotted boar for the last two years; he has become so fat that he can barely stand on his legs.' 'The third riddle is: "What is the softest thing in the world?"' 'That's well known. Eider down — you cannot think of anything softer.' 'The fourth riddle is:

"What is the loveliest thing in the world?"' 'The loveliest thing in the world is my grandson Ivanushka.' 'Thank you, god-mother, you have advised me well. I shall be grateful to you for the rest of my life.'

As for the poor brother, he shed bitter tears and went home. He was met by his seven-year-old daughter – she was his only child – who said: 'Why are you sighing and shedding tears, Father?' 'How can I help sighing and shedding tears? The tsar has proposed four riddles to me, and I shall never be able to solve them.' 'Tell me, what are these riddles?' 'Here they are, my little daughter: "What is the strongest and swiftest thing in the world? What is the fattest thing, what is the softest thing, and what is the loveliest thing?"' 'Father, go to the tsar and tell him that the strongest and fastest thing in the world is the wind; the fattest is the earth, for she feeds everything that grows and lives; the softest of all is the hand, for whatever a man may lie on, he puts his hand under his head; and there is nothing lovelier in the world than sleep.'

The two brothers, the poor one and the rich one, came to the tsar. The tsar heard their answers to the riddles, and asked the poor man: 'Did you solve these riddles yourself, or did someone solve them for you?' The poor man answered: 'Your Majesty, I have a seven-year-old daughter, and she gave me the answers.' 'If your daughter is so wise, here is a silken thread for her; let her weave an embroidered towel for me by tomorrow morning.' The peasant took the silken thread and came home sad and grieving. 'We are in trouble,' he said to his daughter. 'The tsar has ordered you to weave a towel from this thread.' 'Grieve not, Father,' said the little girl. She broke off a twig from a broom, gave it to her father, and told him: 'Go to the tsar and ask him to find a master who can make a loom from this twig; on it I will weave his towel.' The peasant did as his daughter told him. The tsar listened to him and gave him a hundred and fifty eggs, saying: 'Give these eggs to your daughter; let her hatch one hundred and fifty chicks by tomorrow.'

The peasant returned home, even more sad and grieving than the first time. 'Ah, my daughter,' he said, 'you are barely out of one trouble before another is upon you.' 'Grieve not, Father,' answered the seven-year-old girl. She baked the eggs for dinner and for supper and sent her father to the king. 'Tell him,' she said to her father, 'that one-day grain is needed to feed the chicks. In one day let a field be plowed and the millet sown, harvested, and threshed; our chickens refuse to peck any other grain.' The tsar listened to this and said: 'Since your daughter is so wise, let her appear before me tomorrow morning – and I want her to come neither on foot nor on horseback, neither naked nor dressed, neither with a present nor without a gift.' 'Now,' thought the peasant, 'even my daughter cannot solve such a difficult riddle; we are lost.' 'Grieve not,' his seven-year-old daughter said to him. 'Go to the hunters and buy me a live hare and a live quail.' The father bought her a hare and a quail.

Next morning the seven-year-old girl took off her clothes, donned a net, took the quail in her hand, sat upon the hare, and went to the palace. The tsar met her at the gate. She bowed to him, saying, 'Here is a little gift for you, Your Majesty,' and handed him the quail. The tsar stretched out his hand, but the quail shook her wings and – flap, flap! – was gone. 'Very well,' said the tsar, 'you have done as I ordered you to do. Now tell me – since your father is so poor, what do you live on?' 'My father catches fish on the shore, and he never puts bait in the water; and I make fish soup in my skirt.' 'You are stupid! Fish never live on the shore, fish live in the water.' 'And you – are you wise? Who ever saw a cart bear foals? Not a cart but a mare bears foals.'

The tsar awarded the foal to the poor peasant and took the daughter into his own palace; when she grew up he married her and she became the tsarina.

Blubber Boy
(Eskimo)

NCE there was a girl whose boyfriend drowned in the sea. Her parents could do nothing to console her. Nor did any of the other suitors interest her – she wanted the fellow who drowned and no one else. Finally she took a chunk of blubber and carved it into the shape of her drowned boyfriend. Then she carved the boyfriend's face. It was a perfect likeness.

'Oh, if only he were real!' she thought.

She rubbed the blubber against her genitals, round and round, and suddenly it came alive. Her handsome boyfriend was standing in front of her. How delighted she was! She presented him to her parents, saying:

'As you can see, he didn't drown, after all . . .'

The girl's father gave his daughter permission to marry. Now she went with her blubber boy to a small hut just outside the village. Sometimes it would get very warm inside this hut. And then the blubber boy would start to get quite weary. At which point he would say: 'Rub me, dear.' And the girl would rub his entire body against her genitals. This would revive him.

One day the blubber boy was hunting harbor seals and the sun beat down on him harshly. As he paddled his kayak home, he started to sweat. And as he sweated, he got smaller. Half of him had melted away by the time he reached the shore. Then he stepped out of the kayak and fell to the ground, a mere pile of blubber.

'What a pity,' said the girl's parents. 'And he was such a nice young man, too . . .'

The girl buried the blubber beneath a pile of stones. Then she went into mourning. She plugged up her left nostril. She did not sew. She ate neither the eggs of sea-birds nor walrus meat. Each day she visited the blubber in its grave and talked to it and as she did so, walked around the grave three times in the direction of the sun.

After the period of mourning, the girl took another chunk of blubber and began carving again. Again she carved it into the shape of her drowned boyfriend and again rubbed the finished product against her genitals. Suddenly her boyfriend was standing beside her, saying, 'Rub me again, dear . . .'

The Girl Who Stayed in the Fork of a Tree
(West African)

HIS is what a woman did.

She was then living in the bush, never showing herself to anyone. She had living with her just one daughter, who used to pass the day in the fork of a tree making baskets.

One day there appeared a man just when the mother had gone to kill game. He found the girl making baskets as usual. 'Here now!' he said. 'There are people here in the bush! And that girl, what a beauty! Yet they leave her alone. If the king were to marry her, would not all the other queens leave the place?'

Going back to the town, he went straight to the king's house and said, 'Sire, I have discovered a woman of such beauty that, if you call her to this place, all the queens you have here will make haste to go away.'

The following morning people were called together and set to grind their axes. Then they started for the bush. As they came in view of the place, they found the mother had once more gone to hunt.

Before going, she had cooked porridge for her daughter and hung meat for her. Then only had she started on her expedition.

The people said, 'Let us cut down the tree on which the girl is.'

So they put the axes to it. The girl at once started this song:

'Mother, come back!
Mother, here is a man cutting our shade tree.
Mother, come back!
Mother, here is a man cutting our shade tree.
Cut! Here is the tree falling in which I eat.
Here it is falling.'

The mother dropped there as if from the sky:

'Many as you are, I shall stitch you
with the big needle.
Stitch! Stitch!'

They at once fell to the ground . . . The woman left just one to go back and report.

'Go,' she said, 'and tell the news.' He went . . .

When he came to the town the people asked, 'What has happened?'

'There,' he said, 'where we have been! Things are rather bad!'

Likewise, when he stood before the king, the king asked, 'What has happened?'

'Sire,' he said, 'we are all undone. I alone have come back.'

'*Bakoo!* You are all dead! If that is so, tomorrow go to the kraal over there and bring more people. Tomorrow morning let them go and bring me the woman.'

The slept their fill.

The next morning early, the men ground their axes and went to the place.

They, too, found the mother gone, while the porridge was ready there, and the meat was hanging on the tree . . .

'Bring the axes.' Forthwith they went at the shade tree. But the song had already started:

> '*Mother, come back!*
> *Mother, here is a man cutting our shade tree.*
> *Mother, come back!*
> *Mother, here is a man cutting our shade tree.*
> *Cut! Here is the tree falling in which I eat.*
> *Here it is falling.*'

The mother dropped down among them, singing in her turn:

> '*Many as you are, I shall stitch you*
> *with the big needle.*
> *Stitch! Stitch!*'

They were dead. The woman and her daughter picked up the axes . . .

'*Olo!*' said the king when he was told. 'Today let all those that are pregnant give birth to their children.'

So one woman after another straightway brought forth her child. Soon there was a whole row of them.

Then the whole band departed, making a confused noise.

When the girl saw that, she said, 'There is no joke about it now. There comes a red army with the umbilical cords still hanging on.'

They found her at her own place in the fork of the tree.

'Let us give them some porridge,' thought the girl.

She just plastered the porridge on their heads, but the children did not eat it.

The last-born then climbed up the shade tree, picked up the baskets which the girl was stitching, and said, 'Now bring me an axe.'

The girl shouted once more:

> *'Mother, come back!*
> *Mother, here is a man cutting our shade tree.*
> *Mother, come back!*
> *Mother, here is a man cutting our shade tree.*
> *Cut! Here is the tree falling in which I eat.*
> *Here it is falling.'*

The mother dropped down among the crowd:

> *'Many as you are, I shall stitch you*
> *with the big needle.*
> *Stitch! Stitch!'*

But there was the troop already dragging the girl. They had tied her with their umbilical cords, yes, with their umbilical cords. The mother went on with her incantation:

> *'Many as you are, I shall stitch you*
> *with the big needle.*
> *Stitch! Stitch!'*

In vain! The troop was already in the fields and the *ngururu* went up as far as God's abode, and soon the children were in the town.

As they reached it, the mother said, 'Since you have carried

away my child, I must tell you something. She is not to pound in the mortar, nor to go to fetch water at night. If you send her to do one of these things, mind you! I shall know where to find you.'

Then the mother went back to her abode in the bush.

The following day the king said, 'Let us go hunting.' And to his mother he said, 'My wife must not pound in the mortar. All that she can do is to stitch baskets.'

While the husband was away there in the open flat, the other wives as well as the mother-in-law said, 'Why should not she also pound in the mortar?'

When the girl was told to pound in the mortar, she said, 'No.'

A basket of kafir corn was brought to her.

The mother-in-law herself took away the meal from the mortar, and then the other women in their turn brought corn and put it all there.

So the girl pounded, singing at the same time:

'Pound! At home I do not pound,
Here I pound to celebrate my wedding.
   Yepu! Yepu!
If I pound, I go to God's.'

She began to sink into the ground but she went on singing:

'Pound! At home I do not pound,
Here I pound to celebrate my wedding.
   Yepu! Yepu!
If I pound, I go to God's.'

She was now in the ground as far as her hips, then as far as her chest.

'Pound! At home I do not pound,
Here I pound to celebrate my wedding.
   Yepu! Yepu!
If I pound, I go to God's.'

Soon she was down as far as her neck. Now the mortar went on by itself pounding the grain on the ground, pounding on the ground. Finally the girl disappeared altogether.

When nothing more was seen of her, the mortar still pounded as before on the ground.

The women then said, 'Now what shall we do?'

They went and called a crane, and said, 'Go and break the news to her mother. But, first, let us know, what will you say?'

The crane said, *'Wawani! Wawani!'*

They said, 'That has no meaning, go back. Let us send for the crow.'

The crow was called: 'Now what will you say?'

The crow said, *'Kwa! Kwa! Kwa!'*

'The crow does not know how to call. Go, quail. How will you do?'

The quail said, *'Kwalulu! Kwalulu!'*

'The quail does not know how to do it either. Let us call the doves.'

They said, 'Let us hear, doves, what will you call to her mother?'

Then they heard:

'Kuku! Ku!
She-who-nurses-the-sun is gone,
She-who-nurses-the sun.
You who dig,
She-who-nurses-the-sun is gone,
She-who-nurses-the-sun.'

They said, 'Go, you know how to do it, you.'

The mother went when she heard the doves. There she was going toward the town. She carried medicines on a potsherd, also tails of animals with which she beat the air.

While she was on the road, she met a zebra:

'Zebra, what are you doing?
                    – Nsenkenene.
The wife of my father is dead.
                    – Nsenkenene.
O mother! You shall die.
                    – Nsenkenene.'

The zebra died. The woman went on, went on, went on, and then found people digging:

'You who dig, what are you doing?
                    – Nsenkenene.

The wife of my father is dead.
                    – Nsenkenene.
O mother! You shall die.
                    – Nsenkenene.'

They also died. The woman went on and went on, then she found a man beating a skin:

'You who beat, what are you doing?
                    – Nsenkenene.
The wife of my father is dead.
                    – Nsenkenene.
O mother! You shall die.
                    – Nsenkenene.'

When she reached the town there:

'Let me gather, let me gather
The herd of my mother.
Mwinsa, get up.
Let me gather the herd.

'Let me gather, let me gather
The herd of my father.
Mwinsa, get up.
Let me gather the herd.'

She then heard the mortar still sounding right above the child.
   So she sprayed one medicine, then another.
   There was the child already pounding from under the ground. Little by little the head came out. Then the neck, and the song was heard again:

'Pound! At home I do not pound,
Here I pound to celebrate my wedding.
   Yepu! Yepu!
If I pound, I go to God's.'

The child was now in full view. Finally she stepped outside.
   I have finished.

The Princess in the Suit of Leather
(Egyptian)

NEITHER here nor elsewhere lived a king who had a wife whom he loved with all his heart and a daughter who was the light of his eyes. The princess had hardly reached womanhood when the queen fell ill and died. For one whole year the king kept vigil, sitting with bowed head beside her tomb. Then he summoned the matchmakers, elderly women wise in the ways of living, and said, 'I wish to marry again. Here is my poor queen's anklet. Find me the girl, rich or poor, humble or well-born, whose foot this anklet will fit. For I promised the queen as she lay dying that I would marry that girl and no other.'

The matchmakers traveled up and down the kingdom looking for the king's new bride. But search and search as they would, they could not find a single girl around whose ankle the jewel would close. The queen had been such that there was no woman like her. Then one old woman said, 'We have entered the house of every maiden in the land except the house of the king's own daughter. Let us go to the palace.'

When they slipped the anklet on to the princess's foot, it suited as if it had been made to her measure. Out of the seraglio went the women at a run, straight into the king's presence, and said, 'We have visited every maiden in your kingdom, but none was able to squeeze her foot into the late queen's anklet. None, that is, except the princess your daughter. She wears it as easily as if it were her own.' A wrinkled matron spoke up: 'Why not marry the princess? Why give her to a stranger and deprive yourself?' The words were hardly spoken when the king summoned the *qadi* to pen the papers for the marriage. To the princess he made no mention of his plan.

Now there was a bustle in the palace as the jewelers, the clothiers, and the furnishers came to outfit the bride. The princess was pleased to know that she was to be wed. But who her husband was she had no inkling. As late as the 'night of the entering', when the groom first sees the bride, she remained in ignorance even though the servants with their whispers were busy around her, combing and pinning and making her beautiful. At last the minister's daughter, who had come to admire her in her finery, said, 'Why are you frowning? Were not women created for marriage with men? And is there any man whose standing is higher than the king's?'

'What is the meaning of such talk?' cried the princess. 'I won't tell you,' said the girl, 'unless you give me your golden bangle to keep.' The princess pulled off the bracelet, and the girl explained how everything had come about so that the bridegroom was no other than the princess's own father.

The princess turned whiter than the cloth on her head and trembled like one who is sick with the forty-day fever. She rose to her feet and sent away all who were with her. Then, knowing only that she must escape, she ran on to the terrace and leaped over the palace wall, landing in a tanner's yard which lay below. She pressed a handful of gold into the tanner's palm and said, 'Can you make me a suit of leather to hide me from head to heels, showing nothing but my eyes? I want it by tomorrow's dawn.'

The poor man was overjoyed to earn the coins. He set to work with his wife and children. Cutting and stitching through the night they had the suit ready, before it was light enough to know a white thread from a dark. Wait a little! and here comes our lady, the princess. She put on the suit – such a strange spectacle that anyone looking at her would think he was seeing nothing but a pile of hides. In this disguise she left the tanner and lay down beside the city gate, waiting for the day.

Now to return to my lord the king. When he entered the bridal chamber and found the princess gone, he sent his army into the city to search for her. Time and again a soldier would stumble upon the princess lying at the gate and ask, 'Have you seen the king's daughter?' And she would reply:

My name is Juleidah for my coat of skins,
My eyes are weak, my sight is dim,
My ears are deaf, I cannot hear.
I care for no one far or near.

When it was day and the city gate was unbarred, she shuffled out until she was beyond the walls. Then she turned her face away from her father's city and fled.

Walking and running, one foot lifting her and one foot setting her down, there was a day when, with the setting of the sun, the princess came to another city. Too weary to travel a step farther, she fell to the ground. Now her resting place was in the shadow of the wall of the women's quarters, the harem of the sultan's palace. A slave girl, leaning from the window to toss out the crumbs from the royal table, noticed the heap of skins on the ground and thought nothing of it. But when she saw two bright eyes staring out at her from the middle of the hides, she sprang back in terror and said to the queen, 'My lady, there is something monstrous crouching under our window. I have seen it, and it looks like nothing less than an Afreet!' 'Bring it up for me to see and judge,' said the queen.

The slave girl went down shivering with fear, not knowing which was the easier thing to face, the monster outside or her mistress's rage should she fail to do her bidding. But the princess in her suit made no sound when the slave girl tugged at a corner of the leather. The girl took courage and dragged her all the way into the presence of the sultan's wife.

Never had such an astonishing creature been seen in that country. Lifting both palms in amazement, the queen asked her servant, 'What is it?' and then turned to the monster and asked, 'Who are you?' When the heap of skins answered –

My name is Juleidah for my coat of skins,
My eyes are weak, my sight is dim,
My ears are deaf, I cannot hear.
I care for no one far or near.

– how the queen laughed at the quaint reply! 'Go bring food and drink for our guest,' she said, holding her side. 'We shall keep her to amuse us.' When Juleidah had eaten, the queen said, 'Tell us what you can do, so that we may put you to work about the palace.' 'Anything you ask me to do, I am ready to try,' said Juleidah. Then the queen called, 'Mistress cook! Take this broken-winged soul into your kitchen. Maybe for her sake God will reward us with His blessings.'

So now our fine princess was a kitchen skivvy, feeding the fires and raking out the ashes. And whenever the queen lacked company and felt bored, she called Juleidah and laughed at her prattle.

One day the *wazir* sent word that all the sultan's harem was invited to a night's entertainment in his house. All day long there was a stir of excitement in the women's quarters. As the queen prepared to set out in the evening, she stopped by Juleidah and said, 'Won't you come with us tonight? All the servants and slaves are invited. Aren't you afraid to stay alone?' But Juleidah only repeated her refrain:

> My ears are deaf, I cannot hear.
> I care for no one far or near.

One of the serving girls sniffed and said, 'What is there to make her afraid? She is blind and deaf and wouldn't notice an Afreet even if he were to jump on top of her in the dark!' So they left.

In the women's reception hall of the *wazir*'s house there was dining and feasting and music and much merriment. Suddenly, at the height of the talk and enjoyment, such a one entered that they all stopped in the middle of the word they were speaking. Tall as a cypress, with a face like a rose and the silks and jewels of a king's bride, she seemed to fill the room with light. Who was it? Juleidah, who had shaken off her coat of leather as soon as the sultan's harem had gone. She had followed them to the *wazir*'s, and now the ladies who had been so merry began to quarrel, each wanting to sit beside the newcomer.

When dawn was near, Juleidah took a handful of gold sequins from the fold of her sash and scattered them on the floor. The ladies scrambled to pick up the bright treasure. And while they were occupied, Juleidah left the hall. Quickly, quickly she raced back to the palace kitchen and put on the coat of leather. Soon the others returned. Seeing the heap of hides on the kitchen floor, the queen poked it with the toe of her red slipper and said, 'Truly, I wish you had been with us to admire the lady who was at the entertainment.' But Juleidah only mumbled, 'My eyes are weak, I cannot see . . .' and they all went to their own beds to sleep.

When the queen woke up next day, the sun was high in the sky. As was his habit, the sultan's son came in to kiss his mother's hand and bid her good morning. But she could talk only of the visitor at the *wazir*'s feast. 'O my son,' she sighed, 'it was a woman with such a face and such a neck and such a form that all who saw her said, "She is the daughter of neither a king nor a sultan, but of someone greater yet!"' On and on the queen poured out her praises of the woman, until the prince's heart was on fire. Finally his mother concluded, 'I wish I had asked her father's name so that I could engage her to be your bride.' And the sultan's son replied, 'When you return tonight to continue your entertainment, I shall stand outside the *wazir*'s door and wait until she leaves. I'll ask her then about her father and her station.'

At sunset the women dressed themselves once more. With the folds of their robes smelling of orange blossom and incense and their bracelets chinking on their arms, they passed by Juleidah lying on the kitchen floor and said, 'Will you come with us tonight?' But Juleidah only turned her back on them. Then as soon as they were safely gone, she threw off her suit of leather and hurried after them.

In the *wazir*'s hall the guests pressed close around Juleidah, wanting to see her and ask where she came from. But to all their questions she gave no answer, whether yes or no, although she sat with them until the dawning of the day. Then she threw a fistful of pearls on the marble tiles, and while the women pushed one another to catch them, she slipped away as easily as a hair is pulled out of the dough.

Now who was standing at the door? The prince, of course. He had been waiting for this moment. Blocking her path, he grasped her arm and asked who her father was and from what land she came. But the princess had to be back in her kitchen or her secret would be known. So she fought to get away, and in the scuffle, she pulled the prince's ring clean off his hand. 'At least tell me where you come from!' he shouted after her as she ran. 'By Allah, tell me where!' And she replied, 'I live in a land of paddles and ladles.' Then she fled into the palace and hid in her coat of hides.

In came the others, talking and laughing. The prince told his mother what had taken place and announced that he intended to make a journey. 'I must go to the land of the paddles and ladles,' he said. 'Be patient, my son,' said the queen. 'Give me time to prepare your provisions.' Eager as he was, the prince agreed to delay his departure for two days – 'But not one hour more!'

Now the kitchen became the busiest corner of the palace. The grinding and sieving, the kneading and the baking began and Juleidah stood watching. 'Away with you,' cried the cook, 'this is no work for you!' 'I want to serve the prince our master like the rest!' said Juleidah. Willing and not willing to let her help, the cook gave her a piece of dough to shape. Juleidah began to make a cake, and when no one was watching, she pushed the prince's ring inside it. And when the food was packed Juleidah placed her own little cake on top of the rest.

Early on the third morning the rations were strapped into the saddlebags, and the prince set off with his servants and his men. He rode without slackening until the sun grew hot. Then he said, 'Let us rest the horses while we ourselves eat a mouthful.' A servant, seeing Juleidah's tiny loaf lying on top of all the rest, flung it to one side. 'Why did you throw that one away?' asked the prince. 'It was the work of the creature Juleidah; I saw her make it,' said the servant. 'It is as misshapen as she is.' The prince felt pity for the strange half-wit and asked the servant to bring back her cake. When he tore open the loaf, look, his own ring was inside! The ring he lost the night of the *wazir*'s entertainment. Understanding now where lay the land of ladles and paddles, the prince gave orders to turn back.

When the king and queen had greeted him, the prince said, 'Mother, send me my supper with Juleidah.' 'She can barely see or even hear,' said the queen. 'How can she bring your

supper to you?' 'I shall not eat unless Juleidah brings the food,' said the prince. So when the time came, the cooks arranged the dishes on a tray and helped Juleidah lift it on to her head. Up the stairs she went, but before she reached the prince's room she tipped the dishes and sent them crashing to the floor. 'I told you she cannot see,' the queen said to her son. 'And I will only eat what Juleidah brings,' said the prince.

The cooks prepared a second meal, and when they had balanced the loaded tray upon Juleidah's head, they sent two slave girls to hold her by either hand and guide her to the prince's door. 'Go,' said the prince to the two slaves, 'and you, Juleidah, come.' Juleidah began to say,

> My eyes are weak, my sight is dim,
> I'm called Juleidah for my coat of skins,
> My ears are deaf, I cannot hear,
> I care for no one far or near.

But the prince told her, 'Come and fill my cup.' As she approached, he drew the dagger that hung at his side and slashed her leather coat from collar to hem. It fell into a heap upon the floor – and there stood the maiden his mother had described, one who could say to the moon, 'Set that I may shine in your stead.'

Hiding Juleidah in a corner of the room, the prince sent for the queen. Our mistress cried out when she saw the pile of skins upon the floor. 'Why, my son, did you bring her death upon your neck? The poor thing deserved your pity more than your punishment!' 'Come in, Mother,' said the prince. 'Come and look at our Juleidah before you mourn her.' And he led his mother to where our fine princess sat revealed, her fairness filling the room like a ray of light. The queen threw herself upon the girl and kissed her on this side and on that, and bade her sit with the prince and eat. Then she summoned the *qadi* to write the paper that would bind our lord the prince to the fair princess, after which they lived together in the sweetest bliss.

Now we make our way back to the king, Juleidah's father. When he entered the bridal chamber to unveil his own daughter's face and found her gone, and when he had searched the city in vain for her, he called his minister and his servants and dressed himself for travel. From country to country he journeyed, entering one city and leaving the next, taking with him in chains the old woman who had first suggested to him that he marry his own daughter. At last he reached the city where Juleidah was living with her husband the prince.

Now, the princess was sitting in her window when they entered the gate, and she knew them as soon as she saw them. Straightway she sent to her husband urging him to invite the strangers. Our lord went to meet them and succeeded in detaining them only after much pressing, for they were impatient to continue their quest. They dined in the prince's guest hall, then thanked their host and took leave with the words, 'The proverb says: "Have your fill to eat, but then up, on to your feet!" ' – while he delayed them further with the proverb, 'Where you break your bread, there spread out your bed!'

In the end the prince's kindness forced the tired strangers to lie in his house as guests for the night. 'But why did you single out these strangers?' the prince asked Juleidah. 'Lend me your robes and headcloth and let me go to them,' she said. 'Soon you will know my reasons.'

Thus disguised, Juleidah sat with her guests. When the coffee cups had been filled and emptied, she said, 'Let us tell stories to pass the time. Will you speak first, or shall I?' 'Leave us to our sorrows, my son,' said the king her father. 'We have not the spirit to tell tales.' 'I'll entertain you, then, and distract your mind,' said Juleidah. 'There once was a king,' she began, and went on to tell the history of her own adventures from the beginning to the end. Every now and then the old woman would interrupt and say, 'Can you find no better story than this, my son?' But Juleidah kept right on, and when she had finished she said, 'I am your daughter the princess, upon whom all these troubles fell through the words of this old sinner and daughter of shame!'

In the morning they flung the old woman over a tall cliff into the *wadi*. Then the king gave half his kingdom to his daughter and the prince, and they lived in happiness and contentment until death, the parter of the truest lovers, divided them.

The Hare
(Swahili)

NE day the hare went to the house of the hunter who was away hunting. He said to the hunter's wife: 'Come to my house and live with me; we have meat and vegetables every day.' The woman went with him, but when she saw the lair of the hare and had eaten grass with him and slept in the open with him, she was not satisfied. She said: 'I want to go back.' The hare said: 'You came here by your own choice.' The woman did not know the road in the bush, so she said: 'Come with me and I will cook a nice dinner.' The hare took her to her house. Then she said: 'Get me some firewood.'

The hare went to the forest and collected a load of firewood. The woman lit a fire and put a pot on it. When the water was boiling she put the hare into the pot. When the hunter came home she said: 'I caught a hare for dinner.' The hunter never knew what happened.

Mossycoat
(English Gypsy)

ERE was once a poor ould widder-woman as lived in a little cottage. She'd two daughters; de younger on 'em was about nineteen or twenty, and she was very beautiful. Her mother was busy ivry day, a-spinning of a coat for her.

A hawker came courting dis girl; came reg'lar he did, and kept on a-bringing of her dis thing and dat. He was in love wid her, and badly wanted her to marry him. But she wasn't in love wid him; it didn't fall out like dat; and she was in a puzzlement what she'd best do about him. So one day she ext her mother. 'Let he come,' her mother telt her, 'and git what you can out'n him, while I finish dis coat, after when you won't have no need 'n him, nor his presents neether. So tell him, girl, as you won't marry him, unless he gits you a dress o' white satin with sprigs o' goold on it as big as a man's hand; and mind as you tells him it mus' fit exac'ly.'

Next time de hawker cam round, and ext her to wed him, de girl telt him just dis, de wery same as her mother'd said. He took stock 'n her size and build, de hawker did; and inside of a week he was back wid de dress. It answered de describance all right, an when de girl went upstairs wid her mother, and tried it on, it fit 'n exac'ly.

'What should I do now, Mother?' she ext.

'Tell him,' her mother says, 'as you won't marry him unless he gits you a dress med o' silk de color o' all de birds o' de air; and as afore, it must fit you exac'ly .'

De girl telt de hawker dis, and in two or three days he was back at de cottage, wid dis colored silk dress de girl ed exted for; and being as he knowed de size from de t'other un, in course it fit her exac'ly.

'Now what should I do, Mother?' she ext.

'Tell him,' her mother says, 'as you won't marry him unless he gits you a pair o' silver slippers as fits you exac'ly.'

De girl telt de hawker so, and in a few days he called round wid 'em. Her feet was only about three inches long, but de slippers fit her exac'ly; dey was not too tight, neether was dey too loose. Agen de girl ext her mother what she should do now. 'I can finish de coat tonight,' her mother said, 'so you can tell de hawker as you'll marry him tomorrow, and he's to be here at 10 o'clock.' So de girl telt him dis. 'Think-on, my dear,' she says, '10 o'clock in de morning.' 'I'll be dere, my love,' he says, 'by God, I will.'

That night her mother was at work on de coat till late, but she finished it all right. Green moss and goold thread, dat's what it was med on; just dem two things. 'Mossycoat,' she called it, and give de name to de younger daughter, as she'd med it for. It was a magic coat, she said, a wishing coat, she telt her daughter; when she'd got it on, she telt her she'd only to wish to be somewhere, and she'd be dere dat wery instant, and de same if she wanted to change hersel' into summat else, like to be a swan or a bee.

Next morning de mother was up by it was light. She called her younger daughter, and telt her she mus' now go into de world and seek her fortune, and a handsome fortune it was to be. She was a foreseer, de owld mother was, and know'd what was a-coming. She give her daughter mossycoat to put on, and a goold crown to tek wid her, and she telt her to tek as well de two dresses and de silver slippers she'd had off'n de hawker. But she was to go in de clo'es as she wore ivery day, her working clo'es dat is. And now she's ready for to start, Mossycoat is. Her mother den tells her she is to wish herself a hundred miles away, and den walk on till she comes to a big hall, and dere she's to ext for a job. 'You won't hev far to walk, my blessed,' she says – dat's de mother. 'And dey'll be sure to find you work at dis big hall.'

Mossycoat did as her mother telt her, and soon she foun' herself in front of a big gentleman's house. She knocked at de front door and said as she was looking for work. Well, de long and de short of it was as de mistress hersel' come to see her; and she liked de look 'n her, de lady did.

'What work can you do?' she ext.

'I can cook, your ladyship,' said Mossycoat. 'In fact, I'm in de way o' being a wery good cook, from what peoples 'es remarked.'

'I can't give you a job as cook,' de lady tells her, 'being as I got one already; but I'd be willing to imploy you to help de cook, if so as you'd be satisfied wid dat.'

49

'Thank you, ma'am,' says Mossycoat. 'I s'd be real glad 'n de place.'

So it was settled as she was to be undercook. And after when de lady'd showed her up to her bedroom, she took her to de kitchen, and interdoosed her to de t'other sarvants.

'Dis is Mossycoat,' she tells 'em, 'and I've engaged her,' she says, 'to be undercook.'

She leaves 'em den, de mistress does; and Mossycoat she goes up to her bedroom agen, to unpack her things, and hide away her goold crown and silver slippers, and her silk and satin dresses.

It goes wi'out saying as de t'other kitchen girls was fair beside theirsels wid jealousy; and it didn't mend matters as de new girl was a dam' sight beautifuller nor what any of dem was. Here was dis wagrant i' rags put above dem, when all she was fit for at best was to be scullery girl. If anybody was to be undercook, it stands to sense it sud'er been one o' dem as really knowed about things, not dis girl i' rags and tatters, picked up off'n de roads. But dey'd put her in her place, dey would. So dey goes on and on, like what women will, till Mossycoat come down ready to start work. Den dey sets on her. 'Who de devil did she think she was, setting hersel' above dem? She'd be undercook, would she? No dam' fear . . . dey relow of dat. What she'd hev to do, and all she was fit for, was to scour de pans, clean de knives, do de grates and suchlike; and all she'd git was dis.' And down come de skimmer on top of her head, pop, pop, pop. 'Dat's what you deserves,' dey tell her, 'and dat's what you can expect, my lady.'

And dat's how it was wid Mossycoat. She was put to do all de dirtiest work, and soon she was up to de ears in grease, and her face as black as soot. And ivery now and agen, first one and then another o' de sarvants, 'ld pop, pop, pop her a-top o' de head wid de skimmer, till de poor girls' head was dat sore, she couldn't hardly bide it.

Well, it got on, and it got on, and still Mossycoat was at her pans, and knives, and grates; and still de sarvants was pop, pop, popping her on de head wid de skimmer. Now dere was a big dance coming on, as was to last three nights, wid hunting and other sports in de daytime. All de headmost people for miles round was to be dere; and de master, and mistress, and de young master – dey'd niver had but one child – in course dey was a-going. It was all de talk among de sarvants, dis dance was. One was wishing she could be dere; another'd like to dance wid some 'n de young lords; a third 'ld like to see de ladies' dresses, and so dey went on, all excepting Mossycoat. If only dey'd de clo'es, dey'd be al right, dey thought, as dey considered deirselves as good as high-titled ladies any day. 'And you, Mossycoat, you'd like to go, wouldn't you now?' dey says. 'A fit person you'd be to be dere in all your rags and dirt,' dey says, and down comes de skimmer on her head, pop, pop, pop. Den dey laughs at her; which goes to show what a low class o' people dey was.

Now Mossycoat, as I've said afore, was wery handsome, and rags and dirt couldn't hide dat. De t'other sarvants might think as it did, but de young master'd hed his eyes on her, and de master and mistress, dey'd al'ays taken partic'lar notice o' her, on account of her good looks. When de big dance was coming on, dey thought as it'd be nice to ex her to go to it; so dey sent for her to see if she'd like to. 'No, thank you,' she says, 'I'd niver think o' such a thing. I knows my place better'n dat,' she says. 'Besides, I'd greasy all de one side o' de coach,' she tells 'em, 'and anybody's clo'es as I comed up agen.' Dey make light on dat, and presses her to go, de master and mistress does. It's wery kind on 'em, Mossycoat says, but she's not for going, she says. And she sticks to dat. When she gets back into de kitchen, you may depend on it, de t'other sarvants wants to know why she'd bin sent for. Had she got notice, or what was it? So she telt 'em de master and mistress 'ed ext her would she like to go to the dance wid 'em. 'What? You?' dey says, 'it's unbelievable. If it had been one o' we, now, dat'd be different. But you! Why, you'd niver be relowed in, as you'd greasy all the gentlemen's clo'es, if dere were any as 'ed dance wid a scullery girl; and de ladies, dey'd be forced to howld dere noses w'en dey passed by you, to be sure dey would.' No, dey couldn't believe, dey said, as de master and mistress had iver ext *her* to go to de ball wid 'em. She must be lying, dey said, and down come de skimmer a-top of her head, pop, pop, pop.

Next night, de master and de mistress and dere son, dis time, ext her to go to de dance. It was a grand affair de night before, dey said, and she sud ev bin dere. It was going to be still grander tonight, dey said, and dey begged of her to come wid 'em, especially de young master. But no, she says, on account of her rags and her grease, and dirt, she couldn't and she wouldn't; and even de young master couldn't persuade her, though it wasn't for de want o' trying. The t'other sarvants just didn't believe her when she telt 'em about her being invited agen to de dance, and about de young master being wery pressing.

'Hark to her!' they says, 'What'll de upstart say next? And all dam' lies,' dey says. Den one o' dem, wid a mouth like a pig-trough, and legs like a cart horse, catches hold o' de skimmer, and down it comes, pop, pop, pop, on Mossycoat's head.

Dat night, Mossycoat decided as she'd go to de dance, in right proper style, all on her own, and wi'out nobody knowing it. De first thing she does is to put all de t'other sarvants into a trance; she just touches each on 'em, unnoticed, as she moves about, and dey all falls asleep under a spell as soon as she does, and can't wake up agen on deir own; de spell has to be broke by somebody wid de power, same as she has through her magic coat, or has got it some other way. Next Mossycoat has a real good wash: she'd niver been relowed to afore, sin' she'd bin at de hall as the other sarvants was retermined to mek and to keep her as greasy and dirty as dey could. Den she goes upstairs to her bedroom, throws off her working clo'es and shoes, and puts on her white satin dress wid de gowld sprigs, her silver slippers, and her gowld crown. In course, she had mossy coat on underneath. So as soon as she was ready, she jus' wished hersel' at de dance, and dere she was, wery near as soon as de wish was spoke. She did jus' feel hersel' rising up and flying through de elements but only for a moment. Den she was in de ballroom.

De young master sees her standing dere, and once he catched sight on her he can't tek his eyes off her; he'd niver seen anybody as han'some afore, or as beautifully dressed. 'Who is she?' he exes his mother; but she doesn't know, she tells him.

'Can't you find out, Mother?' he says. 'Can't you go and talk to her?' His mother sees as he'll niver rest till she does, so she goes and interdooses hersel' to de young lady, and exes her who she is, where she comes from, and such as dat; but all she could git out'n her was as she come from a place where dey hit her on de head wid de skimmer. Den presently, de young master he goes over and interdooses hissel', but she doesn't tell him her name nor nothing; and when he exes her to hev a dance wid him, she says no, she'd rather not. He stops aside of her though, and keeps exing her time and agen, and at de finish she says as she will, and links up wid him. Dey dances once, up and down de room; den she says she must go. He presses her to stop, but it's a waste o' breath; she's retermined to go, dere and den.

'All right,' he says – dere was nothing else he could say – 'I'll come and see you off.' But she jus' wished she was at home, and dere she was. No seeing of her off for de young master, dere warn't, she jus' went from his side in de twinkle of an eye, leaving him standing dere gaping wid wonderment. Thinking she might be in de hall, or de porch, a-waiting of her carriage, he goes to see, but dere's no sign on her anywheres inside or out, and nobody as he exed seen her go. He went back to de ballroom, but he can't think of nothing or nobody but her and all de time he's a-wanting to go home.

When Mossycoat gets back home, she meks sure as all de t'other sarvants is still in a trance. Den she goes up and changes into her working get-up; and after when she'd done dat, she come down into de kitchen agen, and touches each 'n de sarvants. Dat wakens 'em, as you might say; anyway, dey starts up, wondering whatever time o' day it is, and how long dey bin asleep. Mossycoat tells 'em, and drops a hint as she may have to let de mistress know. Dey begs on her not to let on about 'em, and most'n 'em thinks to give her things if she won't. Owld things, dey was, but wid a bit o' wear in 'em still – a skirt, a pair o' shoes, stockings, stays, and what not. So Mossycoat promises as she won't tell on 'em. An' dat night, dey don't hit her on de head wid de skimmer.

All next day de young master is unrestful. He can't settle his mind to nothing but de young lady as he'd fell in love wid last night at de wery first sight 'n her. He was wondering all de time would she be dere agen tonight, and would she vanish de same as she done last night; and thinking how he could stop her, or catch up wid her if she was for doing dis a second time. He must find out where she lives, he thinks, else how's he to go on after when de dance is over. He'd die, he tells his mother, if he can't git her for his wife; he's dat madly in love wid her. 'Well,' says his mother, 'I thought as she was a nice modest girl, but she wouldn't say who or what she was, or where she come from, except it was a place where dey hit her on de head wid de skimmer.'

'She's a bit of a mystery, I know,' says de young master, 'but dat don't signify as I want her any de less. I must hev her, Mother,' he says, 'whoiver and whativer she is; and dat's de dear God's truth, Mother, strike me dead if it ain't.'

Women sarvants 'es long ears, and big mouths, and you may be sure as it wasn't long afore de young master and dis wonderful han'some lady he'd fell in love wid was all de talk in de kitchen.

'And fancy you, Mossycoat, thinking as he specially wanted *you* to go to de dance,' dey says, and starts in on her proper, meking all manner o' nasty sarcastical remarks, and hitting her on de head wid de skimmer, pop, pop, pop, for lying to 'em (as dey said). It was de same agen later on, after when de master and mistress hed sent for her, and exed her once more to go to de dance wid 'em, and once more she'd defused. It was her last chance, dey said – dat was de sarvants – an' a lot more besides, as ain't worth repeating. And down came de skimmer a-top of her head, pop, pop, pop. Den she put de whole devil's breed 'n 'em into a trance like she done de night afore, and got hersel' ready to go to de dance, de only difference being as dis time she put her t'other dress on, de one med o' silk de color of all de birds o' de air.

She's in de ballroom now, Mossycoat is. De young master, he's waiting and watching for her. As soon as he sees her, he exes his father to send for de fastest horse in his stable, and hev it kept standing ready saddled at de door. Den he exes his mother to go over and talk to de young lady for a bit. She does dat, but can't larn no more about her 'an she did the night afore. Den de young master hears as his horse is ready at de door; so he goes over to de young lady, and exes her for a dance. She says jus' de same as de night afore, 'No,' at first, but 'Yes,' at de finish, and jus' as den, she says she mus' go after when dey've danced only once de length o' de room an' back. But dis time, he keeps howld 'n her till dey gets outside. Den she wishes hersel' at home, and is dere nearly as soon as she's spoken. De young master felt her rise into de air, but couldn't do nothing to stop her. But p'raps he did jus' touch her foot, as she dropped one slipper; I couldn't be sure as he did; it looks a bit like it though. He picks de slipper up; but as for catching up wid her, it would be easier by far to catch up wid de wind on a blowy night. As soon as she gits home, Mossycoat changes back into her owld things; den she looses de t'other sarvants from de spell she'd put on 'em. Dey've been asleep agen, dey thinks, and offers her one a shilling, another a half a crown, a third a week's wage, if she won't tell on 'em; and she promises as she won't.

De young master's in bed next day, a-dying for de love of de lady as lost one 'n her silver slippers de night afore. De doctors can't do him not de leastest good. So it was give out what his state was, and as it was only de lady able to wear de slipper as could save his life; and if she'd come forrad, he'd marry her. De slippers, as I said earlier on, was only but three inches long, or dereabouts. Ladies came from near and far, some wid big feet and some wid small, but none small enough to git it on howiver much dey pinched and squeezed. Poorer people came as well, but it was jus' de same wid dem. And in course, all de sarvants tried, but dey was out'n altogether. De young master was a-dying. Was dere nobody else, his mother exed, nobody at all, rich or poor? 'No,' dey telt her, everybody'd tried it excepting it was Mossycoat.

'Tell her to come at once,' says de mistress.

So dey fetched her.

'Try dis slipper on,' she says – dat's de mistress.

Mossycoat slips her foot into it easy enough; it fits her exac'ly. De young master jumps out o' bed, and is jus' a-going to tek her in his arms.

'Stop' she says, and runs off; but afore long she's back agen in her satin dress wid gowld sprigs, her gowld crown, and both her silver slippers. De young master is jus' a-going to tek her in his arms.

'Stop,' she says, and agen she runs off. Dis time she comes back in her silk dress de color of all de birds o' de air. She don't stop him dis time, and as de saying used to be, he nearly eats her.

After when dey's all settled down agen, and is talking quiet-like, dere's one or two things as de master and mistress and de young master'ld like to know. How did she get to dance, and back agen, in no time, they exed her. 'Jus' wishing,' she says, and she tells 'em all as I've telt you about the magic coat her mother 'ed med for her, and de powers it give her if she cared to use 'em. 'Yes, dat explains everything,' dey says. Den dey bethinks theirselves of her saying as she came from where dey hit her on de head wid de skimmer. What did she mean by dat, dey wants to know. She meant jus' what she said, she telt 'em; it was always coming down on her head, pop, pop, pop. They were right angry when dey heard dat, and de whole of de kitchen sarvants was telt to go, and de dogs sent arter dem to drive de varmints right away from de place.

As soon as dey could Mossycoat and de young master got married, and she'd a coach and six to ride in, ai, ten if she liked, for you may be sure as she'd everything as she fancied. Dey lived happy ever after, and had a basketful o' children. I was dere when de owld son comed of age, a-playing de fiddle. But dat was many years back, and I shouldn't wonder if de owld master and mistress isn't dead by now, though I've niver heerd tell as dey was.

Vasilisa the Priest's Daughter
(Russian)

N a certain land, in a certain kingdom, there was a priest named Vasily who had a daughter named Vasilisa Vasilyevna. She wore man's clothes, rode horseback, was a good shot with the rifle, and did everything in a quite unmaidenly way, so that only very few people knew that she was a girl; most people thought that she was a man and called her Vasily Vasilyevich, all the more so because Vasilisa Vasilyevna was very fond of vodka, and this, as is well known, is entirely unbecoming to a maiden. One day, King Barkhat (for that was the name of the king of that country) went to hunt game, and he met Vasilisa Vasilyevna. She was riding horseback in man's clothes and was also hunting. When he saw her, King Barkhat asked his servants: 'Who is that young man?' One servant answered him: 'Your Majesty, that is not a man, but a girl; I know for a certainty that she is the daughter of the priest Vasily and that her name is Vasilisa Vasilyevna.'

As soon as the king returned home he wrote a letter to the priest Vasily asking him to permit his son Vasily Vasilyevich to come to visit him and eat at the king's table. Meanwhile he himself went to the little old back yard witch and began to question her as to how he could find out whether Vasily Vasilyevich was really a girl. The little old witch said to him: 'On the right side of your chamber hang up an embroidery frame, and on the left side a gun; if she is really Vasilisa Vasilyevna, she will first notice the embroidery frame; if she is Vasily Vasilyevich, she will notice the gun.' King Barkhat followed the little old witch's advice and ordered his servants to hang up an embroidery frame and a gun in his chamber.

As soon as the king's letter reached Father Vasily and he showed it to his daughter, she went to the stable, saddled a gray horse with a gray mane, and went straight to King Barkhat's palace. The king received her; she politely said her prayers, made the sign of the cross as is prescribed, bowed low to all four sides, graciously greeted King Barkhat, and entered the palace with him. They sat together at table and began to drink heady drinks and eat rich viands. After dinner, Vasilisa Vasilyevna walked with King Barkhat through the palace chambers; as soon as she saw the embroidery frame she began to reproach King Barkhat: 'What kind of junk do you have here, King Barkhat? In my father's house there is no trace of such womanish fiddle-faddle, but in King Barkhat's palace womanish fiddle-faddle hangs in the chambers!' Then she politely said farewell to King Barkhat and rode home. The king had not found out whether she was really a girl.

And so two days later – no more – King Barkhat again sent a letter to the priest Vasily, asking him to send his son Vasily Vasilyevich to the palace. As soon as Vasilisa Vasilyevna heard about this, she went to the stable, saddled a gray horse with a gray mane, and rode straight to King Barkhat's palace. The king received her. She graciously greeted him, politely said her prayers to God, made the sign of the cross as is prescribed, and bowed low to all four sides. King Barkhat had been advised by the little old back yard witch to order kasha cooked for supper and to have it stuffed with pearls. The little old witch had told him that if the youth was really Vasilisa Vasilyevna he would put the pearls in a pile, and if he was Vasily Vasilyevich he would throw them under the table.

Supper time came. The king sat at table and placed Vasilisa Vasilyevna on his right hand, and they began to drink heady drinks and eat rich viands. Kasha was served after all the other dishes, and as soon as Vasilisa Vasilyevna took a spoonful of it and discovered a pearl, she flung it under the table together with the kasha and began to reproach King Barkhat. 'What kind of trash do they put in your kasha?' she said. 'In my father's house there is no trace of such womanish fiddle-faddle, yet in King Barkhat's house womanish fiddle-faddle is put in the food!' Then she politely said farewell to King Barkhat and rode home. Again the king had not found out whether she was really a girl, although he badly wanted to know.

Two days later, upon the advice of the little old witch, King Barkhat ordered that his bath be heated; she had told him that if the youth really was Vasilisa Vasilyevna he would refuse to go to the bath with him. So the bath was heated.

Again King Barkhat wrote a letter to the priest Vasily, telling him to send his son Vasily Vasilyevich to the palace for a visit.

As soon as Vasilisa Vasilyevna heard about it, she went to the stable, saddled her gray horse with the gray mane, and galloped straight to King Barkhat's palace. The king went out to receive her on the front porch. She greeted him civilly and entered the palace on a velvet rug; having come in, she politely said her prayers to God, made the sign of the cross as is prescribed, and bowed very low to all four sides. Then she sat at table with King Barkhat, and began to drink heady drinks and eat rich viands.

After dinner the king said: 'Would it not please you, Vasily Vasilyevich, to come with me to the bath?' 'Certainly, Your Majesty,' Vasilisa Vasilyevna answered, 'I have not had a bath for a long time and should like very much to steam myself.' So they went together to the bathhouse. While King Barkhat undressed in the anteroom, she took her bath and left. So the king did not catch her in the bath either. Having left the bathhouse, Vasilisa Vasilyevna wrote a note to the king and ordered the servants to hand it to him when he came out. And this note ran: 'Ah, King Barkhat, raven that you are, you could not surprise the falcon in the garden! For I am not Vasily Vasilyevich, but Vasilisa Vasilyevna.' And so King Barkhat got nothing for all his trouble; for Vasilisa Vasilyevna was a clever girl, and very pretty too!

The Pupil
(Swahili)

SHEIKH Ali was an old teacher and Kibwana was his pupil. One day the teacher went out and the teacher's wife called Kibwana: 'You, young man, come quickly.' 'What for?' 'Stupid, you are hungry and you don't know how to eat!' 'All right,' said Kibwana when he at last understood. He went inside and lay with his teacher's wife. The teacher's wife taught him what the teacher did not teach him.

The Rich Farmer's Wife
(Norwegian)

THERE was once a rich farmer who owned big property; silver was stowed away in his chest, and he had money in the bank besides; but he felt something was wanting, for he was a widower. One day his neighbor's daughter was working for him, and he took a great fancy to her. As her parents were poor, he thought he had only to hint at marriage, and she would jump at the chance. So he told her he had really been thinking of getting married again.

'Oh, yes, one can think all kinds of things,' said the girl, chuckling to herself.

She thought the ugly old fellow might have thought of something that suited him better than getting married.

'Well, you see, I thought you might be my wife,' said the farmer.

'No, thank you,' said the girl, 'I can't see much in that.'

The farmer was not used to hearing 'No', and the less she wanted him, the crazier he was to have her.

As he did not get anywhere with the girl, he sent for her father and told him, if he could manage to make her consent, he need not pay back the money he had borrowed off the farmer and he might have the field that lay next to his meadow into the bargain.

Well, the father thought he would soon bring his daughter to her senses. 'She is only a child,' he said, 'and doesn't know what is best for her.'

But all his talking and coaxing did no good. She would not have the farmer, not even if he was plastered all over with gold right up to his ears.

The farmer waited day after day. Finally he grew so angry and impatient that he said to the girl's father, if he were going to keep his promise, matters would have to be fixed at once, for he would not wait any longer.

The father saw no way out of it except for the rich farmer to get everything ready for the wedding, and, when the parson and the wedding guests were there, to send for the girl just as

61

if she were wanted for some work on the farm. When she came, he would have to marry her in a hurry, so she would have no chance to change her mind.

The rich farmer thought this was all right, so he set to brewing and baking and getting ready for the wedding in grand style. When the guests had come, the rich farmer called one of his boys and told him to run down to the neighbor's and ask him to send what he had promised.

'But if you're not back right away,' he said, shaking his fist at the boy, 'I'll . . .' he didn't have a chance to say more, for the boy was off like a flash.

'My boss wants you to send what you've promised him,' said the boy when he got to the neighbor's, 'but you've got to hustle, for he's in an awful hurry today.'

'All right, run down to the meadow and take her along, for there you'll find her,' said the neighbor.

The boy hurried off, and when he got to the meadow, he found the daughter raking.

'I came to fetch what your father has promised my boss,' he said.

'Ah, ha, is that the way you're going to fool me?' thought the girl.

'Is that what you're after?' she said. 'I suppose it is that little bay mare of ours. You must go over and get her; she's tethered on the other side of the peas.'

The boy jumped on the back of the little bay mare and rode her home at full gallop.

'Have you got her with you?' said the rich farmer.

'She's down at the door,' said the boy.

'Take her up to my mother's room,' said the farmer.

'Goodness gracious, how are you going to manage that?' said the boy.

'You just do as I tell you,' said the farmer. 'If you can't manage it alone, get the others to help you.' He thought the girl might make trouble.

When the boy saw his master's face, he knew there was no use arguing. So he got all the help and hurried down. Some tugged at the head, and some pushed behind, and at last they got the mare upstairs and into the bedroom. There lay the wedding finery all ready.

'Well, I've finished the job, boss,' said the boy, 'but it was no easy matter, the very worst I've ever had to do on this farm.'

'All right, you shan't have done it for nothing,' said the farmer. 'Now send the women folk up to dress her.'

'But, my goodness gracious!' said the boy.

'No nonsense,' said the farmer; 'tell them to dress her and to forget neither wreath nor crown.'

The boy hurried down into the kitchen.

'Now, listen, girls,' he said, 'hurry upstairs and dress the little bay mare as a bride. I guess the boss wants to make the wedding guests snicker.'

Well, the girls dressed the little bay mare in everything that was there. Then the boy went down and said she was ready, with wreath and crown and all.

'All right, bring her down,' said the rich farmer. 'I'll receive her myself at the door.'

There was a terrible clatter on the stairs, for this bride did not come down in satin slippers. But when the door was opened, and the rich farmer's bride came into the parlor, there was plenty of giggling and snickering.

And as for the rich farmer, he was so pleased with his bride that he did not go courting again.

Keep Your Secrets
(West African)

CERTAIN girl was given by her parents to a young man in marriage. She did not care for the youth, so she refused and said that she would choose a husband for herself. Shortly after there came to the village a fine young man of great strength and beauty. The girl fell in love with him at first sight and told her parents that she had found the man she wished to marry, and as the latter was not unwilling the marriage soon took place.

Now it happened that the young man was not a man at all, but a hyena, for although as a rule women change into hyenas and men into hawks, the hyena can change itself into either man or woman as it may please.

During the first night the two newly married ones were sleeping together the husband said: 'Supposing that when we go to my town we chance to quarrel on the road, what would you do?' The wife answered that she would change herself into a tree. The man said that he would be able to catch her even then.

She said that if that was the case she would turn into a pool of water. 'Oh! that would not trouble me,' said the hyena man, 'I should catch you all the same.'

'Why, then I should turn into a stone,' replied his spouse. 'Still I should catch you,' remarked the man.

Just at that moment the girl's mother shouted from her room, for she had heard the conversation: 'Keep quiet, my daughter; is it thus that a woman tells all her secrets to her man?' So the girl said no more.

Next morning, when the day was breaking, the husband told his wife to rise up as he was returning to his home. He bade her make ready to accompany him a short way down the road to see him off. She did as he told her, and as soon as ever the couple were out of sight of the village the husband turned himself into a hyena and tried to catch the girl, who changed herself into a tree, then into a pool of water, then into a stone, but the hyena almost tore the tree down, nearly drank all the water and half swallowed the stone.

Then the girl changed herself into that thing which the night before her mother had managed to stop her from betraying. The hyena looked and looked everywhere and at last, fearing the villagers would come and kill him, made off.

At once the girl changed into her own proper form and ran back to the village.

The Three Measures of Salt
(Greek)

HERE was once a king with nine sons; he was faced by another king with nine daughters: in those days everyone was a king. Every morning each king used to go out to his frontier to greet the other. Once as they met at the frontier and greeted one another the king with the nine daughters said to the other: 'Good day, my lord king, you with your nine boys, and may you never get a wife for any of them!' When the other heard this he was smitten to the heart, and sat in a corner of his palace deep in thought. One of his sons came up: 'What is the matter, Father, that you are so sorrowful?' 'Nothing, my son.' The next brother asked him: 'Nothing, my son; I have a headache.' The third one came: 'But why won't you tell us what is the matter?' The king said not a word. Not to make too long a story, they all asked him and to none of them would he say what was the matter. The boys left him. Midday came and the king had no appetite to eat. God brought the day to its evening; then the dawn; but the king was still wrapt in thought. The eldest son came to him again: 'But, Father, this cannot be endured; a day and a night you are here fasting and sorrowful, and yet you won't tell us what is the matter.' He said: 'But what can I say, my son?' He told him what had happened between him and the other king: 'When he saw me yesterday morning he said to me: "Good day, king, with your nine sons, and may you never get a wife for any of them!"' 'And is it this that has filled you with such great bitterness, Father? Tomorrow when you meet, you must say to him: "Good morning, my lord king, with your nine daughters, and may you never get a husband for any of them."' Next day very early the king went out to his frontier and when he saw the other king he said: 'Good day, my lord king, with your nine daughters, and may you never get a husband for any of them.' When the other king heard this, how vexed he was! He too went and sat in a corner of his palace all full of trouble.

One of his daughters came and said: 'What is the matter, Father?' 'Nothing, my daughter.' Then the next daughter asked him: 'Nothing at all but a headache.' Then came the third. The king said: 'I told you there is nothing the matter.' Thus not to make a long story, all the nine came and asked him and he would tell none of them. Then his daughters left him. Midday came, but he would not eat. God brought the day to its evening; then the dawn; still he was wrapt in care. Then at last his daughters said: 'But this cannot be endured: for him to sit all by himself a day and a night; to put not even a crumb of church bread in his mouth, and to refuse to breathe a word of what is the matter, but just to put us off with stories!' The eldest went again to her father: 'Dear Father, why please won't you tell us what is the matter?' 'If you want to know, my daughter, the king over the way said to me: "Good day, my lord king, with your nine daughters, and a husband for none of them may you never have!"' She was a clever girl and said: 'Are you grieved for that, Father? Tomorrow you must answer him and say: "Since I have no husband for my girls, why, give me one of your sons: my eldest daughter can very easily rub three measures of salt on his face and he be none the wiser."' As the girl had told him, so he did.

Next day when they greeted one another very early, he said to the other king: 'Since I have no husband for any of my girls, give me one of your sons; my eldest daughter is a match for him; very easily can she rub three measures of salt on his face and he be none the wiser.' So they made the match and married the eldest son with the eldest daughter. When they lay down in bed the first evening the prince said to his newly wed princess: 'You have managed it very well, you clever girl, and now we are married; but tell me what are these three measures of salt which you would rub on my head and I be none the wiser?' She said: 'I won't tell you.' 'Tell me or I will go away and leave you.' 'Go then; only let me know where you are going so that I can send you a letter sometimes.' 'I am going to Salonika.' So the youth made all ready. She too went off in a ship and reached that same place before him.

By the shore she met an old woman who said to her: 'You must be newly come here. If you like, I have a house I can let you have near the sea, a house for a king's daughter.' The girl went up into the house and then she said to the old woman: 'A prince will be coming here in a day or two and you must bring him here.' 'At your orders, my lady,' said the old woman. Next day the prince arrived. The old woman went down to the shore and said to him: 'I can bring you to a house fit for a prince; you will also have there a girl to kiss.' He went up into the house and saw the princess. 'Good day, and you are very much like my wife: what am I to think of it?' 'Well, well, my good Christian,' says she: 'Man to man and thing to thing, likenesses there are everywhere.' But of course the woman was the wife herself. All day they talked and in the evening they lay down together. She became with child and had a boy baby: when he was born the room was full of light, for on his brow was the star of morning. Within the year the prince wanted to go away, and she said: 'And won't you leave some present for your child?' Then he took out his gold watch and hung it on the baby, and to the old woman he gave a present of a thousand gold pieces. When he had gone, his wife embarked in a ship and came to her country before him. The boy she handed over to a nurse and he was brought up in a golden room below the earth which she had constructed in her father's palace. She warned all the maidservants that they must say nothing to the prince when he came back about her being away; only that she had had a cold and been ill all the year. Next day the prince arrived; he asked how his wife was. They said: 'As I could wish your ill-wishers were, and this all because of your absence.' Then he came to find her and they kissed one another, and he said: 'I am told that you have been ill because of our separation, but it was all your fault because you would not tell me about those three measures of salt which you said you would rub on me and I be none the wiser. Now tell me,' said he. 'No, I won't tell you.' 'Obstinate are you? Well, so am I. Either you will tell me or I shall go away and leave you.' 'Go then; only tell me where you will be that I may be able some time to send you a letter.' 'In Aigina,' said he.

When he went off, she too went by another way and took ship and came to Aigina before him. There on the shore she found the same old woman – it was really her Fate – and again she went with her to a house on the shore. Next day the prince also arrived and the old woman took him to the same house and left him there and then went off. As soon as the prince saw the woman in the house he ran and kissed her. She said: 'And what makes you so passionate just from seeing me?' 'I have a wife just like you and she came to my mind.' 'Man to man and thing to thing, likenesses there are everywhere.' All day they were there talking and in the evening they lay down together and so every evening, until she was with child and had a boy baby; when he was born the room was full of light, for on his brow was the shining moon. Before a year was over he gave the boy his gold walking-stick for a remembrance: he kissed him; gave the old woman another thousand gold pieces as a present and went away. Thus he went off and his wife after him. She came first to her house and handed over this second child to the same nurse and gave the servants a present not to tell that she had been away; in the palace she again played the part of the sorrowful woman. When her husband came next day, he questioned the servants about his wife, and they told him that all the year she had shut herself up in sorrow. The servants went back again and the prince came to his wife and said: 'Whatever you may have suffered, it is all the fault of your ladyship. But now do tell me what are those three measures of salt you would rub on my face and I be none the wiser: if you won't, I shall be off again.' 'And a good journey to you; only tell me where you are going and I shall know if at any time I want to send you any news.' 'I'm going to Venice.'

Again he took ship and she followed, arriving before him. The same old woman appeared and took her to a great big palace on the shore. In two or three days the prince arrived. The old woman said to him: 'You are welcome, prince. Pray be so good as to come to my house and stay there as long as you please, because I have a girl there for you.' 'Wonderful,' said he. Then he went and again he saw the woman; he said: 'Oh, how like you are to my wife!' 'Man to man and thing to thing, likenesses there are everywhere.' Not to make a long story, she became with child and bore a daughter; the room was full of light, for on her forehead was the shining of the sun. They christened the child and called her Alexandra. Before the year was out the prince wanted to go away and the princess said to him: 'Won't you at least make the baby some present for her to remember you?' Says he: 'Of course. Even without you telling me I had been thinking of it.' He went to the shops and bought a string of precious stones of all sorts, a thing beyond price – when you say from Venice, you can imagine what it was – and he hung it on the baby's neck; also he bought a dress all of gold, and he took off his ring and gave it to her. Then he kissed the baby and gave the old woman a thousand gold pieces as a present and went off. The princess starting after him arrived at her house before him; she handed the child over to the nurse with money for her trouble and made a present to the women servants not to tell of her. Again she shut herself up in the palace pretending to be full of grief. In two or three days her husband came and asked the servants: 'How is my wife?' said he. 'As I would wish your ill-wishers were, and all for your absence.' He went and found her in a sad state. He said: 'And whom can you blame? You have asked for what has happened to you. Why wouldn't you tell me what are those three measures of salt which you would smear over my face and I be none the wiser? But tell me now.' 'I won't tell you.' 'This cannot be endured. Tell me or I will leave you and take another wife.' 'Well, go and marry again and I will come and give you my blessing.' Then he made up a match with another princess nearby and fixed say next Sunday for the wedding.

All the world went to give them their blessing and the instruments of music were playing. Then his first wife dressed herself in her best and fitted out her three children finely; to the eldest she gave the watch, to the second the walking-stick, and the youngest she adorned with the string of jewels and the ring. The nurse brought them and they all went to join in the blessings at the marriage service. All the women danced in the hall and their eyes were upon the children and the mother because all the room was bright as lightning from the morning star and the sun and the moon, all on the children's foreheads. All said: 'Joy and delight to the mother who bore them!' The prince too left the girl whom he was going to marry and stared at the children; the young bride was full of jealousy. Then the two boys were heard talking to their sister, who was not yet I suppose a year old and was being carried by the nurse, the boys being in front of her: 'Little lady, little lady,' said the boys, 'little Alexandra, listen to the watch, tick tick tick: mother in the room all decked with gold.' When the prince heard this he could endure no longer and right in the middle of the marriage service he left his new bride and ran up to the children. He looked at them and saw the string of jewels and the watch and the ring, and so he recognized them.

His former wife was standing by and he asked whose

children these were. 'Yours and mine; one of them we had at Salonika, the second at Aigina, and the youngest at Venice. The woman whom you met in all those three places, each of them was I, and when I left the place I always got ahead of you. And to think that you should not know your own children! These were the three measures of salt which I was to smear on your face and you be none the wiser.' He lifted up the children and in his delight kissed them all. He took them to his former house and their mother too with them. And so the new bride was left there with the bath grown cold and she half-married.

The Resourceful Wife
(Indian Tribal)

 WOMAN was so mad with love for her lover that she gave him all the rice in the bin, and had to fill it with chaff so that her husband would not notice what she had done. By and by the days for sowing came round, and the woman knew she could no more deceive her husband.

One day her husband went to plough his field which lay near a tank. The next morning his wife went very early to the tank, made herself naked and smeared mud all over her body. She sat down in the grass waiting for him. When he came, she suddenly stood up and in a loud voice cried, 'I am going to take away your two bullocks. But if you need them you can give me the grain in your bin and I will fill it with chaff instead. But one or the other I must have, for I am hungry.'

The man at once said that the Goddess – for so he thought her – should take the grain, for he knew he would be ruined if he lost his bullocks. 'Very well,' said the wife. 'Go back now to your house, and you will find that I have taken your grain, but I have put chaff in its place.' So saying she disappeared into the tank.

The man ran home and found in fact that all the grain was gone and his bin was full of chaff. His wife quickly bathed and changed her clothes, and came home by way of the well where she told the other women the story with great pride.

Aunt Kate's Goomer-Dust
(North American: Ozarks)

ONE time there was a farm boy named Jack and he wanted to marry a rich girl that lived in town, but her pappy was against it. 'Listen, Minnie,' says the old man, 'this feller ain't house-broke, scarcely! He's got cowdung on his boots! He cain't even write his own name!' Minnie didn't turn no answer, but she knowed what Jack could do, and it suited her fine. Book-learning is all right, but it ain't got nothing to do with picking out a good husband. Minnie had done made up her mind to marry Jack, no matter what anybody said.

Jack wanted to run off and get married regardless, but Minnie says no, because she don't figure on being poor all her life. She says we got to make Pappy give us a big farm with a good house on it. Jack he just laughed, and they didn't do no more talking for awhile. Finally he says well, I'll go out to Honey Mountain tomorrow, and see what Aunt Kate thinks.

Aunt Kate knowed a lot of things that most folks never heard tell of. Jack told her what a fix him and Minnie was in, but Aunt Kate says she can't do nothing without silver. So Jack gave her two dollars, and it was all the money he had. Then she fetched him a little box like a pepper-duster, with some yellow powder in it. 'That's goomer-dust,' she says. 'Don't get it on you, and be careful not to get none on Minnie. But you tell her to sprinkle a little on her pappy's pants.'

Late that night Minnie dusted some powder on the old man's britches, where he had hung 'em on the bedpost. Next morning he broke wind right at breakfast, so loud it rattled the pictures on the wall and scared the cat plumb out of the kitchen. The old man thought it must be something he et. But pretty soon he ripped out another one, and it wasn't no time at all till he was making so much noise that Minnie shut the windows for fear the neighbours would hear it. 'Ain't you goin' down to the office, Pappy?' says she. But just then the old man turned loose the awfullest blow-out a body ever heard, and he says, 'No, Minnie. I'm going to bed. And I want you should fetch Doc Holton right away.'

When Doc got there Pappy was feeling better, but pretty white and shaky. 'Soon as I got in bed the wind died down,' he says, 'but it was terrible while it lasted,' and he told Doc all about what happened. Doc examined Pappy a long time and give him some medicine to make him sleep. Minnie follered Doc out on the porch, and Doc says, 'Did you hear them loud noises he keeps talkin' about, like somebody breakin' wind?' Minnie says no, she didn't hear nothing like that. 'Just as I thought,' says Doc. 'He just imagined the whole thing. There ain't nothing wrong with your pappy, only his nerves.'

Pappy slept pretty good, on account of the medicine Doc give him. But next morning, soon as he got up and put his clothes on, he begun to break wind worse than ever. Finally he fired off a blast that sounded like a ten-bore shotgun, so Minnie helped him back in bed and sent for the doctor. Doc give him a shot in the arm this time. 'Keep that man in bed,' says he, 'till I get Doctor Culberson to come over and look at him.' Both of them doctors examined Pappy from head to foot, but they couldn't find nothing wrong with him. They just shuck their heads, and give him some more sleeping medicine.

Things went along like that for three days a-running, and finally Doc says Pappy better stay in bed all the time for awhile, and take medicine every four hours, and maybe he would be happier in a institution. 'Put me in the asylum, just because I got wind on the guts?' yelled Pappy. And with that he begun to raise such a row the doctor had to give him another shot in the arm.

Next morning Pappy set up in bed a-hollering how the doctors are all damn fools, and Minnie says she knows a fellow that can cure him in five minutes. Pretty soon Jack come a-walking in. 'Yes, I can cure you easy,' he says, 'but you got to let me and Minnie get married, and give us one of them big farms.' Pappy wouldn't even speak to Jack. 'If this halfwit cures me,' he says to Minnie, 'you can have any goddam thing you want.' Minnie walked over and stirred up the coals in the fireplace. Soon as it got to burning good, Jack took the tongs and throwed Pappy's britches right in the fire.

When Pappy seen them pants a-burning he was plumb speechless. He just laid there weak as a cat, and Jack marched out like a regular doctor. But after while the old man got up and put on his Sunday clothes. He never broke wind, neither.

Minnie fixed him a fine breakfast, and he et every bite of it and never even belched. Then he walked round the house three times, without feeling no gas on his innards. 'Well, by God,' he says, 'I believe to my soul that damn fool did cure me!' On the way down town he stopped in to see Doc Holton. 'I finally got well, without no thanks to you,' says he. 'If you had your way, I'd be in the crazy-house this minute!'

Soon as he got Doc told, Pappy went over to the bank and deeded his best farm to Minnie. He give her some money to buy horses and cows and machinery. And so her and Jack got married, and they done all right. Some folks say they lived happy ever after.

The Battle of the Birds
(Scots Gaelic)

HERE was once a time when every creature and bird was gathering to battle. The son of the king of Tethertown said, that he would go to see the battle, and that he would bring sure word home to his father the king, who would be king of the creatures this year. The battle was over before he arrived all but one fight, between a great black raven and a snake, and it seemed as if the snake would get the victory over the raven. When the king's son saw this, he helped the raven, and with one blow takes the head off the snake. When the raven had taken breath, and saw that the snake was dead, he said, 'For thy kindness to me this day, I will give thee a sight. Come up now on the root of my two wings.' The king's son mounted upon the raven, and, before he stopped, he took him over seven Bens, and seven Glens, and seven Mountain Moors.

'Now,' said the raven, 'seest thou that house yonder? Go now to it. It is a sister of mine that makes her dwelling in it; and I will go bail that thou art welcome. And if she asks thee, Wert thou at the battle of the birds? say thou that thou wert. And if she asks, Didst thou see my likeness? say that thou sawest it. But be sure that thou meetest me tomorrow morning here, in this place.' The king's son got good and right good treatment this night. Meat of each meat, drink of each drink, warm water to his feet, and a soft bed for his limbs.

On the next day the raven gave him the same sight over seven Bens, and seven Glens, and seven Mountain moors. They saw a bothy far off, but, though far off, they were soon there. He got good treatment this night, as before – plenty of meat and drink, and warm water to his feet, and a soft bed to his limbs – and on the next day it was the same thing.

On the third morning, instead of seeing the raven as at the other times, who should meet him but the handsomest lad he ever saw, with a bundle in his hand. The king's son asked this lad if he had seen a big black raven. Said the lad to him, 'Thou wilt never see the raven again, for I am that raven. I was put under spells; it was meeting thee that loosed me, and for that thou art getting this bundle. Now,' said the lad, 'thou wilt turn back on the self-same steps, and thou wilt lie a night in each house, as thou wert before; but thy lot is not to lose the bundle which I gave thee, till thou art in the place where thou wouldst most wish to dwell.'

The king's son turned his back to the lad, and his face to his father's house; and he got lodging from the raven's sisters, just as he got it when going forward. When he was nearing his father's house he was going through a close wood. It seemed to him that the bundle was growing heavy, and he thought he would look what was in it.

When he loosed the bundle, it was not without astonishing himself. In a twinkling he sees the very grandest place he ever saw. A great castle, and an orchard about the castle, in which was every kind of fruit and herb. He stood full of wonder and regret for having loosed the bundle – it was not in his power to put it back again – and he would have wished this pretty place to be in the pretty little green hollow that was opposite his father's house; but, at one glance, he sees a great giant coming towards him.

'Bad's the place where thou hast built thy house, king's son,' says the giant. 'Yes, but it is not here I would wish it to be, though it happened to be here by mishap,' says the king's son. 'What's the reward thou wouldst give me for putting it back in the bundle as it was before?' 'What's the reward thou wouldst ask?' says the king's son. 'If thou wilt give me the first son thou hast when he is seven years of age,' says the giant. 'Thou wilt get that if I have a son,' said the king's son.

In a twinkling the giant put each garden, and orchard, and castle in the bundle as they were before. 'Now,' says the giant, 'take thou thine own road, and I will take my road; but mind thy promise, and though thou shouldst forget, I will remember.'

The king's son took to the road, and at the end of a few days he reached the place he was fondest of. He loosed the bundle, and the same place was just as it was before. And when he opened the castle-door he sees the handsomest maiden he ever cast eye upon. 'Advance, king's son,' said the pretty maid; 'everything is in order for thee, if thou wilt marry me this very night.' 'It's I am the man that is willing,' said the king's son. And on the same night they married.

But at the end of a day and seven years, what great man is seen coming to the castle but the giant. The king's son minded his promise to the giant, and till now he had not told his promise to the queen. 'Leave thou the matter between me and the giant,' says the queen.

'Turn out thy son,' says the giant; 'mind your promise.' 'Thou wilt get that,' says the king, 'when his mother puts him in order for his journey.' The queen arrayed the cook's son, and she gave him to the giant by the hand. The giant went away with him; but he had not gone far when he put a rod in the hand of the little laddie. The giant asked him – 'If thy father had that rod what would he do with it?' 'If father had that rod he would beat the dogs and the cats, if they would be going near the king's meat,' said the little laddie. 'Thou'rt the cook's son,' said the giant. He catches him by the two small ankles and knocks him – 'Sgleog' – against the stone that was beside him. The giant turned back to the castle in rage and madness, and he said that if they did not turn out the king's son to him, the highest stone in the castle would be the lowest. Said the queen to the king, 'we'll try it yet; the butler's son is of the same age as our son.' She arrayed the butler's son, and she gives him to the giant by the hand. The giant had not gone far when he put the rod in his hand. 'If thy father had that rod,' says the giant, 'what would he do with it?' 'He would beat the dogs and the cats when they would be coming near the king's bottles and glasses.' 'Thou art the son of the butler,' says the giant, and dashed his brains out too. The giant returned in very great rage and anger. The earth shook under the soles of his feet, and the castle shook and all that was in it. 'OUT HERE THY SON,' says the giant, 'or in a twinkling the stone that is highest in the dwelling will be the lowest.' So needs must they had to give the king's son to the giant.

The giant took him to his own house, and he reared him as his own son. On a day of days when the giant was from home, the lad heard the sweetest music he ever heard in a room at the top of the giant's house. At a glance he saw the finest face he had ever seen. She beckoned to him to come a bit nearer to her, and she told him to go this time, but to be sure to be at the same place about that dead midnight.

And as he promised he did. The giant's daughter was at his side in a twinkling, and she said, 'Tomorrow thou wilt get the choice of my two sisters to marry; but say thou that thou wilt not take either, but me. My father wants me to marry the son of the king of the Green City, but I don't like him.' On the morrow the giant took out his three daughters, and he said, 'Now son of the king of Tethertown, thou hast not lost by living with me so long. Thou wilt get to wife one of the two eldest of my daughters, and with her leave to go home with her the day after the wedding.' 'If thou wilt give me this pretty little one,' says the king's son, 'I will take thee at thy word.'

The giant's wrath kindled, and he said, 'Before thou gett'st her thou must do the three things that I ask thee to do.' 'Say on,' says the king's son. The giant took him to the byre. 'Now,' says the giant, 'the dung of a hundred cattle is here, and it has not been cleansed for seven years. I am going from home today, and if this byre is not cleaned before night comes, so clean that a golden apple will run from end to end of it, not only thou shalt not get my daughter, but 'tis a drink of thy blood that will quench my thirst this night.' He begins cleaning the byre, but it was just as well to keep baling the great ocean. After midday, when sweat was blinding him, the giant's young daughter came where he was, and she said to him, 'Thou art being punished, king's son.' 'I am that,' says the king's son. 'Come over,' says she, 'and lay down thy weariness.' 'I will do that,' says he, 'there is but death awaiting me, at any rate.' He sat down near her. He was so tired that he fell asleep beside her. When he awoke, the giant's daughter was not to be seen, but the byre was so well cleaned that a golden apple would run from end to end of it. In comes the giant, and he said, 'Thou hast cleaned the byre, king's son?' 'I have cleaned it,' says he. 'Somebody cleaned it,' says the giant. 'Thou didst not clean it, at all events,' said the king's son. 'Yes, yes!' says the giant, 'since thou wert so active today, thou wilt get to this time tomorrow to thatch this byre with birds' down – birds with no two feathers of one colour.' The king's son was on foot before the sun; he caught up his bow and his quiver of arrows to kill the birds. He took to the moors, but if he did, the birds were not so easy to take. He was running after them till the sweat was blinding him. About midday who should come but the giant's daughter. 'Thou art exhausting thyself, king's son,' says she. 'I am,' said he. 'There fell but these two blackbirds, and both of one colour.' 'Come over and lay down thy weariness on this pretty hillock,' says the giant's daughter. 'It's I am willing,' said he. He thought she would aid him this time, too, and he sat down near her, and he was not long there till he fell asleep.

When he awoke, the giant's daughter was gone. He thought he would go back to the house, and he sees the byre thatched with the feathers. When the giant came home, he said, 'Thou hast thatched the byre, king's son?' 'I thatched it,' says he. 'Somebody thatched it,' says the giant. 'Thou didst not thatch it,' says the king's son. 'Yes, yes!' says the giant. 'Now,' says the giant, 'there is a fir-tree beside that loch down there, and there is a magpie's nest in its top. The eggs thou wilt find in the nest. I must have them for my first meal. Not one must be burst or broken, and there are five in the nest.' Early in the morning the king's son went where the tree was, and that tree was not hard to hit upon. Its match was not in the whole wood. From the foot to the first branch was five hundred feet. The king's son was going all round the tree. She came who was always bringing help to him. 'Thou art losing the skin of thy hands and feet.' 'Ach! I am,' says he. 'I am no sooner up than down.' 'This is no time for stopping,' says the giant's daughter. She thrust finger after finger into the tree, till she made a ladder for the king's son to go up to the magpie's nest. When he was at the nest, she said, 'Make haste now with the eggs, for my father's breath is burning my back.' In his hurry she left her little finger in the top of the tree. 'Now,' says she, 'thou wilt go home with the eggs quickly, and thou wilt get me to marry tonight if thou canst know me. I and my two sisters will be arrayed in the same garments, and made like each other, but look at me when my father says, go to thy wife, king's son; and thou wilt see a hand without a little finger.' He gave the eggs to the giant. 'Yes, yes!' says the giant, 'be making ready for thy marriage.'

Then indeed there was a wedding, and it *was* a wedding! Giants and gentlemen, and the son of the king of the Green City was in the midst of them. They were married, and the dancing began, and that was a dance? The giant's house was shaking from top to bottom. But bed time came, and the giant said, 'It is time for thee to go to rest, son of the king of Tethertown; take thy bride with thee from amidst those.'

She put out the hand off which the little finger was, and he caught her by the hand.

'Thou hast aimed well this time too; but there is no knowing but we may meet thee another way,' said the giant.

But to rest they went. 'Now,' says she, 'sleep not, or else thou diest. We must fly quick, quick, or for certain my father will kill thee.'

Out they went, and on the blue gray filly in the stable they mounted. 'Stop a while,' says she, 'and I will play a trick to the old hero.' She jumped in, and cut an apple into nine shares, and she put two shares at the head of the bed, and two shares at the foot of the bed, and two shares at the door of the kitchen, and two shares at the big door, and one outside the house.

The giant awoke and called, 'Are you asleep?' 'We are not yet,' said the apple that was at the head of the bed. At the end of a while he called again. 'We are not yet,' said the apple that was at the foot of the bed. A while after this he called again. 'We are not yet,' said the apple at the kitchen door. The giant called again. The apple that was at the big door answered. 'You are now going far from me,' says the giant. 'We are not yet,' says the apple that was outside the house. 'You are flying,' says the giant. The giant jumped on his feet, and to the bed he went, but it was cold – empty.

'My own daughter's tricks are trying me,' said the giant. 'Here's after them,' says he.

In the mouth of day, the giant's daughter said that her father's breath was burning her back. 'Put thy hand, quick,' said she, 'in the ear of the gray filly, and whatever thou findest in it, throw it behind thee.' 'There is a twig of sloe tree,' said he. 'Throw it behind thee,' said she.

No sooner did he that, than there were twenty miles of black thorn wood, so thick that scarce a weasel could go through it. The giant came headlong, and there he is fleecing his head and neck in the thorns.

'My own daughter's tricks are here as before,' said the giant; 'but if I had my own big axe and wood knife here, I would not be long making a way through this.' He went home for the big axe and the wood knife, and sure he was not long on his journey, and he was the boy behind the big axe. He was not long making a way through the black thorn. 'I will leave the axe and the wood knife here till I return,' says he. 'If thou leave them,' said a hoodie that was in a tree, 'we will steal them.'

'You will do that same,' says the giant, 'but I will get them home.' He returned and left them at the house. At the heat of day the giant's daughter felt her father's breath burning her back.

'Put thy finger in the filly's ear, and throw behind thee whatever thou findest in it.' He got a splinter of gray stone, and in a twinkling there were twenty miles, by breadth and height, of great gray rock behind them. The giant came full pelt, but past the rock he could not go.

'The tricks of my own daughter are the hardest things that ever met me,' says the giant; 'but if I had my lever and my mighty mattock, I would not be long making my way through this rock also.' There was no help for it, but to turn the chase for them; and he was the boy to split the stones. He was not long making a road through the rock. 'I will leave the tools here, and I will return no more.' 'If thou leave them,' says the hoodie, 'we will steal them.' 'Do that if thou wilt; there is no time to go back.' At the time of breaking the watch, the giant's daughter said that she was feeling her father's breath burning her back. 'Look in the filly's ear, king's son, or else we are lost.' He did so, and it was a bladder of water that was in her ear this time. He threw it behind him and there was a fresh-water loch, twenty miles in length and breadth, behind them.

The giant came on, but with the speed he had on him, he was in the middle of the loch, and he went under, and he rose no more.

On the next day the young companions were come in sight of his father's house. 'Now,' said she, 'my father is drowned, and he won't trouble us any more; but before we go further,' says she, 'go thou to thy father's house, and tell that thou hast the like of me; but this is thy lot, let neither man nor creature kiss thee, for if thou dost thou wilt not remember that thou hast ever seen me.' Everyone he met was giving him welcome and luck, and he charged his father and mother not to kiss him; but as mishap was to be, an old greyhound was in and she knew him, and jumped up to his mouth, and after that he did not remember the giant's daughter.

She was sitting at the well's side as he left her, but the king's son was not coming. In the mouth of night she climbed up into a tree of oak that was beside the well, and she lay in the fork of the tree all that night. A shoemaker had a house near the well, and about midday on the morrow, the shoemaker asked his wife to go for a drink for him out of the well. When the shoemaker's wife reached the well, and when she saw the shadow of her that was in the tree, thinking of it that it was her own shadow – and she never thought till now that she was so handsome – she gave a cast to the dish that was in her hand, and it was broken on the ground, and she took herself to the house without vessel or water.

'Where is the water, wife?' said the shoemaker. 'Thou shambling, contemptible old carle, without grace, I have stayed too long thy water and wood slave.' 'I am thinking, wife, that thou has turned crazy. Go thou, daughter, quickly, and fetch a drink for thy father.' His daughter went, and in the same way so it happened to her. She never thought till now that she was so loveable, and she took herself home. 'Up with the drink,' said her father. 'Thou home-spun shoe carle, dost thou think that I am fit to be thy slave.' The poor shoemaker thought that they had taken a turn in their understandings, and he went himself to the well. He saw the shadow of the maiden in the well, and he looked up to the tree, and he sees the finest woman he ever saw. 'Thy seat is wavering, but thy face is fair,' said the shoemaker. 'Come down, for there is need of thee for a short while at my house.' The shoemaker understood that this was the shadow that had driven his people mad. The shoemaker took her to his house, and he said that he had but a poor bothy, but that she should get a share of all that was in it. At the end of a day or two came a leash of gentlemen lads to the shoemaker's house for shoes to be made them, for the king had come home, and he was going to marry. The lads saw the giant's daughter, and they never saw one so pretty as she. ''Tis thou hast the pretty daughter, here,' said the lads to the shoemaker. 'She is pretty, indeed,' says the shoemaker, 'but she is no daughter of mine.' 'St Nail!' said one of them, 'I would give a hundred pounds to marry her.' The two others said the very same. The poor shoemaker said that he had nothing to do with her. 'But,' said they, 'ask her tonight, and send us word tomorrow.' When the gentles went away, she asked the shoemaker – 'What's that they were saying about me?' The shoemaker told her. 'Go thou after them,' said she; 'I will marry one of them, and let him bring his purse with him.' The youth returned, and he gave the shoemaker a hundred pounds for tocher. They went to rest, and when she had laid down, she asked the lad for a drink of water from a tumbler that was on the board on the further side of the chamber. He went; but out of that he could not come, as he held the vessel of water the length of the night. 'Thou lad,' said she, 'why wilt thou not lie down?' but out of that he could not drag till the bright morrow's day was. The shoemaker came to the door of the chamber, and she asked him to take away that lubberly boy. This wooer went and betook himself to his home, but he did not tell the other two how it happened to him. Next came the second chap, and in the same way, when she had gone to rest – 'Look,' she said, 'if the latch is on the door.' The latch laid hold of his hands, and out of that he could not come the length of the night, and out of that he did not come till the morrow's day was bright. He went, under shame and disgrace. No matter, he did not tell the other chap how it had happened, and on the third night he came. As it happened to the two others, so it happened to him. One foot stuck to the floor; he could neither come nor go, but so he was the length of the night. On the morrow, he took his soles out of that, and he was not seen looking behind him. 'Now,' said the girl to the shoemaker, 'thine is the sporran of gold; I have no need of it. It will better thee, and I am no worse for thy kindness to me.' The shoemaker had the shoes ready, and on that very day the king was to be married. The shoemaker was going to the castle with the shoes of the young people, and the girl said to the shoemaker, 'I would like to get a sight of the king's son before he marries.' 'Come with me,' says the shoemaker, 'I am well acquainted with the servants at the caastle, and thou shalt get a sight of the king's son and all the company.' And when the gentles saw the pretty woman that was here they took her to the wedding-room, and they filled for her a glass of wine. When she was going to drink what is in it, a flame went up out of the glass, and a golden pigeon and a silver pigeon sprung out of it. They were flying about when three grains of barley fell on the floor. The silver pigeon sprang, and he eats that. Said the golden pigeon to him, 'If thou hadst mind when I cleared the byre, thou wouldst not eat that without giving me a share.' Again fell three other grains of barley, and the silver pigeon sprang, and he eats that, as before. 'If thou hadst mind when I thatched the byre, thou wouldst not eat that without

giving me my share,' says the golden pigeon. Three other grains fell, and the silver pigeon sprang, and he eats that. 'If thou hadst mind when I harried the magpie's nest, thou wouldst not eat that without giving me my share,' says the golden pigeon; 'I lost my little finger bringing it down, and I want it still.' The king's son minded, and he knew who it was he had got. He sprang where she was, and kissed her from hand to mouth. And when the priest came they married a second time. And there I left them.

Parsley-girl
(Italian)

NCE upon a time, when it was winter, a woman said: 'I've a real craving for some parsley. There's lots of parsley in the Holy Sisters' garden. I'll go and get some.'

The first time, she took one sprig of parsley and she didn't spy a soul. The second time, she took two sprigs and nobody spotted her. But the third time, just as she was picking herself a whole bunch, a hand fell on her shoulder and there was a great big nun.

'What are you doing?' asked the nun.

'Picking some parsley. I've a real craving for some parsley because I'm going to have a baby.'

'Take all the parsley you want, but when you've had your baby you must call him Parsley-boy if he's a boy or Parsley-girl if she's a girl, and when the baby grows up you must give it to us. That is the price of your parsley.'

Although she laughed it off at the time, when the woman's little girl was born she called her Parsley-girl. Sometimes Parsley-girl went to play beside the convent wall. One day one of the nuns called out to her: 'Parsley-girl! Ask your mother when she's going to give it to us.'

'All right,' said Parsley-girl.

She went home and said to her mother: 'The nun was asking me, when are you going to give it to them?'

Her mother laughed and said: 'Tell them to come and take it themselves.'

When Parsley-girl went back to play bside the convent wall, the nun said: 'Parsley-girl, did you ask your mother?'

'Yes,' said Parsley-girl. 'And she said you must take it yourself.'

So the nun stretched out her long arm and picked Parsley-girl up by the scruff.

'Not me!'

'Yes, you!'

And the nun told Parsley-girl about the parsley and the promise. Parsley-girl burst out crying. 'Naughty Mummy! She never said a thing!' When they went inside the convent, the nun said: 'Put a big pot of water on the fire, Parsley-girl, and when it comes to the boil, in you go! You'll make us a nice little supper.'

Parsley-girl burst out crying all over again. Up popped a little old man out of a casserole.

'Why are you crying, Parsley-girl?'

'I'm crying because the nuns are going to eat me for supper.'

'They're not nuns, they're mean old witches. Put the pot of water on the fire and stop crying.'

'Why should I stop crying? The nuns are going to eat me.'

'Oh, no, they're not. Take this magic wand. When they come to see if the pot is boiling, give them a little tap with it and they'll all jump in like frogs into a pond.'

Although she thought: 'The little old man only said that to stop me crying,' she felt a bit better. When the pot boiled, she called out: 'Sisters! Sisters! The pot is boiling!'

They all came to see, crying: 'Oh, what a lovely supper we're going to have!' Parsley-girl was scared stiff so she picked up the magic wand and hit them all on their big, fat bottoms and, yes! they all jumped, splash, into the pot.

'Take the pot off the fire, Parsley-girl! We were only joking!'

'Oh, no, you weren't! You're not nuns at all, you're witches! You stay there until you're good and done, but don't think I'm going to do you the honour of eating you, you're much too old and tough. I'll look on the stove to see what else you've got.'

She went to the stove and there, in a casserole, she found a fine young man.

'Hello, fine young man. I'm hungry.'

'Don't make fun of me. I'm not young at all, I'm old and ugly.'

'Oh, no, you're not.' And she showed him his fine reflection in the washing-up bowl. 'But as for me, I'm just a little girl, worse luck.'

'You're not a little girl at all,' he said. 'I'll show you.'

And he measured her up against the wall to show her how tall she'd grown. Then Parsley-girl said: 'I'm going to make you a proposition.'

'Whatever can it be?'

'Let's get married.'

'But you're so pretty and I'm so plain.'

'I think you're very good-looking, personally.'

'All right. If you want to get married, I'll marry you.'

'Then let's have some supper and go to bed. We can find a priest tomorrow.'

'But don't let's stay in the convent, because the nuns put the devil in the place where Jesus ought to be.'

They went to look for the devil but he had turned back into Jesus because of the magic wand. Parsley-girl said: 'You do realize I've killed all the witches, don't you?'

They looked inside the pot. It was full of corpses.

'Let's dig a hole and bury them and then let's get out of here.'

They had supper, then they went to bed. They went to the priest in the morning and got married.

Clever Gretel
(German)

 HERE was once a cook named Gretel, who wore shoes with red heels, and when she went out in them, she whirled this way and that way and was as happy as a lark. 'You really are quite pretty!' she would say to herself. And when she returned home, she would drink some wine out of sheer delight. Since the wine would whet her appetite, she would take the best things she was cooking and taste them until she was content. Then she would say, 'The cook must know what the food tastes like!'

One day her master happened to say to her, 'Gretel, tonight I'm having a guest for dinner. Prepare two chickens for me and make them as tasty as possible.'

'I'll take care of it, sir,' Gretel responded. So she killed two chickens, scalded them, plucked them, stuck them on a spit, and toward evening placed them over a fire to roast. The chickens began to turn brown and were almost ready, but the guest did not make his appearance. So Gretel called to her master, 'If the guest doesn't come soon, I'll have to take the chickens off the fire. It would be a great shame if they weren't eaten now, while they're still at their juiciest.'

'Then I'll run and fetch the guest myself,' said the master.

When the master had left the house, Gretel laid the spit with the chickens to one side and thought, if I keep standing by the fire, I'll just sweat and get thirsty. Who knows when they'll come? Meanwhile, I'll hop down into the cellar and take a drink.

She ran downstairs, filled a jug with wine, and said, 'May God bless it for you, Gretel!' and she took a healthy swig. 'The wine flows nicely,' she continued talking, 'and it's not good to interrupt the flow.' So she took another long swig. Then she went upstairs and placed the chickens back over the fire, basted them with butter, and merrily turned the spit. Since the roast chickens smelled so good, Gretel thought, perhaps something's missing. I'd better taste them to see how they are. She touched one of them with her finger and said, 'Goodness!

The chickens are really good! It's a crying shame not to eat them all at once!' She ran to the window to see if her master was on his way with the guest, but when she saw no one coming, she returned to the chickens and thought. That one wing is burning. I'd better eat it up.

So she cut if off, ate it, and enjoyed it. When she had finished, she thought, I'd better eat the other wing or else my master will notice that something's missing. After she had consumed the two wings, she returned to the window, looked for her master, but was unable to see him. Who knows, it suddenly occurred to her, perhaps they've decided not to come and have stopped somewhere along the way. Then she said to herself, 'Hey, Gretel, cheer up! You've already taken a nice chunk. Have another drink and eat it all up! When it's gone, there'll be no reason for you to feel guilty. Why should God's good gifts go to waste?'

Once again she ran down into the cellar, took a good honest drink, and then went back to eat up the chicken with relish. When the one chicken had been eaten and her master still had not returned. Gretel looked at the other bird and said, 'Where one is, the other should be too. The two of them belong together: whatever's right for one is right for the other. I think if I have another drink, it won't do me any harm.' Therefore she took another healthy swig and let the second chicken run to join the other.

Just as she was in the midst of enjoying her meal, her master came back and called, 'Hurry, Gretel, the guest will soon be here!'

'Yes, sir, I'll get everything ready,' answered Gretel.

Meanwhile, the master checked to see if the table was properly set and took out the large knife with which he wanted to carve the chickens and began sharpening it on the steps in the hallway. As he was doing that the guest came and knocked nicely and politely at the door. Gretel ran and looked to see who was there, and when she saw the guest, she put her finger to her lips and whispered, 'Shhh, be quiet! Get out of here as quick as you can! If my master catches you, you'll be done for. It's true he invited you to dinner, but he really wants to cut off both your ears. Listen to him sharpening his knife!'

The guest heard the sharpening and hurried back down the steps as fast as he could. Gretel wasted no time and ran screaming to her master. 'What kind of guest did you invite!' she cried.

'Goodness gracious, Gretel! Why do you ask? What do you mean?'

'Well,' she said, 'he snatched both chickens just as I was about to bring them to the table, and he's run away with them!'

'That's not at all a nice way to behave!' said her master, and he was disappointed by the loss of the fine chickens. 'At least he could have left me one of them so I'd have something to eat.'

He then shouted after the guest to stop running, but the guest pretended not to hear. So the master ran after him, with the knife still in his hand, and screamed, 'Just one, just one!' merely meaning that the guest should at least leave him one of the chickens and not take both. But the guest thought that his host was after just one of his ears, and to make sure that he would reach home safely with both his ears, he ran as if someone had lit a fire under his feet.

The Furburger
(North American)

LADY went into a pet shop to buy a rare exotic animal, one that no one else had. When she told the storekeeper what she wanted, he proceeded to show her everything that he had in the line of rare and exotic animals. After much distress, the lady hadn't found anything quite unusual enough to suit her taste. She made one last plea to the storekeeper. Out of desperation, the storekeeper said, 'I do have one animal left that you haven't seen yet; however, I am somewhat reluctant to show it to you.' 'Oh, please do,' cried the lady.

So the storekeeper went back into the backroom of the store, and after a little bit returned with a cage. Putting the cage on the counter, the storekeeper proceeded to open the cage and take out the animal and set it on the counter. The lady looked, but all she saw was a piece of fur, not a head or a tail, no eyes, nothing. 'What in the world is that thing?' said the lady. 'It's a furburger,' said the storekeeper very nonchalantly. 'But what does it do?' asked the lady. 'Watch very carefully, madam,' said the storekeeper. Then the storekeeper looked down at the furburger and said, 'Furburger, the wall!' And immediately the animal flew over and hit the wall like a ton of bricks, completely destroying the wall and leaving nothing but dust. Then, just as swiftly as before, the furburger flew back and sat on the counter again. Then the storekeeper said, 'Furburger, the door!' And immediately the animal flew over and hit the door like a ton of bricks, completely demolishing the entire door and doorframe. Then, just as quickly as before, the furburger flew back and sat on the counter.

'I'll take it,' said the lady. 'All right, if you really want it,' said the storekeeper. And so, as the lady was leaving the store with her furburger, the storekeeper said, 'Pardon me, ma'am, but what are you going to do with your furburger?' And the lady looked back and said, 'Well, I've been having trouble with my husband lately, and so tonight when I get home, I'm going to put the furburger in the middle of the kitchen floor. And when my husband comes home from work, he will come in the door and look down and say to me, "What in the hell is that?" and I'm going to say, "Why, dear, that's a furburger." And my husband will look at me and say, "Furburger, my ass!"'

Part Three

SILLIES

A Pottle o' Brains
(English)

NCE in these parts, and not so long gone neither, there was a fool that wanted to buy a pottle o' brains, for he was ever getting into scrapes through his foolishness, and being laughed at by everyone. Folk told him that he could get everything he liked from the wise woman that lived on the top o' the hill, and dealt in potions and herbs and spells and things, and could tell thee all as'd come to thee or thy folk. So he told his mother, and asked her if he could seek the wise woman and buy a pottle o' brains.

'That ye should,' says she: 'thou'st sore need o' them, my son; and if I should die, who'd take care o' a poor fool such's thou, no more fit to look after thyself than an unborn baby? but mind thy manners, and speak her pretty, my lad; for they wise folk are gey and light mispleased.'

So off he went after his tea, and there she was, sitting by the fire, and stirring a big pot.

'Good e'en, missis,' says he, 'it's a fine night.'

'Aye,' says she, and went on stirring.

'It'll maybe rain,' says he, and fidgeted from one foot to t'other.

'Maybe,' says she.

'And m'appen it won't,' says he, and looked out o' the window.

'M'appen,' says she.

And he scratched his head and twisted his hat.

'Well,' says he, 'I can't mind nothing else about the weather, but let me see; the crops are getting on fine.'

'Fine,' says she.

'And – and – the beasts is fattening,' says he.

'They are,' says she.

'And – and – says he, and comes to a stop – 'I reckon we'll tackle business now, having done the polite like. Have you any brains for to sell?'

'That depends,' says she, 'if thou wants king's brains, or soldier's brains, or schoolmaster's brains, I dinna keep 'em.'

'Hout no,' says he, 'jist ordinary brains – fit for any fool – same as everyone has about here; something clean common-like.'

'Aye so,' says the wise woman, 'I might manage that, if so be thou'lt help thyself.'

'How's that for, missis?' says he.

'Jest so,' says she, looking in the pot; 'bring me the heart of the thing thou likest best of all, and I'll tell thee where to get thy pottle o' brains.'

'But,' says he, scratching his head, 'how can I do that?'

'That's no for me to say,' says she, 'find out for thyself, my lad! if thou doesn't want to be a fool all thy days. But thou'll have to read me a riddle so as I can see thou'st brought the right thing, and if thy brains is about thee. And I've something else to see to,' says she, 'so gode'en to thee,' and she carried the pot away with her into the back place.

So off went the fool to his mother, and told her what the wise woman said.

'And I reckon I'll have to kill that pig,' says he, 'for I like fat bacon better than anything.'

'Then do it, my lad,' said his mother, 'for certain 'twill be a strange and good thing fur thee, if thou canst buy a pottle o' brains, and be able to look after thy own self.'

So he killed his pig, and next day off he went to the wise woman's cottage, and there she sat, reading in a great book.

'Gode'en, missis,' says he, 'I've brought thee the heart o' the thing I like best of all; and I put it hapt in paper on the table.'

'Aye so?' says she, and looked at him through her spectacles. 'Tell me this then, what runs without feet?'

He scratched his head, and thought, and thought, but he couldn't tell.

'Go thy ways,' says she, 'thou'st not fetched me the right thing yet. I've no brains for thee today.' And she clapt the book together, and turned her back.

So off the fool went to tell his mother.

But as he got nigh the house, out came folk running to tell him that his mother was dying.

And when he got in, his mother only looked at him and smiled as if to say she could leave him with a quiet mind since he had got brains enough now to look after himself – and then she died.

So down he sat and the more he thought about it the badder he felt. He minded how she'd nursed him when he was a tiddy brat, and helped him with his lessons, and cooked his dinners, and mended his clouts, and bore with his foolishness; and he felt sorrier and sorrier, while he began to sob and greet.

'Oh, Mother, Mother!' says he, 'who'll take care of me now! Thou shouldn't have left me alone, for I liked thee better than everything!'

And as he said that, he thought of the words of the wise woman. 'Hi, yi!' says he, 'must I take Mother's heart to her?'

'No! I can't do that,' says he. 'What'll I do! What'll I do to get that pottle of brains, now I'm alone in the world?' So he thought and thought and thought, and next day he went and borrowed a sack, and bundled his mother in, and carried it on his shoulder up to the wise woman's cottage.

'Gode'en, missis,' says he, 'I reckon I've fetched thee the right thing this time, surely,' and he plumped the sack down kerflap! in the doorsill.

'Maybe,' says the wise woman, 'but read me this, now, what's yellow and shining but isn't gold?'

And he scratched his head, and thought, and thought, but he couldn't tell.

'Thou'st not hit the right thing, my lad,' says she. 'I doubt thou'rt a bigger fool than I thought!' and shut the door in his face.

'See there!' says he, and set down by the road side and greets.

'I've lost the only two things as I cared for, and what else can I find to buy a pottle of brains with!' and he fair howled, till the tears ran down into his mouth. And up came a lass that lived near at hand, and looked at him.

'What's up with thee, fool?' says she.

'Oo, I've killed my pig, and lost my mother, and I'm nobbut a fool myself,' says he, sobbing.

'That's bad,' says she; 'and haven't thee anybody to look after thee?'

'No,' says he, 'and I canna buy my pottle of brains, for there's nothing I like best left!'

'What art talking about!' says she.

And down she sets by him, and he told her all about the wise woman and the pig, and his mother and the riddles, and that

he was alone in the world.

'Well,' says she, 'I wouldn't mind looking after thee myself.'

'Could thee do it?' says he.

'Ou, ay!' says she; 'folk says as fools make good husbands, and I reckon I'll have thee, if thou'rt willing.'

'Can'st cook?' says he.

'Ay, I can,' says she.

'And scrub?' says he.

'Surely,' says she.

'And mend my clouts?' says he.

'I can that,' says she.

'I reckon thou'lt do then as well as anybody,' says he; 'but what'll I do about this wise woman?'

'Oh, wait a bit,' says she, 'something may turn up, and it'll not matter if thou'rt a fool, so long's thou'st got me to look after thee.'

'That's true,' says he, and off they went and got married. And she kept his house so clean and neat, and cooked his dinner so fine, that one night he says to her: 'Lass, I'm thinking I like thee best of everything after all.'

'That's good hearing,' says she, 'and what then?'

'Have I got to kill thee, dost think, and take thy heart up to the wise woman for that pottle o' brains?'

'Law, no!' says she, looking skeered, 'I winna have that. But see here; thou didn't cut out thy mother's heart, did thou?'

'No; but if I had, maybe I'd have got my pottle o' brains,' says he.

'Not a bit of it,' says she; 'just thou take me as I be, heart and all, and I'll wager I'll help thee read the riddles.'

'Can thee so?' says he, doubtful like; 'I reckon they're too hard for women folk.'

'Well,' says she, 'let's see now. Tell me the first.'

'What runs without feet?' says he.

'Why, water!' says she.

'It do,' says he, and scratched his head.

'And what's yellow and shining but isn't gold?'

'Why, the sun!' says she.

'Faith, it be!' says he. 'Come, we'll go up to the wise woman at once,' and off they went. And as they came up the pad, she was sitting at the door, twining straws.

'Gode'en, missis,' says he.

'Gode'en, fool,' says she.

'I reckon I've fetched thee the right thing at last,' says he.

The wise woman looked at them both, and wiped her spectacles.

'Canst tell me what that is as has first no legs, and then two legs, and ends with four legs?'

And the fool scratched his head, and thought and thought, but he couldn't tell.

And the lass whispered in his ear:

'It's a tadpole.'

'M'appen,' says he then, 'it may be a tadpole, missis.'

The wise woman nodded her head.

'That's right,' says she, 'and thou'st got thy pottle o' brains already.'

'Where be they?' says he, looking about and feeling in his pockets.

'In thy wife's head,' says she. 'The only cure for a fool is a good wife to look after him, and that thou'st got, so gode'en to thee!' And with that she nodded to them, and up and into the house.

So they went home together, and he never wanted to buy a pottle o' brains again, for his wife had enough for both.

Young Man in the Morning
(African American)

AN old lady lived in the country was anxious to get married, but was too old, like me. And there was a young man come through the yard mornings, who she wanted to marry. So he told her, 'If you wet your sheet and wrap it around you, and stay on the roof all night tonight, I'll marry you in the morning.'

And she was fool enough to try it. She wrapped the wet sheet around her and went upon the roof, and sat there and shivered. The young man stayed in the house to make sure she stayed on the roof. Through the night he could hear her shivering and saying:

Oooooh, oooooh,
Young man in the morning.

She meant she'd just make it till morning, if she didn't freeze. (She sure was dumb.) Every time she said it she'd get weaker. So about three o'clock in the morning the sheet was ice, and the young man heard her rolling off the roof of the house and hit the ground in the yard, froze stiff. And when she landed he says, 'What a blessing. No old woman for me.'

Now I Should Laugh,
If I Were Not Dead
(Icelandic)

NCE two married women had a dispute about which of their husbands was the biggest fool. At last they agreed to try if they were as foolish as they seemed to be. One of the women then played this trick. When her husband came home from his work, she took a spinning-wheel and carders, and sitting down, began to card and spin, but neither the farmer nor anyone else saw any wool in her hands. Her husband, observing this, asked if she was mad to scrape the teazles together and spin the wheel, without having the wool, and prayed her to tell what this meant. She said it was scarcely to be expected that he should see what she was doing, for it was a kind of linen too fine to be seen with the eye. Of this she was going to make him clothes. He thought this a very good explanation, and wondered much at how clever his good wife was, and was not a little glad in looking forward to the joy and pride he would feel in having on these marvellous clothes. When his wife had spun, as she said, enough for the clothes, she set up the loom, and wove the stuff. Her husband used, now and then, to visit her, wondering at the skill of his good lady. She was much amused at all this, and made haste to carry out the trick well. She took the cloth from the loom, when it was finished, and first washed and fulled it, and last, sat down to work, cutting it and sewing the clothes out of it. When she had finished all this, she bade her husband come and try the clothes on, but did not dare let him put them on alone, wherefore she would help him. So she made believe to dress him in his fine clothes, and although the poor man was in reality naked, yet he firmly believed that it was all his own mistake, and thought his clever wife had made him these wondrous-fine clothes, and so glad he was at this, that he could not help jumping about for joy.

Now we turn to the other wife. When her husband came home from his work, she asked him why in the world he was up, and going about upon his feet. The man was startled at this question, and said: 'Why on earth do you ask this?' She persuaded him that he was very ill, and told him he had better go to bed. He believed this, and went to bed as soon as he could. When some time had passed, the wife said she would do the last services for him. He asked why, and prayed her by all means not to do so. She said: 'Why do you behave like a fool; don't you know that you died this morning? I am going, at once, to have your coffin made.' Now the poor man, believing this to be true, rested thus till he was put into his coffin. His wife then appointed a day for the burial, and hired six coffin-carriers, and asked the other couple to follow her dear husband to his grave. She had a window made in one side of the coffin, so that her husband might see all that passed round him. When the hour came for removing the coffin, the naked man came there, thinking that everybody would admire his delicate clothes. But far from it; although the coffin-bearers were in a sad mood, yet nobody could help laughing when they saw this naked fool. And when the man in the coffin caught a glance of him, he cried out as loud as he could: 'Now I should laugh, if I were not dead!' The burial was put off, and the man let out of the coffin.

The Three Sillies
(English)

NCE upon a time there was a farmer and his wife who had one daughter, and she was courted by a gentleman. Every evening he used to come and see her, and stop to supper at the farmhouse, and the daughter used to be sent down into the cellar to draw the beer for supper. So one evening she had gone down to draw the beer, and she happened to look up at the ceiling while she was drawing, and she saw a mallet stuck in one of the beams. It must have been there a long, long time, but somehow or other she had never noticed it before, and she began a-thinking. And she thought it was very dangerous to have that mallet there, for she said to herself: 'Suppose him and me was to be married, and we was to have a son, and he was to grow up to be a man, and come down into the cellar to draw the beer, like I'm doing now, and the mallet was to fall on his head and kill him, what a dreadful thing it would be!' And she put down the candle and the jug, and sat herself down and began a-crying.

Well, they began to wonder upstairs how it was that she was so long drawing the beer, and her mother went down to see after her, and she found her sitting on the settle crying, and the beer running over the floor. 'Why, whatever is the matter?' said her mother. 'Oh, Mother!' says she, 'look at that horrid mallet! Suppose we was to be married, and was to have a son, and he was to grow up, and was to come down into the cellar to draw the beer, and the mallet was to fall on his head and kill him, what a dreadful thing it would be.'

'Dear, dear! what a dreadful thing it would be!' said the mother, and she sat down aside of the daughter, and started a-crying too. Then after a bit the father began to wonder that they didn't come back, and he went down into the cellar to look after them himself, and there they two sat a-crying, and the beer running all over the floor. 'Whatever is the matter?' says he. 'Why,' says the mother, 'look at that horrid mallet. Just suppose, if our daughter and her sweetheart was to be married, and was to have a son, and he was to grow up, and

104

was to come down into the cellar to draw the beer, and the mallet was to fall on his head and kill him, what a dreadful thing it would be !'

'Dear, dear, dear! so it would!' said the father, and he sat himself down aside of the other two, and started a-crying.

Now the gentleman got tired of stopping up in the kitchen by himself, and at last he went down into the cellar too, to see what they were after; and there they three sat a-crying side by side, and the beer running all over the floor.

And he ran straight and turned the tap. Then he said: 'Whatever are you three doing, sitting there crying, and letting the beer run all over the floor?'

'Oh,' says the father, 'look at that horrid mallet! Suppose you and our daughter was to be married, and was to have a son, and he was to grow up, and was to come down into the cellar to draw the beer, and the mallet was to fall on his head and kill him!' And then they all started a-crying worse than before.

But the gentleman burst out a-laughing, and reached up and pulled out the mallet, and then he said: 'I've travelled many miles, and I never met three such big sillies as you three before; and now I shall start out on my travels again, and when I can find three bigger sillies than you three, then I'll come back and marry your daughter.' So he wished them goodbye, and started off on his travels, and left them all crying because the girl had lost her sweetheart.

Well, he set out, and he travelled a long way, and at last he came to a woman's cottage that had some grass growing on the roof. And the woman was trying to get her cow to go up a ladder to the grass, and the poor thing durst not go. So the gentleman asked the woman what she was doing. 'Why, lookye,' she said, 'look at all that beautiful grass. I'm going to get the cow on to the roof to eat it. She'll be quite safe, for I shall tie a string round her neck and pass it down the chimney, and tie it to my wrist as I go about the house, so she can't fall off without my knowing it.' 'Oh, you poor silly!' said the gentleman, 'you should cut the grass and throw it down to the cow!' But the woman thought it was easier to get the cow up the ladder than to get the grass down, so she pushed her and coaxed her and got her up, and tied a string round her neck, and passed it down the chimney, and fastened it to her own wrist. And the gentleman went on his way, but he hadn't gone

far when the cow tumbled off the roof, and hung by the string tied round her neck, and it strangled her. And the weight of the cow tied to her wrist pulled the woman up the chimney, and she stuck fast halfway, and was smothered in the soot.

Well, that was one big silly.

And the gentleman went on and on, and he went to an inn to stop the night, and they were so full at the inn that they had to put him in a double-bedded room, and another traveller was to sleep in the other bed. The other man was a very pleasant fellow, and they got very friendly together; but in the morning, when they were both getting up, the gentleman was surprised to see the other hang his trousers on the knobs of the chest of drawers and run across the room and try to jump into them, and he tried over and over again, and he couldn't manage it; and the gentleman wondered whatever he was doing it for. At last he stopped and wiped his face with his handkerchief. 'Oh dear,' he says, 'I do think trousers are the most awkwardest kind of clothes that ever were. I can't think who could have invented such things. It takes me the best part of an hour to get into mine every morning, and I get so hot! How do you manage yours?' So the gentleman burst out a-laughing, and showed him to put them on; and he was very much obliged to him, and said he should never have thought of doing it that way.

So that was another big silly.

Then the gentleman went on his travels again; and he came to a village, and outside the village there was a pond, and round the pond was a crowd of people. And they had got rakes, and brooms, and pitchforks, reaching into the pond; and the gentleman asked what was the matter. 'Why,' they say, 'matter enough! Moon's tumbled into the pond, and we can't rake her out anyhow!' So the gentleman burst out a-laughing, and told them to look up into the sky, and that it was only the shadow in the water. But they wouldn't listen to him, and abused him shamefully, and he got away as quick as he could.

So there was a whole lot of sillies bigger than them three sillies at home.

So the gentleman turned back home again, and married the farmer's daughter, and if they don't live happy for ever after, that's nothing to do with you or me.

The Boy Who Had Never Seen Women
(African American)

THERE was a boy in Alabama, I think, they raised never to see a girl till he was twenty-one – they was kind of 'sperimenting. He was raised by mens. So when he was twenty-one his daddy carried him to where the high school children would pass by when they came home for dinner at noon. And he seen them from the windows coming along so pretty, with their ribbons and long hair ('cause they had long hair in those days), and smiling and playing. And he said, 'Daddy, Daddy, come here. Looky looky, what are those?' 'Those are ducks.' 'Give me one, Daddy.' 'Which one do you want?' 'It don't make no difference, Daddy, any one.'

So it's better to let them grow up with each other, so they can pick a little.

The Old Woman Who Lived in a Vinegar Bottle
(English)

ONCE upon a time there was an old woman who lived in a vinegar bottle. One day a fairy was passing that way, and she heard the old woman talking to herself.

'It is a shame, it is a shame, it is a shame,' said the old woman. 'I didn't ought to live in a vinegar bottle. I ought to live in a nice little cottage with a thatched roof, and roses growing all up the wall, that I ought.'

So the fairy said, 'Very well, when you go to bed tonight you turn round three times, and shut your eyes, and in the morning you'll see what you will see.'

So the old woman went to bed, and turned round three times, and shut her eyes, and in the morning there she was, in a pretty little cottage with a thatched roof, and roses growing up the walls. And she was very surprised, and very pleased, but she quite forgot to thank the fairy.

And the fairy went north, and she went south, and she went east, and she went west, all about the business she had to do. And presently she thought, 'I'll go and see how that old woman is getting on. She must be very happy in her little cottage.'

And as she got up to the front door, she heard the old woman talking to herself.

'It is a shame, it is a shame, it is a shame,' said the old woman. 'I didn't ought to live in a little cottage like this, all by myself. I ought to live in a nice little house in a row of houses, with lace curtains at the windows, and a brass knocker on the door, and people calling mussels and cockles outside, all merry and cheerful.'

The fairy was rather surprised; but she said: 'Very well. You go to bed tonight, and turn round three times, and shut your eyes, and in the morning you shall see what you shall see.'

So the old woman went to bed, and turned round three times, and shut her eyes, and in the morning there she was in a nice little house, in a row of little houses, with lace curtains at the windows, and a brass knocker on the door, and people calling mussels and cockles outside, all merry and cheerful. And she was very much surprised, and very much pleased. But she quite forgot to thank the fairy.

And the fairy went north, and she went south, and she went east, and she went west, all about the business she had to do; and after a time she thought to herself, 'I'll go and see how that old woman is getting on. Surely she must be happy now.'

And when she got to the little row of houses, she heard the old woman talking to herself. 'It is a shame, it is a shame, it is a shame,' said the old woman. 'I didn't ought to live in a row of houses like this, with common people on each side of me. I ought to live in a great mansion in the country, with a big garden all round it, and servants to answer the bell.'

And the fairy was very surprised, and rather annoyed, but she said: 'Very well, go to bed and turn round three times, and shut your eyes, and in the morning you will see what you will see.'

And the old woman went to bed, and turned round three times, and shut her eyes, and in the morning there she was, in a great mansion in the country, surrounded by a fine garden, and servants to answer the bell. And she was very pleased and very surprised, and she learned how to speak genteelly, but she quite forgot to thank the fairy.

And the fairy went north, and she went south, and she went east, and she went west, all about the business she had to do; and after a time she thought to herself, 'I'll go and see how that old woman is getting on. Surely she must be happy now.'

But no sooner had she got near the old woman's drawing-room window than she heard the old woman talking to herself in a genteel voice.

'It certainly is a very great shame,' said the old woman, 'that I should be living alone here, where there is no society. I ought to be a duchess, driving in my own coach to wait on the Queen, with footmen running beside me.'

The fairy was very much surprised, and very much disappointed, but she said: 'Very well. Go to bed tonight, and turn round three times, and shut your eyes; and in the morning you shall see what you shall see.'

So the old woman went to bed, and turned round three times, and shut her eyes; and in the morning, there she was, a duchess with a coach of her own, to wait on the Queen, and footmen running beside her. And she was very much surprised, and very much pleased. BUT she quite forgot to thank the fairy.

And the fairy went north, and she went south, and she went east, and she went west, all about the business she had to do; and after a while she thought to herself: 'I'd better go and see how that old woman is getting on. Surely she is happy, now she's a duchess.'

But no sooner had she come to the window of the old woman's great town mansion, than she heard her saying in a more genteel tone than ever: 'It is indeed a very great shame that I should be a mere Duchess, and have to curtsey to the Queen. Why can't I be a queen myself, and sit on a golden throne, with a golden crown on my head, and courtiers all around me.'

The fairy was very much disappointed and very angry; but she said: 'Very well. Go to bed and turn round three times, and shut your eyes, and in the morning you shall see what you shall see.'

So the old woman went to bed, and turned round three times, and shut her eyes; and in the morning there she was in a royal palace, a queen in her own right, sitting on a golden throne, with a golden crown on her head, and her courtiers all around her. And she was highly delighted, and ordered them right and left. BUT she quite forgot to thank the fairy.

And the fairy went north, and she went south, and she went east, and she went west, all about the business she had to do; and after a while she thought to herself: 'I'll go and see how that old woman is getting on. Surely she must be satisfied now!'

But as soon as she got near the Throne Room, she heard the old woman talking.

'It is a great shame, a very great shame,' she said, 'that I should be Queen of a paltry little country like this instead of ruling the whole round world. What I am really fitted for is to be *Pope*, to govern the minds of everyone on Earth.'

'Very well,' said the fairy. 'Go to bed. Turn round three times, and shut your eyes, and in the morning you shall see what you shall see.'

So the old woman went to bed, full of proud thoughts. She turned round three times, and shut her eyes. And in the morning she was back in her vinegar bottle.

Tom Tit Tot
(English)

NCE upon a time there was a woman, and she baked five pies. And when they came out of the oven, they were that overbaked the crusts were too hard to eat. So she says to her daughter:

'Darter,' says she, 'put you them there pies on the shelf, and leave 'em there a little, and they'll come again.' — She meant, you know, the crust would get soft.

But the girl, she says to herself: 'Well, if they'll come again, I'll eat 'em now.' And she set to work and ate 'em all, first and last.

Well, come supper-time the woman said: 'Go you, and get one o' them there pies. I dare say they've come again now.'

The girl went and she looked, and there was nothing but the dishes. So back she came and says she: 'Noo, they ain't come again.'

'Not one of 'em?' says the mother.

'Not one of 'em,' says she.

'Well, come again, or not come again,' said the woman, 'I'll have one for supper.'

'But you can't, if they ain't come,' said the girl.

'But I can,' says she. 'Go you, and bring the best of 'em.'

'Best or worst,' says the girl, 'I've ate 'em all, and you can't have one till that's come again.'

Well, the woman she was done, and she took her spinning to the door to spin, and as she span she sang:

'My darter ha' ate five, five pies today.
My darter ha' ate five, five pies today.'

The king was coming down the street, and he heard her sing, but what she sang he couldn't hear, so he stopped and said:

'What was that you were singing, my good woman?'

The woman was ashamed to let him hear what her daughter had been doing, so she sang, instead of that:

'My darter ha' spun five, five skeins today.
My darter ha' spun five, five skeins today.'

'Stars o' mine!' said the king, 'I never heard tell of anyone that could do that.'

Then he said: 'Look you here, I want a wife, and I'll marry your daughter. But look you here,' says he, 'eleven months out of the year she shall have all she likes to eat, and all the gowns she likes to get, and all the company she likes to keep; but the last month of the year she'll have to spin five skeins every day, and if she don't I shall kill her.'

'All right,' says the woman; for she thought what a grand marriage that was. And as for the five skeins, when the time came, there'd be plenty of ways of getting out of it, and likeliest, he'd have forgotten all about it.

Well, so they were married. And for eleven months the girl had all she liked to eat, and all the gowns she liked to get, and all the company she liked to keep.

But when the time was getting over, she began to think about the skeins and to wonder if he had 'em in mind. But not one word did he say about 'em, and she thought he'd wholly forgotten 'em.

However, the last day of the last month he takes her to a room she'd never set eyes on before. There was nothing in it but a spinning-wheel and a stool. And says he: 'Now, my dear, here you'll be shut in tomorrow with some victuals and some flax, and if you haven't spun five skeins by the night, your head'll go off.'

And away he went about his business.

Well, she was that frightened, she'd always been such a gatless girl, that she didn't so much as know how to spin, and what was she to do tomorrow with no one to come nigh her to help her? She sat down on a stool in the kitchen, and law! how she did cry!

However, all of a sudden she heard a sort of knocking low down on the door. She upped and oped it, and what should she see but a small little black thing with a long tail. That looked up at her right curious, and that said:

'What are you a-crying for?'

'What's that to you?' says she.

'Never you mind,' that said, 'but tell me what you're a-crying for.'

'That won't do me no good if I do,' says she.

'You don't know that,' that said, and twirled that's tail round.

'Well,' says she, 'that won't do no harm, if that don't do no good,' and she upped and told about the pies, and the skeins, and everything.

'This is what I'll do,' says the little black thing, 'I'll come to your window every morning and take the flax and bring it spun at night.'

'What's your pay?' says she.

That looked out of the corner of that's eyes, and that said: 'I'll give you three guesses every night to guess my name, and if you haven't guessed it before the month's up you shall be mine.'

Well, she thought she'd be sure to guess that's name before the month was up. 'All right,' says she, 'I agree.'

'All right,' that says, and law! how that twirled that's tail.

Well, the next day, her husband took her into the room, and there was the flax and the day's food.

'Now there's the flax,' says he, 'and if that ain't spun up this night, off goes your head.' And then he went out and locked the door.

He'd hardly gone, when there was a knocking against the window.

She upped and she oped it, and there sure enough was the little old thing sitting on the ledge.

'Where's the flax?' says he.

'Here it be,' says she. And she gave it to him.

Well, come the evening a knocking came again to the window. She upped and she oped it, and there was the little old thing with five skeins of flax on his arm.

'Here it be,' says he, and he gave it to her.

'Now, what's my name?' says he.

'What, is that Bill?' says she.

'Noo, that ain't,' says he, and he twirled his tail.

'Is that Ned?' says she.

'Noo, that ain't,' says he, and he twirled his tail.

'Well, is that Mark?' says she.

'Noo, that ain't,' says he, and he twirled his tail harder, and away he flew.

Well, when her husband came in, there were the five skeins ready for him. 'I see I shan't have to kill you tonight, my dear,' says he; 'you'll have your food and your flax in the morning,' says he, and away he goes.

Well, every day the flax and the food were brought, and every day that there little black impet used to come mornings and evenings. And all the day the girl sat trying to think of names to say to it when it came at night. But she never hit on the right one. And as it got towards the end of the month, the impet began to look so maliceful, and that twirled that's tail faster and faster each time she gave a guess.

At last it came to the last day but one. The impet came at night along with the five skeins, and that said:

'What, ain't you got my name yet?'

'Is that Nicodemus?' says she.

'Noo, t'ain't,' that says.

'Is that Sammle?' says she.

'Noo, t'ain't,' that says.

'A-well, is that Methusaleh?' says she.

'Noo, t'ain't that neither,' that says.

Then that looks at her with that's eyes like a coal o' fire and that says: 'Woman, there's only tomorrow night, and then you'll be mine!' And away it flew.

Well, she felt that horrid. However, she heard the king coming along the passage. In he came, and when he sees the five skeins, he says, says he:

'Well, my dear,' says he. 'I don't see but what you'll have your skeins ready tomorrow night as well, and as I reckon I shan't have to kill you, I'll have supper in here tonight.' So they brought supper, and another stool for him and down the two sat.

Well, he hadn't eaten but a mouthful or so, when he stops and begins to laugh.

'What is it?' says she.

'A-why,' says he, 'I was out a-hunting today and I got away to a place in the wood I'd never seen before. And there was an old chalk-pit. And I heard a kind of a sort of a humming. So I got off my hobby, and I went right quiet to the pit, and I looked down. Well, what should there be but the funniest little black thing you ever set eyes on. And what was that doing, but that had a little spinning-wheel, and that was spinning wonderful fast, and twirling that's tail. And as that span that sang:

"*Nimmy nimmy not*
My name's Tom Tit Tot."'

116

Well, when the girl heard this, she felt as if she could have jumped out of her skin for joy, but she didn't say a word.

Next day that there little thing looked so maliceful when he came for the flax. And when night came, she heard that knocking against the window-panes. She oped the window, and that come right in on the ledge. That was grinning from ear to ear, and Oo! that's tail was twirling round so fast.

'What's my name?' that says, as that gave her the skeins.

'Is that Solomon?' she says, pretending to be afeard.

'Noo, t'ain't,' that says, and that came further into the room.

'Well, is that Zebedee?' says she again.

'Noo, t'ain't,' says the impet. And then that laughed and twirled that's tail till you couldn't hardly see it.

'Take time, woman,' that says; 'next guess, and you're mine.' And that stretched out that's black hands at her.

Well, she backed a step or two, and she looked at it, and then she laughed out, and says she, pointing her finger at it:

'Nimmy nimmy not
Your name's Tom Tit Tot!'

Well, when that heard her, that gave an awful shriek and away that flew into the dark, and she never saw it any more.

The Husband Who Was to Mind the House

(Norwegian)

HERE was once a man so surly and cross that he never thought his wife did anything right in the house. So one evening, in hay-making time, he came home, scolding and swearing, and showing his teeth and making a dust.

'Dear love, don't be so angry, there's a good man,' said his goody; 'tomorrow let's change our work. I'll go out with the mowers and mow, and you shall mind the house at home.'

Yes, the husband thought that would do very well. He was quite willing, he said.

So, early next morning, his goody took a scythe over her neck, and went out into the hay-field with the mowers and began to mow; but the man was to mind the house, and do the work at home.

First of all he wanted to churn the butter; but when he had churned a while, he got thirsty, and went down to the cellar to tap a barrel of ale. So, just when he had knocked in the bung, and was putting the tap into the cask, he heard overhead the pig come into the kitchen. Then off he ran up the cellar steps, with the tap in his hand, as fast as he could, to look after the pig, lest it should upset the churn; but when he got up, and saw the pig had already knocked the churn over, and stood there, routing and grunting amongst the cream which was running all over the floor, he got so wild with rage that he quite forgot the ale-barrel, and ran at the pig as hard as he could. He caught it, too, just as it ran out of doors, and gave it such a kick that piggy lay for dead on the spot. Then all at once he remembered he had the tap in his hand; but when he got down to the cellar, every drop of ale had run out of the cask.

Then he went into the dairy and found enough cream left to fill the churn again, and so he began to churn, for butter they must have at dinner. When he had churned a bit, he remembered that their milking cow was still shut up in the byre, and hadn't had a bit to eat or a drop to drink all the morning, though the sun was high. Then all at once he thought 'twas too

118

far to take her down to the meadow, so he'd just get her up on the house-top – for the house, you must know, was thatched with sods, and a fine crop of grass was growing there. Now their house lay close up against a steep down, and he thought if he laid a plank across to the thatch at the back he'd easily get the cow up.

But still he couldn't leave the churn, for there was his little babe crawling about on the floor, and 'if I leave it,' he thought, 'the child is safe to upset it.' So he took the churn on his back, and went out with it; but then he thought he'd better first water the cow before he turned her out on the thatch; so he took up a bucket to draw water out of the well; but, as he stooped down at the well's brink, all the cream ran out of the churn over his shoulders, and so down into the well.

Now it was near dinner-time, and he hadn't even got the butter yet; so he thought he'd best boil the porridge, and filled the pot with water, and hung it over the fire. When he had done that, he thought the cow might perhaps fall off the thatch and break her legs or her neck. So he got up on the house to tie her up. One end of the rope he made fast to the cow's neck, and the other he slipped down the chimney and tied round his own thigh; and he had to make haste, for the water now began to boil in the pot, and he had still to grind the oatmeal.

So he began to grind away; but while he was hard at it, down fell the cow off the house-top after all, and as she fell, she dragged the man up the chimney by the rope. There he stuck fast; and as for the cow, she hung halfway down the wall, swinging between heaven and earth, for she could neither get down nor up.

And now the goody had waited seven lengths and seven breadths for her husband to come and call them home to dinner; but never a call they had. At last she thought she'd waited long enough, and went home. But when she got there and saw the cow hanging in such an ugly place, she ran up and cut the rope in two with her scythe. But as she did this, down came her husband out of the chimney; and so when his old dame came inside the kitchen, there she found him standing on his head in the porridge pot.

Part Four

GOOD GIRLS
AND WHERE IT GETS THEM

East o' the Sun and West o' the Moon
(Norwegian)

ONCE on a time there was a poor husbandman who had so many children that he hadn't much of either food or clothing to give them. Pretty children they all were, but the prettiest was the youngest daughter, who was so lovely there was no end to her loveliness.

So one day, 'twas on a Thursday evening late at the fall of the year, the weather was so wild and rough outside, and it was so cruelly dark, and rain fell and wind blew, till the walls of the cottage shook again. There they all sat round the fire busy with this thing and that. But just then, all at once something gave three taps on the window-pane. Then the father went out to see what was the matter; and, when he got out of doors, what should he see but a great big White Bear.

'Good evening to you,' said the White Bear.

'The same to you,' said the man.

'Will you give me your youngest daughter? If you will, I'll make you as rich as you are now poor,' said the Bear.

Well, the man would not be at all sorry to be so rich; but still he thought he must have a bit of a talk with his daughter first; so he went in and told them how there was a great White Bear waiting outside, who had given his word to make them so rich if he could only have the youngest daughter.

The lassie said 'No!' outright. Nothing could get her to say anything else; so the man went out and settled it with the White Bear, that he should come again the next Thursday evening and get an answer. Meantime he talked his daughter over, and kept on telling her of all the riches they would get, and how well off she would be herself; and so at last she thought better of it, and washed and mended her rags, made herself as smart as she could, and was ready to start. I can't say her packing gave her much trouble.

Next Thursday evening came the White Bear to fetch her, and she got upon his back with her bundle, and off they went. So, when they had gone a bit of the way, the White Bear said –

'Are you afraid?'

'No! she wasn't.'

'Well! mind and hold tight by my shaggy coat, and then there's nothing to fear,' said the Bear.

So she rode a long, long way, till they came to a great steep hill. There, on the face of it, the White Bear gave a knock, and a door opened, and they came into a castle, where there were many rooms all lit up; rooms gleaming with silver and gold; and there too was a table ready laid, and it was all as grand as grand could be. Then the White Bear gave her a silver bell; and when she wanted anything, she was only to ring it, and she would get it at once.

Well, after she had eaten and drunk, and evening wore on, she got sleepy after her journey, and thought she would like to go to bed, so she rang the bell; and she had scarce taken hold of it before she came into a chamber, where there was a bed made, as fair and white as anyone would wish to sleep in, with silken pillows and curtains, and gold fringe. All that was in the room was gold or silver; but when she had gone to bed, and put out the light, a man came and laid himself alongside her. That was the White Bear, who threw off his beast shape at night; but she never saw him, for he always came after she had put out the light, and before the day dawned he was up and off again. So things went on happily for a while, but at last she began to get silent and sorrowful; for there she went about all day alone, and she longed to go home to see her father and mother, and brothers and sisters. So one day, when the White Bear asked what it was that she lacked, she said it was so dull and lonely there, and how she longed to go home to see her father and mother, and brothers and sisters, and that was why she was so sad and sorrowful, because she couldn't get to them.

'Well, well!' said the Bear, 'perhaps there's a cure for all this; but you must promise me one thing, not to talk alone with your mother, but only when the rest are by to hear; for she'll take you by the hand and try to lead you into a room alone to talk; but you must mind and not do that, else you'll bring bad luck on both of us.'

So one Sunday the White Bear came and said now they could set off to see her father and mother. Well, off they started, she sitting on his back; and they went far and long. At last they came to a grand house, and there her brothers and sisters were running about out of doors at play, and everything was so pretty, 'twas a joy to see.

'This is where your father and mother live now,' said the White Bear; 'but don't forget what I told you, else you'll make us both unlucky.'

'No! bless her, she'd not forget;' and when she had reached the house, the White Bear turned right about and left her.

Then when she went in to see her father and mother, there was such joy, there was no end to it. None of them thought they could thank her enough for all she had done for them. Now, they had everything they wished, as good as good could be, and they all wanted to know how she got on where she lived.

Well, she said, it was very good to live where she did; she had all she wished. What she said beside I don't know; but I don't think any of them had the right end of the stick, or that they got much out of her. But so in the afternoon, after they had done dinner, all happened as the White Bear had said. Her mother wanted to talk with her alone in her bedroom; but she minded what the White Bear had said, and wouldn't go up stairs.

'Oh, what we have to talk about will keep,' she said, and put her mother off. But somehow or other, her mother got round her at last, and she had to tell her the whole story. So she said, how every night, when she had gone to bed, a man came and lay down beside her as soon as she had put out the light, and how she never saw him, because he was always up and away before the morning dawned; and how she went about woeful and sorrowing, for she thought she should so like to see him, and how all day long she walked about there alone, and how dull, and dreary, and lonesome it was.

'My!' said her mother; 'it may well be a Troll you slept with! But now I'll teach you a lesson how to set eyes on him. I'll give you a bit of candle, which you can carry home in your bosom; just light that while he is asleep, but take care not to drop the tallow on him.'

Yes! she took the candle, and hid it in her bosom, and as night drew on, the White Bear came and fetched her away.

But when they had gone a bit of the way, the White Bear asked if all hadn't happened as he had said.

'Well, she couldn't say it hadn't.'

'Now, mind,' said he, 'if you have listened to your mother's

advice, you have brought bad luck on us both, and then, all
that has passed between us will be as nothing.'

'No,' she said, 'she hadn't listened to her mother's advice.'

So when she reached home, and had gone to bed, it was the
old story over again. There came a man and lay down beside
her; but at dead of night, when she heard he slept, she got up
and struck a light, lit the candle, and let the light shine on him,
and so she saw that he was the loveliest Prince one ever set eyes
on, and she fell so deep in love with him on the spot, that she
thought she couldn't live if she didn't give him a kiss there and
then. And so she did, but as she kissed him, she dropped three
hot drops of tallow on his shirt, and he woke up.

'What have you done?' he cried; 'now you have made us both
unlucky, for had you held out only this one year, I had been
freed. For I have a stepmother who has bewitched me, so that I
am a White Bear by day, and a Man by night. But now all ties
are snapt between us; now I must set off from you to her. She
lives in a castle which stands east o' the sun and west o' the
moon, and there, too, is a Princess, with a nose three ells long,
and she's the wife I must have now.'

She wept and took it ill, but there was no help for it; go he
must.

Then she asked if she mightn't go with him.

No, she mightn't.

'Tell me the way, then,' she said, 'and I'll search you out; *that*
surely I may get leave to do.'

'Yes, she might do that,' he said; 'but there was no way to
that place. It lay east o' the sun and west o' the moon, and
thither she'd never find her way.'

So next morning, when she woke up, both Prince and castle
were gone, and then she lay on a little green patch, in the midst
of the gloomy thick wood, and by her side lay the same bundle
of rags she had brought with her from her old home.

So when she had rubbed the sleep out of her eyes, and wept
till she was tired, she set out on her way, and walked many,
many days, till she came to a lofty crag. Under it sat an old hag,
and played with a gold apple which she tossed about. Her the
lassie asked if she knew the way to the Prince, who lived with
his stepmother in the castle that lay east o' the sun and west o'
the moon, and who was to marry the Princess with a nose three
ells long.

'How did you come to know about him?' asked the old hag; 'but maybe you are the lassie who ought to have had him?'

Yes, she was.

'So, so; it's you, is it?' said the old hag. 'Well, all I know about him is, that he lives in the castle that lies east o' the sun and west o' the moon, and thither you'll come, late or never; but still you may have the loan of my horse, and on him you can ride to my next neighbour. Maybe she'll be able to tell you; and when you get there, just give the horse a switch under the left ear, and beg him to be off home; and, stay, this gold apple you may take with you.'

So she got upon the horse, and rode a long long time, till she came to another crag, under which sat another old hag, with a gold carding-comb. Her the lassie asked if she knew the way to the castle that lay east o' the sun and west o' the moon, and she answered, like the first old hag, that she knew nothing about it, except it was east o' the sun and west o' the moon.

'And thither you'll come, late or never; but you shall have the loan of my horse to my next neighbour; maybe she'll tell you all about it; and when you get there, just switch the horse under the left ear, and beg him to be off home.'

And this old hag gave her the golden carding-comb; it might be she'd find some use for it, she said. So the lassie got up on the horse, and rode a far far way, and a weary time; and so at last she came to another great crag, under which sat another old hag, spinning with a golden spinning-wheel. Her, too, she asked if she knew the way to the Prince, and where the castle was that lay east o' the sun and west o' the moon. So it was the same thing over again.

'Maybe it's you who ought to have had the Prince?' said the old hag.

Yes, it was.

But she, too, didn't know the way a bit better than the other two. 'East o' the sun and west o' the moon it was,' she knew – that was all.

'And thither you'll come, late or never; but I'll lend you my horse, and then I think you'd best ride to the East Wind and ask him; maybe he knows those parts, and can blow you thither. But when you get to him, you need only give the horse a switch under the left ear, and he'll trot home of himself.'

And so, too, she gave her the gold spinning-wheel.

'Maybe you'll find a use for it,' said the old hag.

Then on she rode many many days, a weary time, before she got to the East Wind's house, but at last she did reach it, and then she asked the East Wind if he could tell her the way to the Prince who dwelt east o' the sun and west o' the moon. Yes, the

East Wind had often heard tell of it, the Prince and the castle, but he couldn't tell the way, for he had never blown so far.

'But, if you will, I'll go with you to my brother the West Wind, maybe he knows, for he's much stronger. So, if you will just get on my back, I'll carry you thither.'

Yes, she got on his back, and I should just think they went briskly along.

So when they got there, they went into the West Wind's house, and the East Wind said the lassie he had brought was the one who ought to have had the Prince who lived in the castle east o' the sun and west o' the moon: and so she had set out to seek him, and how he had come with her, and would be glad to know if the West Wind knew how to get to the castle.

'Nay,' said the West Wind, 'so far I've never blown; but if you will, I'll go with you to our brother the South Wind, for he's much stronger than either of us, and he has flapped his wings far and wide. Maybe he'll tell you. You can get on my back, and I'll carry you to him.'

Yes! she got on his back, and so they travelled to the South Wind, and weren't so very long on the way, I should think.

When they got there, the West Wind asked him if he could tell her the way to the castle that lay east o' the sun and west o' the moon, for it was she who ought to have had the Prince who lived there.

'You don't say so! That's she, is it?' said the South Wind.

'Well, I have blustered about in most places in my time, but so far have I never blown; but if you will, I'll take you to my brother the North Wind; he is the oldest and strongest of the whole lot of us, and if he don't know where it is, you'll never find anyone in the world to tell you. You can get on my back, and I'll carry you thither.'

Yes! she got on his back, and away he went from his house at a fine rate. And this time, too, she wasn't long on her way.

So when they got to the North Wind's house, he was so wild and cross, cold puffs came from him a long way off.

'BLAST YOU BOTH, WHAT DO YOU WANT?' he roared out to them ever so far off, so that it struck them with an icy shiver.

'Well,' said the South Wind, 'you needn't be so foul-mouthed, for here I am, your brother, the South Wind, and here is the lassie who ought to have had the Prince who dwells in the castle that lies east o' the sun and west o' the moon, and now she wants to ask you if you ever were there, and can tell her the way, for she would be so glad to find him again.'

'YES, I KNOW WELL ENOUGH WHERE IT IS,' said the North Wind; 'once in my life I blew an aspen-leaf thither, but I was so tired I couldn't blow a puff for ever so many days after. But if you really wish to go thither, and aren't afraid to come along with me, I'll take you on my back and see if I can blow you thither.'

Yes! with all her heart; she must and would get thither if it were possible in any way; and as for fear, however madly he went, she wouldn't be at all afraid.

'Very well, then,' said the North Wind, 'but you must sleep here tonight, for we must have the whole day before us, if we're to get thither at all.'

Early next morning the North Wind woke her, and puffed himself up, and blew himself out, and made himself so stout and big, 'twas gruesome to look at him; and so off they went high up through the air, as if they would never stop till they got to the world's end.

Down here below there was such a storm; it threw down long tracts of wood and many houses, and when it swept over the great sea, ships foundered by hundreds.

So they tore on and on, – no one can believe how far they went, – and all the while they still went over the sea, and the North Wind got more and more weary, and so out of breath he could scarce bring out a puff, and his wings drooped and drooped, till at last he sunk so low that the crests of the waves dashed over his heels.

'Are you afraid?' said the North Wind.

'No!' she wasn't.

But they weren't very far from land; and the North Wind had still so much strength left in him that he managed to throw her up on the shore under the windows of the castle which lay east o' the sun and west o' the moon; but then he was so weak and worn out, he had to stay there and rest many days before he could get home again.

Next morning the lassie sat down under the castle window, and began to play with the gold apple; and the first person she saw was the Long-nose who was to have the Prince.

'What do you want for your gold apple, you lassie?' said the Long-nose, and threw up the window.

'It's not for sale, for gold or money,' said the lassie.

'If it's not for sale for gold or money, what is it that you will sell it for? You may name your own price,' said the Princess.

'Well! if I may get to the Prince, who lives here, and be with him tonight, you shall have it,' said the lassie whom the North Wind had brought.

Yes! she might; that could be done. So the Princess got the gold apple; but when the lassie came up to the Prince's bedroom at night he was fast asleep; she called him and shook him, and between whiles she wept sore; but all she could do she couldn't wake him up. Next morning as soon as day broke, came the Princess with the long nose, and drove her out again.

So in the daytime she sat down under the castle windows and began to card with her golden carding-comb, and the same thing happened. The Princess asked what she wanted for it; and she said it wasn't for sale for gold or money, but if she might get leave to go up to the Prince and be with him that night, the Princess should have it. But when she went up she found him fast asleep again, and all she called, and all she shook, and wept, and prayed, she couldn't get life into him; and as soon as the first gray peep of day came, then came the Princess with the long nose, and chased her out again.

So in the daytime the lassie sat down outside under the castle window, and began to spin with her golden spinning-wheel, and that, too, the Princess with the long nose wanted to have. So she threw up the window and asked what she wanted for it. The lassie said, as she had said twice before, it wasn't for sale for gold or money; but if she might go up to the Prince who was there, and be with him alone that night, she might have it.

Yes! she might do that and welcome. But now you must know there were some Christian folk who had been carried off thither, and as they sat in their room, which was next the Prince, they had heard how a woman had been in there, and wept and prayed, and called to him two nights running, and they told that to the Prince.

That evening, when the Princess came with her sleepy drink, the Prince made as if he drank, but threw it over his shoulder, for he could guess it was a sleepy drink. So, when the lassie came in, she found the Prince wide awake; and then she told him the whole story how she had come thither.

'Ah,' said the Prince, 'you've just come in the very nick of time, for tomorrow is to be our wedding-day; but now I won't have the Long-nose, and you are the only woman in the world who can set me free. I'll say I want to see what my wife is fit for, and beg her to wash the shirt which has the three spots of tallow on it; she'll say yes, for she doesn't know 'tis you who put them there; but that's a work only for Christian folk, and not for such a pack of Trolls, and so I'll say that I won't have any other for my bride than the woman who can wash them out, and ask you to do it.'

So there was great joy and love between them all that night. But next day, when the wedding was to be, the Prince said –

'First of all, I'd like to see what my bride is fit for.'

'Yes!' said the stepmother, with all her heart.

'Well,' said the Prince, 'I've got a fine shirt which I'd like for my wedding shirt, but somehow or other it has got three spots of tallow on it, which I must have washed out; and I have sworn never to take any other bride than the woman who's able to do that. If she can't, she's not worth having.'

Well, that was no great thing they said, so they agreed, and she with the long nose began to wash away as hard as she could, but the more she rubbed and scrubbed, the bigger the spots grew.

'Ah!' said the old hag, her mother, 'you can't wash; let me try.'

But she hadn't long taken the shirt in hand, before it got far worse than ever, and with all her rubbing, and wringing, and scrubbing, the spots grew bigger and blacker, and the darker and uglier was the shirt.

Then all the other Trolls began to wash, but the longer it lasted, the blacker and uglier the shirt grew, till at last it was as black all over as if it had been up the chimney.

'Ah!' said the Prince, 'you're none of you worth a straw: you can't wash. Why there, outside, sits a beggar lassie, I'll be bound she knows how to wash better than the whole lot of you. COME IN, LASSIE!' he shouted.

Well, in she came.

'Can you wash this shirt clean, lassie, you?' said he.

'I don't know,' she said, 'but I think I can.'

And almost before she had taken it and dipped it in the water, it was as white as driven snow, and whiter still.

'Yes; you are the lassie, for me,' said the Prince.

At that the old hag flew into such a rage, she burst on the spot, and the Princess with the long nose after her, and the whole pack of Trolls after her, – at least I've never heard a word about them since.

As for the Prince and Princess, they set free all the poor Christian folk who had been carried off and shut up there; and they took with them all the silver and gold, and flitted away as far as they could from the castle that lay east o' the sun and west o' the moon.

The Good Girl and the Ornery Girl
(North American: Ozarks)

NE time there was an old woman lived away out in the timber, and she had two daughters. One of them was a good girl and the other one was ornery, but the old woman liked the ornery one best. So they made the good girl do all the work, and she had to split wood with a dull axe. The ornery girl just laid a-flat of her back all day and never done nothing.

The good girl went out to pick up sticks, and pretty soon she seen a cow. The cow says, 'For God's sake milk me, my bag's about to bust!' So the good girl milked the cow, but she didn't drink none of the milk. Pretty soon she seen a apple tree, and the tree says, 'For God's sake pick these apples, or I'll break plumb down!' So the good girl picked the apples, but she didn't eat none. Pretty soon she seen some cornbread a-baking, and the bread says, 'For God's sake take me out, I'm a-burning up!' So the good girl pulled the bread out, but she didn't taste a crumb. A little old man come along just then, and

he throwed a sack of gold money so it stuck all over her. When the good girl got home she shed gold pieces like feathers off a goose.

Next day the ornery girl went out to get her some gold too. Pretty soon she seen a cow, and the cow says, 'For God's sake milk me, my bag's about to bust!' But the ornery girl just kicked the old cow in the belly, and went right on. Pretty soon she seen a apple tree, and the tree says, 'For God's sake pick these apples, or I'll break plumb down!' But the ornery girl just laughed, and went right on. Pretty soon she seen some cornbread a-baking, and the bread says, 'For God's sake take me out, I'm a-burning up!' But the ornery girl didn't pay no mind, and went right on. A little old man come along just then, and he throwed a kettle of tar so it stuck all over her. When the ornery girl got home she was so black the old woman didn't know who it was.

The folks tried everything they could, and finally they got most of the tar off. But the ornery girl always looked kind of ugly after that, and she never done any good. It served the little bitch right, too.

The Armless Maiden
(Russian)

IN a certain kingdom, not in our land, there lived a wealthy merchant; he had two children, a son and a daughter. The father and mother died. The brother said to the sister: 'Let us leave this town, little sister; I will rent a shop and trade, and find lodgings for you; we will live together.' They went to another province. When they came there, the brother inscribed himself in the merchants' guild, and rented a shop of woven cloths. The brother decided to marry and took a sorceress to wife. One day he went to trade in his shop and said to his sister: 'Keep order in the house, sister.' The wife felt offended because he said this to his sister. To revenge herself she broke all the furniture and when her husband came back she met him and said: 'See what a sister you have; she has broken all the furniture in the house.' 'Too bad, but we can get some new things,' said the husband.

The next day when leaving for his shop he said farewell to his wife and his sister and said to his sister: 'Please, little sister, see to it that everything in the house is kept as well as possible.' The wife bided her time, went to the stables, and cut off the head of her husband's favorite horse with a saber. She awaited him on the porch. 'See what a sister you have,' she said. 'She has cut off the head of your favorite horse.' 'Ah, let the dogs eat what is theirs,' answered the husband.

On the third day the husband again went to his shop, said farewell, and said to his sister: 'Please look after my wife, so that she does not hurt herself or the baby, if by chance she gives birth to one.' When the wife gave birth to her child, she cut off his head. When her husband came home he found her sitting and lamenting over her baby. 'See what a sister you have! No sooner had I given birth to my baby than she cut off his head with a saber.' The husband did not say anything; he wept bitter tears and turned away.

Night came. At the stroke of midnight he rose and said: 'Little sister, make ready; we are going to mass.' She said: 'My beloved brother, I do not think it is a holiday today.' 'Yes, my

135

sister, it is a holiday; let us go.' 'It is still too early to go, brother,' she said. 'No,' he answered, 'young maidens always take a long time to get ready.' The sister began to dress; she was very slow and reluctant. Her brother said: 'Hurry, sister, get dressed.' 'Please,' she said, 'it is still early, brother.' 'No, little sister, it is not early, it is high time to be gone.'

When the sister was ready they sat in a carriage and set out for mass. They drove for a long time or a short time. Finally they came to a wood. The sister said: 'What wood is this?' He answered: 'This is the hedge around the church.' The carriage caught in a bush. The brother said: 'Get out, little sister, disentangle the carriage.' 'Ah, my beloved brother, I cannot do that, I will dirty my dress.' 'I will buy you a new dress, sister, a better one than this.' She got down from the carriage, began to disentangle it, and her brother cut off her arms to the elbows, struck his horse with the whip, and drove away.

The little sister was left alone; she burst into tears and began to walk in the woods. She walked and walked, a long time or a short time; she was all scratched, but could not find a path leading out of the woods. Finally, after several years, she found a path. She came to a market town and stood beneath the window of the wealthiest merchant to beg for alms. This merchant had a son, an only one, who was the apple of his father's eye. He fell in love with the beggar woman and said: 'Dear Father and Mother, marry me.' 'To whom shall we marry you?' 'To this beggar woman.' 'Ah, my dear child, do not the merchants of our town have lovely daughters?' 'Please marry me to her,' he said. 'If you do not, I will do something to myself.' They were distressed, because he was their only son, their life's treasure. They gathered all the merchants and clerics and asked them to judge the matter: should they marry their son to the beggar woman or not? The priest said: 'Such must be his fate, and God gives your son his sanction to marry the beggar woman.'

So the son lived with her for a year and then another year. At the end of that time he went to another province, where her brother had his shop. When taking his leave he said: 'Dear Father and Mother, do not abandon my wife; as soon as she gives birth to a child, write to me that very hour.' Two or three months after the son left, his wife gave birth to a child; his arms were golden up to the elbows, his sides were studded with

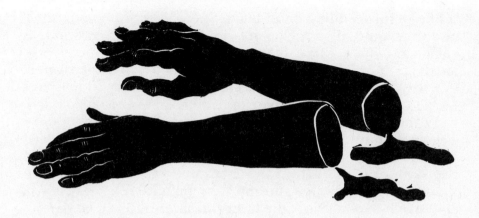

stars, there was a bright moon on his forehead and a radiant sun near his heart. The grandparents were overjoyed and at once wrote their beloved son a letter. They dispatched an old man with this note in all haste. Meanwhile the wicked sister-in-law had learned about all this and invited the old messenger into her house: 'Come in, little father,' she said, 'and take a rest.' 'No, I have no time, I am bringing an urgent message.' 'Come in, little father, take a rest, have something to eat.'

She sat him down to dinner, took his bag, found the letter in it, read it, tore it into little pieces, and wrote another letter instead: 'Your wife,' it said, 'has given birth to a half dog and half bear that she conceived with beasts in the woods.' The old messenger came to the merchant's son and handed him the letter; he read it and burst into tears. He wrote in answer, asking that his son be not molested till he returned. 'When I come back,' he said, 'I will see what kind of baby it is.' The sorceress again invited the old messenger into her house. 'Come in, sit down, take a rest,' she said. Again she charmed him with talk, stole the letter he carried, read it, tore it up, and instead ordered that her sister-in-law be driven out the moment the letter was received. The old messenger brought this letter; the father and mother read it and were grieved. 'Why does he cause us so much trouble?' they said. 'We married him to the girl, and now he does not want his wife!' They pitied not so much the wife as the babe. So they gave their blessing to her and the babe, tied the babe to her breast, and sent her away.

She went, shedding bitter tears. She walked, for a long time or a short time, all in the open field, and there was no wood or village anywhere. She came to a dale and was very thirsty. She looked to the right and saw a well. She wanted to drink from it but was afraid to stoop, lest she drop her baby. Then she fancied that the water came closer. She stooped to drink and her baby fell into the well. She began to walk around the well, weeping, and wondering how to get her child out of the well. An old man came up to her and said: 'Why are you weeping, you slave of God?' 'How can I help weeping? I stooped over the well to drink water and my baby fell into it.' 'Bend down and take him out.' 'No, little father, I cannot; I have no hands, only stumps.' 'Do as I tell you. Take your baby.' She went to the well, stretched out her arms, and God helped, for suddenly she had her hands, all whole. She bent down, pulled her baby out, and began to give thanks to God, bowing to all four sides.

She said her prayers, went on farther, and came to the house where her brother and husband were staying, and asked for shelter. Her husband said: 'Brother, let the beggar woman in; beggar women can tell stories and recount real happenings.' The wicked sister-in-law said: 'We have no room for visitors, we are overcrowded.' 'Please, brother, let her come; there is nothing I like better than to hear beggar women tell tales.' They let her in. She sat on the stove with her baby. Her husband said: 'Now, little dove, tell us a tale – any kind of story.'

She said: 'I do not know any tales or stories, but I can tell the truth. Listen, here is a true happening that I can recount to you.' And she began: 'In a certain kingdom, not in our land, lived a wealthy merchant; he had two children, a son and a daughter. The father and mother died. The brother said to the sister: "Let us leave this town, little sister." And they came to another province. The brother inscribed himself in the merchants' guild and took a shop of woven cloth. He decided to marry and took a sorceress to wife.' At this point the sister-in-law muttered: 'Why does she bore us with her stories, that hag?' But the husband said: 'Go on, go on, little mother, I love such stories more than anything!'

'And so,' the beggar woman went on, 'the brother went to trade in his shop and said to his sister: "Keep order in the house, sister." The wife felt offended because he had said this to his sister and out of spite broke all the furniture.' And then she went on to tell how her brother took her to mass and cut off her hands, how she gave birth to a baby, how her sister-in-law lured the old messenger – and again the sister-in-law interrupted her, crying: 'What gibberish she is telling!' But the husband said: 'Brother, order your wife to keep quiet; it is a wonderful story, is it not?'

She came to the point when her husband wrote to his parents ordering that the baby be left in peace until his return, and the sister-in-law mumbled: 'What nonsense!' Then she reached the point when she came to their house as a beggar woman, and the sister-in-law mumbled: 'What is this old bitch gibbering about!' And the husband said: 'Brother, order her to keep quiet; why does she interrupt all the time?' Finally she came to the point in the story when she was let in and began to tell the truth instead of a story. And then she pointed at them and said: 'This is my husband, this is my brother, and this is my sister-in-law.'

Then her husband jumped up to her on the stove and said: 'Now, my dear, show me the baby. Let me see whether my father and mother wrote me the truth.' They took the baby, removed its swaddling clothes – and the whole room was illumined! 'So it is true that she did not tell us just a tale; here is my wife, and here is my son – golden up to the elbows – his sides studded with stars, a bright moon on his forehead, and a radiant sun near his heart!'

The brother took the best mare from his stable, tied his wife to its tail, and let it run in the open field. The mare dragged her on the ground until she brought back only her braid; the rest was strewn on the field. Then they harnessed three horses and went home to the young husband's father and mother; they began to live happily and to prosper. I was there and drank mead and wine; it ran down my mustache, but did not go into my mouth.

Part Five

WITCHES

The Chinese Princess
(Kashmiri)

N the reign of the Mughal Emperor Shah Jahan the Valley of Kashmir was under the rule of a governor named Ali Mardan Khan. He was very fond of hunting. One day he was in search of game in a forest not far from the beautiful Dal Lake when he saw a stag. Leaving his companions behind, he gave chase to it. After some time the stag eluded him and disappeared into some bushes.

Ali Mardan drew rein, and waited in the hope that it would come out of its hiding place; but there was no sign of it. Tired and disappointed he was returning to his companions when suddenly he heard some one crying. He went in the direction of the sound, and there he found seated under a tree a damsel of surpassing beauty, richly dressed and bejewelled. It was obvious that she did not belong to this country.

Ali Mardan was dazzled by her beauty. He dismounted and inquired of her as to who she was and why she was crying.

'Oh, Sir,' she replied 'I am the daughter of a Chinese King. My father fell in a battle between him and the ruler of a neighbouring province. Many of our noblemen were taken prisoner; but I, somehow, managed to escape. Since then I have been wandering from place to place until I reached here.'

'Fair maiden,' Ali Mardan replied, consoling her, 'Now you need wander no more. No harm will come to you, for I am the ruler of this country.'

The Chinese princess wept on hearing this.

'Oh my lord,' she said, 'I weep for my father, I weep for my mother, I weep for my country and I weep for myself. What will become of me, friendless and homeless, how can I live?'

'Weep no more, lovely one,' the King said compassionately. 'Stay in my palace where you will be safe and comfortable.'

'That gladly will I do,' said the girl, still crying, 'and were you to ask me to become your wife, I should not be able to refuse you.'

On hearing these words Ali Mardan's face brightened. He held the girl's hands.

'Come, my beloved! I will make you my wife,' he said and he took her to his palace and they were married soon after.

Ali Mardan and his wife spent some time happily together when one day she approached him saying:

'Build me a palace by the Lake, where from the balcony I could see my reflection in the water.'

Thereupon Ali Mardan immediately gave orders for the construction of the new palace. Thousands of labourers and masons were engaged to complete the building, and in the shortest possible time a beautiful palace of marble adorned the bank of the Dal Lake. It was enclosed on three sides by gardens full of flowers of the rarest fragrance and beauty, and there beside the lake she lived happily with Ali Mardan whose love for her increased every day.

But their happiness did not last long. One morning Ali Mardan woke up feeling unwell.

'I have a pain in my stomach,' he told his Chinese wife.

He did not worry much about it. But as the pain persisted throughout the day, his wife sent for the royal physician, who examined him and gave him some medicine, but still the pain did not subside. Ali Mardan was confined to his room and the Chinese princess constantly attended to his needs. Many days passed but his malady was no better.

Now it chanced, that a Yogi was passing by way of the Dal Lake carrying a small jar of water. He was surprised to see the new palace.

'I have never seen a palace here before,' he said to himself. 'Who could have built it I wonder.'

As he felt tired and the day was hot, he went into the garden of the palace, and sat down under a tree. So much at peace did he feel among the flowers beds, and so sweetly did the birds sing around him that soon he was lulled to sleep.

Now at this very hour Ali Mardan, feeling slightly better, was having a stroll in the garden. He was walking slowly supported by his courtiers.

Ali Mardan was a man of humble heart and always showed great respect towards holy men irrespective of their belief; so instead of becoming angry with the intruder, he smiled.

'Don't disturb the sleeping Yogi,' he said to his attendants. 'Go bring the best bed you can find, and lay this holy man gently upon it.' Then seeing the jar of water he added:

'Take great care of this too.'

Two hours later when the Yogi awoke he was surprised to find himself on such a comfortable bed.

'Don't worry,' said an attendant who approached, seeing him awake. 'You are the guest of Ali Mardan, the Governor of Kashmir, who desires to see you.'

Then noticing that he was searching for something, the attendant added:

'Your jar of water is in safe custody; rest assured.'

He was then taken to the Governor's room. He found him lying on his bed.

'Have you rested well, holy man.' Ali Mardan asked gently. 'Who are you and from where do you come?'

'Sire,' replied the Yogi, 'I am an humble disciple of my Guru who lives at some distance from here in a forest. My master likes to drink the water of a sacred spring and sends me every now and then to fetch it. The last time I passed this way there was no palace here, so I was surprised to find this one today. But I must now take leave of you as I am already delayed and my master will be anxious if I don't get back before dark.'

The Yogi then thanked him for his kindness, and was just leaving the bedroom when Ali Mardan was seized by a spasm of pain. On inquiring, the Yogi came to know of the Governor's mysterious malady. Then he left the palace.

That evening the Yogi returned to his master, and related to him the events of the day. He particularly mentioned the hospitality shown to him by the Governor. The Guru was very pleased to hear of it. Then the disciple told him of how the Governor was in the grip of a strange illness which no physician had so far been able to cure.

'I am sorry to hear about his illness,' said the Guru. 'Take me to him tomorrow, and we will see if we can do anything to help him.'

Next morning the disciple took his master to the palace and sought an audience with the Governor, who was still confined to his bedroom. The disciple introduced his master to Ali Mardan and also told him the purpose of their visit.

'I am much honoured by your Holy presence, O! Guru,' said Ali Mardan. 'And if you can cure me of this disease I shall be grateful to you all my life.'

'Show me your body,' said the holy man.

Hardly had he uncovered himself, when the Guru inquired:
'Have you recently married?'

'Yes,' said Ali Mardan, and briefly told the holy man of his encounter with the Chinese princess and of his marriage with her.

'Just as I had suspected,' observed the holy man, then in grave tone he said:

'O Governor! you are really very ill, but I can cure you if you do as I tell you.'

The Governor was alarmed and assured the holy man that he would do as he was bidden.

That evening Ali Mardan, as instructed by the Guru, ordered two kinds of *kitcheri* to be cooked, one sweet and the other salty, and placed on one dish in such a way that the salty *kitcheri* was on one side and the sweet on the other. When, as usual, the Governor and his Chinese wife sat down to eat, he turned the salty side of the dish towards her. She found her portion too salty but seeing that her husband was eating with relish she made no remark and ate in silence.

When the time came for them to retire, Ali Mardan, under the instructions of the Guru, had secretly given orders to the attendants that the drinking water should be removed from their bedroom and that the room should be locked from outside.

As was expected the Chinese princess woke up very thirsty in the middle of the night, and finding no water and no way out she became desperate. She looked at her husband to assure herself that he was fast asleep; then she assumed the shape of a snake, slipped through the window, and went down to the Lake to quench her thirst. After a few minutes she returned by the same way and resuming her human shape, lay down beside her husband again.

Ali Mardan, who in fact had been feigning sleep, was horrified at what he had seen, and was unable to sleep for the rest of the night. Early next morning he sought the holy man and told him what had happened in the night.

'Oh! Governor,' said the holy man, 'as you have seen, your wife is no woman but a Lamia – a snake woman.' Then he explained to Ali Mardan:

'If for one hundred years the glance of no human being falls on a snake a crest forms on its head, and it becomes the king of the snakes, and if for another hundred years it comes not within sight of a man it changes into a dragon, and if for three hundred years it has not been looked upon by a human being it becomes a Lamia. A lamia possesses enormous powers and can change its appearance at will. It is very fond of assuming the form of a woman. Such is your wife O! Governor,' he concluded.

'Horrors!' exclaimed the Governor. 'But is there no way of escape from this monster?'

'Yes there is,' replied the holy man; 'only we must act cautiously so as not to arouse her suspicions, for if she suspects even remotely that her secret is disclosed she will destroy not only you, but your country as well. Therefore, do precisely what I tell you.'

Then the Guru told the Governor of his plan which was carried out at once. A house of lac was built at some distance from the palace, which had only a bedroom and kitchen. A big oven with a strong lid was built in the kitchen.

The royal physician then advised Ali Mardan to confine himself in this house for forty days. During this period no one but his wife should be allowed to see him.

His wife was only too glad to have Ali Mardan all to herself. A few days passed during which she happily attended to all his needs. One day Ali Mardan told his wife:

'The physician has prescribed a special loaf for me; kindly cook it for me.'

'I dislike ovens,' she said.

'But my life is in danger,' said the Governor. 'If you really love me, do this for me.'

She had no alternative but to cook the loaf. She went to the kitchen and set to work. Just when she stooped over the mouth of the oven to turn the loaf, Ali Mardan, seizing his opportunity, collected all his strength, pushed her in, and clamped down the lid so that she was unable to escape. He then hurried out and as directed by the holy man, set light to the house which, being made of lac, flared up instantaneously.

'You have done well,' said the Guru, who just then came up. 'Now go to your palace and rest there for two days. On the third day come to me and I will show you something.'

The Governor obeyed. In these two days his health was completely restored. He became as cheerful and strong as he had been on the day he met his fake Chinese princess.

On the third day, as appointed, Ali Mardan and the Guru went to the place where the house of lac had stood. All that was left of it was a heap of ashes.

'Look carefully in the ashes,' said the holy man, 'and you will find a pebble among them.'

Ali Mardan searched for a few minutes.

'Here it is,' he said at last.

'Good,' said the Guru, 'now which will you have, the pebble or the ashes?'

'The pebble,' answered the King.

'All right,' said the holy man. 'Then I will take the ashes.'

Whereupon he carefully wrapped the ashes in the hem of his garment and went away with his disciple.

Ali Mardan soon discovered the virtue of the pebble. It was the philosopher's stone the touch of which can change all metals into gold. But what the worth of the ashes was, remained a secret, for Ali Mardan never saw the Guru or his disciple again.

The Cat-Witch
(African American)

THIS happened in slavery times, in North Carolina. I've heard my grandmother tell it more than enough.

My grandmother was cook and house-girl for this family of slave-owners – they must have been Bissits, 'cause she was a Bissit. Well, Old Marster had sheep, and he sheared his sheep and put the wool upstairs. And Old Miss accused the cook of stealing her wool. 'Every day my wool gets smaller and smaller; somebody's taking my wool.' She knowed nobody could get up there handy but the house-girl. So they took her out and tore up her back about the wool, and Old Marster give her a terrible whipping.

When Grandma went upstairs to clean up, she'd often see a cat laying in the pile of wool. So she thought the cat laying there packed the wool, and made it look small. And she said to herself, she's going to cut off the cat's head with a butcher knife, if she catches her again. And sure enough she did. She grabbed the cat by her foot, her front foot, and hacked her foot with the knife, and cut if off. And the cat went running down the stairs, and out.

So she kilt the foot she cut off, and it turned natural, it turned to a hand. And the hand had a gold ring on the finger, with an initial in the ring. My grandmother carried the hand down to her Mistress, and showed it to her. Grandma could not read nor write, but Old Miss could, and she saw the initial on the ring. So it was an outcry; they begin to talk about it, like people do in a neighborhood, and they look around to see who lost her hand. And they found it was this rich white woman, who owned slaves, and was the wife of a young man hadn't been long married. (Witches don't stay long in one place; they travel.) Next morning she wouldn't get up to cook her husband's breakfast, 'cause she didn't have but one hand. And when he heard the talk, and saw the hand with his wife's gold ring, and found her in bed without a hand, he knew she was the cat-witch. And he said he didn't want her no longer.

So it was a custom of killing old witches. They took and

fastened her to an iron stake, they staked her, and poured tar around her, and set her afire, and burnt her up.

She had studied witchcraft, and she wanted that wool, and could get places, like the wind, like a hant. She would slip out after her husband was in bed, go through keyholes, if necessary be a rat – they can change – and steal things, and bring them back.

My grandma told that for the truth.

The Baba Yaga
(Russian)

NCE upon a time there was an old couple. The husband lost his wife and married again. But he had a daughter by the first marriage, a young girl, and she found no favor in the eyes of her evil stepmother, who used to beat her, and consider how she could get her killed outright. One day the father went away somewhere or other, so the stepmother said to the girl, 'Go to your aunt, my sister, and ask her for a needle and thread to make you a shift.'

Now that aunt was a Baba Yaga. Well, this girl was no fool, so she went to a real aunt of hers first, and says she:

'Good morning, Auntie!'

'Good morning, my dear! What have you come for?'

'Mother has sent me to her sister, to ask for a needle and thread to make me a shift.'

Then her aunt instructed her what to do. 'There is a birch tree there, niece, which would hit you in the eye – you must tie a ribbon round it; there are doors which would creak and bang – you must pour oil on their hinges; there are dogs which would tear you in pieces – you must throw them these rolls; there is a cat which would scratch your eyes out – you must give it a piece of bacon.'

So the girl went away, and walked and walked, till she came to the place. There stood a hut, and in it sat weaving the Baba Yaga, the Bony-Shanks.

'Good morning, Auntie,' says the girl.

'Good morning, my dear,' replies the Baba Yaga.

'Mother has sent me to ask you for a needle and thread to make me a shift.'

'Very well; sit down and weave a little in the meantime.'

So the girl sat down behind the loom, and the Baba Yaga went outside, and said to her servant-maid:

'Go and heat the bath, and get my niece washed; and mind you look sharp after her, I want to breakfast off her.'

Well, the girl sat there in such a fright that she was as much dead as alive. Presently she spoke imploringly to the servant-

151

maid, saying:

'Kinswoman dear, do please wet the firewood instead of making it burn; and fetch the water for the bath in a sieve.' And she made her a present of a handkerchief.

The Baba Yaga waited awhile; then she came to the window and asked:

'Are you weaving, niece? Are you weaving, my dear?'

'Oh yes, dear Aunt, I'm weaving.' So the Baba Yaga went away again, and the girl gave the Cat a piece of bacon, and asked:

'Is there no way of escaping from here?'

'Here's a comb for you and a towel,' said the Cat; 'take them, and be off. The Baba Yaga will pursue you, but you must lay your ear on the ground, and when you hear that she is close at hand, first of all throw down the towel. It will become a wide, wide river. And if the Baba Yaga gets across the river, and tries to catch you, then you must lay your ear on the ground again, and when you hear that she is close at hand, throw down the comb. It will become a dense, dense forest; through that she won't be able to force her way anyhow.'

The girl took the towel and the comb and fled. The dogs would have rent her, but she threw them the rolls, and they let her go by; the doors would have begun to bang, but she poured oil on their hinges, and they let her pass through; the birch tree would have poked her eyes out, but she tied the ribbon round it, and it let her pass on. And the Cat sat down to the loom, and worked away; muddled everything about, if it didn't do much weaving. Up came the Baba Yaga to the window, and asked:

'Are you weaving, niece? Are you weaving, my dear?'

'I'm weaving, dear Aunt, I'm weaving,' gruffly replied the Cat.

The Baba Yaga rushed into the hut, saw that the girl was gone, and took to beating the Cat, and abusing it for not having scratched the girl's eyes out. 'Long as I've served you,' said the Cat, 'you've never given me so much as a bone; but she gave me bacon.' Then the Baba Yaga pounced upon the dogs, on the doors, on the birch tree, and on the servant-maid, and set to work to abuse them all, and to knock them about. Then the dogs said to her, 'Long as we've served you, you've never so much as pitched us a burnt crust; but she gave us rolls to eat.'

And the doors said, 'Long as we've served you, you've never poured even a drop of water on our hinges; but she poured oil on us.' The birch tree said, 'Long as I've served you, you've never tied a single thread round me; but she fastened a ribbon around me.' And the servant-maid said, 'Long as I've served you, you've never given me so much as a rag; but she gave me a handkerchief.'

The Baba Yaga, bony of limb, quickly jumped into the mortar, sent it flying along with the pestle, sweeping away the while all traces of its flight with a broom, and set off in pursuit of the girl. Then the girl put her ear to the ground, and when she heard that the Baba Yaga was chasing her, and was now close at hand, she flung down the towel. And it became a wide, such a wide river! Up came the Baba Yaga to the river, and gnashed her teeth with spite; then she went home for her oxen, and drove them to the river. The oxen drank up every drop of the river, and then the Baba Yaga began the pursuit anew. But the girl put her ear to the ground again, and when she heard that the Baba Yaga was near, she flung down the comb, and instantly a forest sprang up, such an awfully thick one! The Baba Yaga began gnawing away at it, but however hard she worked, she couldn't gnaw her way though it, so she had to go back again.

But by this time the girl's father had returned home, and he asked:

'Where's my daughter?'

'She's gone to her aunt's,' replied her stepmother.

Soon afterwards the girl herself came running home.

'Where have you been?' asked her father.

'Ah, Father!' she said, 'Mother sent me to Aunt's to ask for a needle and thread to make me a shift. But Aunt's a Baba Yaga, and she wanted to eat me!'

'And how did you get away, daughter?'

'Why, like this,' said the girl, and explained the whole matter. As soon as her father had heard all about it, he became wroth with his wife, and shot her. But he and his daughter lived on and flourished, and everything went well with them.

Mrs Number Three
(Chinese)

DURING the T'ang Period there stood, to the west of the city of K'ai Fêng Fu, an inn called the 'Footbridge Tavern', kept by a woman about thirty years of age. No one knew who she was or whence she came, and she was known locally as 'Mrs Number Three'. She was childless, had no relations, and was supposed to be a widow. It was a comfortable, roomy inn; the hostess was in easy circumstances, and had a herd of very fine asses.

Besides this, she had a generous nature. If a traveller were short of money, she would reduce her prices, or board him for nothing; so her inn was never empty.

Sometime between AD 806 and 820, a man called Chao Chi Ho, on his way to Lo Yang (which was then the capital city of China), stopped at the 'Foot-Bridge Tavern' for the night. There was six or seven guests there already, each of whom had a bed in a large sleeping apartment. Chao, the last arrival, had a bed allotted to him in a corner, against the wall of the hostess's bedroom. Mrs Number Three treated him well, as she did all her guests. At bedtime she offered wine to each, and took a glass with them. Chao alone had none, as he did not generally drink wine. Quite late, when all the guests had gone to bed, the hostess retired to her room, shut the door and blew out the light.

The other guests were soon snoring peacefully, but Chao felt restless.

About midnight he heard the hostess moving things about in her room, and peeped through a crack in the wall. She lit a candle, and took out of a box an ox, a drover and a plough, little wooden models about six or seven inches high. She placed them near the hearth, on the beaten-clay floor of the room, took some water in her mouth, and sprayed it over the figures. Immediately they came to life. The drover goaded the ox, which drew the plough, back and forth, furrowing the floor over a space about equal to that of an ordinary mat. When the ploughing was done, she handed the drover a packet of buckwheat grains. He sowed them, and they at once began to sprout. In a few minutes they flowered, and then bore ripe grain. The drover gathered the grain, threshed it, and handed it to Mrs Number Three, who made him grind it in a little mill. Then she put the drover, his ox and his plough – which had again become little wooden figures – back into their box and used the buckwheat to make cakes.

At cockcrow the guests arose and prepared to leave, but the hostess said, 'You must not go without breakfast,' and set the buckwheat cakes before them.

Chao was very uneasy, so he thanked her and walked out of the inn. Looking over his shoulder, he saw each guest, the moment he tasted the cakes, drop down on all fours and begin to bray. Each had turned into a fine strong donkey; and the hostess forthwith drove them into her stable, and took possession of their belongings.

Chao did not tell a soul about his adventure; but a month later, when his business in Lo Yang was finished, he returned,

and stopped one evening at the 'Foot-Bridge Tavern'. He had with him some fresh buckwheat cakes, of the same size and shape as those made at the time of his former visit by Mrs Number Three.

The inn happened to be empty, and she made him very comfortable. Before he went to bed, she asked him if he wished to order anything.

'Not tonight,' he replied, 'but I should like something to eat first thing in the morning, before I go.'

'You shall have a good meal,' said the hostess.

During the night, the usual magic growth of buckwheat took place, and the next morning she placed before Chao a dish of buckwheat cakes. While she was away for a few minutes, Chao took one of the magic cakes off the dish, replaced it by one of his own, and waited for her to return. When she came back, she said, 'You are not eating anything.'

'I was waiting for you,' he replied. 'I have some cakes. If you will not try one of mine, I shall not eat those you have given me.'

'Give me one,' said Mrs Number Three.

Chao handed her the magic cake he had taken from the dish, and the moment she put her teeth into it she went down on all fours and began to bray. She had become a fine, strong she-ass.

Chao harnessed her, and rode home on her back, taking with him the box of wooden figures; but as he did not know the spell, he was unable to make them move, or to turn other people into asses.

Mrs Number Three was the strongest and most enduring donkey imaginable. She could travel 100 li a day on any road.

Four years later, Chao was riding her past a temple dedicated to Mount Hua, when an old man suddenly began clapping his hands and laughing, crying out, 'Now, Mrs Number Three of the Foot-Bridge, what's happened to you, eh?' Then, seizing the bridle, he said to Chao, 'She has tried to do you a wrong, I grant, but she has performed sufficient penance for her sins. Let me now set her free!' Then he took the halter off her head, and immediately she shed the ass's skin and stood upright in human form. She saluted the old man and vanished. No one has ever heard of her since.

Part Six

UNHAPPY FAMILIES

The Girl Who Banished Seven Youths
(Moroccan)

THERE was a woman who had seven sons. When-ever she felt her labor pains begin, she said, 'This time I shall bear a daughter.' But it always was a boy.

Say that she carried again and her month came round. Her husband's sister came to help as her time drew near. Her seven sons went out to hunt, but before they left they told their aunt: 'If our mother gives birth to a girl, hang the spindle over the door. When we see it, we shall spin around and come home. If she gives birth to another boy, hang up the sickle. When we see it, we shall cut loose and go.' The woman hated her nephews, so although the child was indeed a girl, she hung the sickle over the door. When they saw it, the seven went off into the desert.

The child was given the name Wudei'a Who Sent Away Subei'a, or The Girl Who Banished Seven. She grew and began to play with the other girls. One day she quarreled with her friends, and they said to her, 'If there was any good in you, would your seven brothers have left for the desert on the day you were born?'

Wudei'a ran home to her mother. 'Is it true that I have seven brothers?' she asked. 'Seven brothers you have,' her mother said, 'but on the day you were born, they went out hunting, and – O sadness and affliction – we have heard nothing of them since.' 'Then I shall go out and find them,' said the girl. 'How can you do so, when we have not seen them these fifteen years?' asked her mother. 'I'll search the world from its beginning to its end until I find them,' said Wudei'a.

So her mother gave her a camel to ride and sent with her a manservant and a maid. A while after they had set out, the manservant said, 'Get off the camel and let the maid ride.' 'Ya Ummi, O my mother,' called Wudei'a. And her mother replied, 'Why do you call?' 'The servant wants me to get off the camel,' said Wudei'a. Her mother told the servant to let Wudei'a ride, and they traveled on a little further. Again the servant tried to make Wudei'a dismount, and again she called

'Ya Ummi!' for her mother to help. The third time, however, her mother did not reply to her call, for they were too far away to be heard. So now the servant forced her off the camel and let the maid ride. Wudei'a walked on the ground with the blood pouring from her bare feet, for she was not used to walking so far.

Three days they traveled in this way, the maidservant riding high on the camel's back while Wudei'a walked below, weeping and tying cloths around her feet. On the third day they met a merchant's caravan. The servant said, 'O lords of this caravan, have you seen seven men hunting in the wilderness?' 'You will reach them before noon; their castle is on the road,' they answered.

Now the manservant heated pitch in the sun, and with it he rubbed the girl Wudei'a until all her skin was dark. Leading the camel to the castle gate, he called out, 'Good news, masters! I have brought your sister to you.' The seven brothers ran to greet their father's servant, but they said, 'We have no sister; our mother gave birth to a son!' The servant made the camel kneel and pointed to the maid. 'Your mother gave birth to a girl, and here she has come.' The brothers had never seen their sister; how could they know? They believed their father's servant when he told them that the maid was their sister and that Wudei'a was their sister's slave girl.

Next day the brothers said, 'Today we shall sit with our sister; we shall not go to hunt.' The oldest brother said to the black slave girl, 'Come and look through my hair for lice.' So Wudei'a laid her brother's head on her knee and wept as she combed his hair. A tear fell on to her arm. Her brother rubbed the spot, and the white flesh beneath the pitch appeared. 'Tell me your story,' said her eldest brother. Sobbing and talking Wudei'a told her tale. Her brother took his sword in his hand, went into the castle and cut off the heads of the servant and the maid. He heated water and brought out soap and Wudei'a washed herself until her skin was white again. Her brothers said, 'Now she looks like our true sister.' And they kissed her and stayed with her that day and the next. But on the third day they said, 'Sister, lock the castle gate, for we are going hunting and will not come back till seven days have passed. Lock the cat in with you and take care of her. Do not eat anything without giving a share to her.'

Seven days Wudei'a waited in the castle with the cat. On the eighth her brothers returned with game. They asked, 'Were you afraid?' 'What should I fear?' said Wudei'a. 'My room has seven doors, six of wood and the seventh made of iron.' After a time the brothers went away to hunt again. 'No one dares to approach our castle,' they told her. 'Be careful only of the cat; whatever you eat, give her half of it. And should anything happen, she knows our hunting grounds – she and the dove on the windowsill.'

Cleaning the rooms while she waited for her brothers to return, Wudei'a found a broad bean on the ground and picked it up. 'What are you eating?' asked the cat. 'Nothing. I found a broad bean among the sweepings,' said Wudei'a. 'Why didn't you give me half?' asked the cat. 'I forgot,' said Wudei'a. 'Watch and see how I'll repay you,' said the cat. 'All for half a bean?' asked Wudei'a. But the cat ran to the kitchen, pissed on the fire, and put it out.

There was no fire now to cook the food. Wudei'a stood on the castle wall, looking till she saw a light far off. She set out in that direction, and when she reached the place she found a Ghoul sitting at his fire. His hair was so long that one whisker was a pallet beneath him and the other a blanket above. 'Greetings, father Ghoul,' said Wudei'a. And the Ghoul replied.

> *By Allah, had not your greeting*
> *Come first before your speaking.*
> *By now the hills around would hear*
> *Your young bones crack and your flesh tear!*

'I need a fire,' said Wudei'a. The Ghoul answered,

> *If you want a large ember, you must give a strip of skin*
> *From your tallest finger to just below your chin.*
> *Or if the ember you want is a small one.*
> *From your ear down to your thumb.*

Wudei'a took the large ember and began to walk back, the blood flowing from her wound. A raven followed behind her throwing earth on each bloodstain to bury it. When she reached her gate, the bird flew up to the top of the wall. Wudei'a was startled and she scolded. 'May God give you cause to feel fear as you have frightened me.' 'Is this how kindness is rewarded?' said the raven. Down from the wall he dropped and ran along the ground, baring the blood he had covered all the way from her doorstep to the Ghoul's camp.

In the middle of the night the Ghoul woke up and followed the trail of blood until he came to the brothers' castle. He charged through the gate but he found the girl's room shut with seven doors – six made of wooden panels and the seventh a door of iron. He said,

> *Wudei'a Who Sent Away Subei'a,*
> *What was your old father doing when you came?*

She answered,

> *Lying on a gold bed frame,*
> *Of fine silk his counterpane*
> *And his mattress of the same.*

The Ghoul laughed and smashed down one of the wooden doors. Then he went away. But the next night and the next, the same thing happened until he had broken all six doors of wood. Only the seventh door was left, the door of iron.

Now Wudei'a was afraid. She wrote a message on a piece of paper and tied the paper around the neck of her brothers' dove with a thread. 'O dove, whom my brothers love,' she said, 'carry my words to them through the air above.' The tame bird flew off and did not alight until it sat in the lap of the oldest of the brothers. He read from his sister's paper.

> *Six doors are broken down; only the seventh remains.*
> *Come quickly if you want to see your sister again.*

The seven youths jumped into their saddles, and before the middle of the afternoon they had returned home. The castle gate was broken, the six wooden doors of their sister's room were splintered. Through the seventh door of iron they shouted, 'Sister, sister, we are your brothers; unlock your door and tell us how it happened.'

When she had repeated her tale, they said, 'May Allah grant you wisdom, did we not tell you never to eat without giving the cat its share? How could you forget?' Then they prepared themselves for the visit of the Ghoul. They dug a deep pit and filled it with firewood. They lit a fire and fed it until the pit was heaped with glowing coals. Then they laid a mat carefully to cover the opening of their trap and waited.

The Ghoul arrived and said,

Wudei'a Who Sent Away Subei'a,
What was your old father doing when you came?

She answered through her door,

He was flaying mules and donkeys,
Drinking blood and sucking entrails.
Matted hair so wild and long
It was his bed to lie upon.
O pray he may fall into the fire
To toast and burn till he expire.

The Ghoul boiled with rage. With a roar he broke down the seventh door and burst in. Wudei'a's brothers met him and said, 'Come neighbor, sit with us a while.' But when the Ghoul folded his legs to squat on the straw mat, he tumbled into the pit of embers. The brothers threw wood on top of him, heaping more and more until he was all burned up, even his bones. Nothing remained of him except the nail of his little finger, which had jumped into the middle of the room. It lay on the floor until later, when Wudei'a bent down to wipe the tiles with a cloth. Then it pricked her finger and slipped under the skin of her hand. That same moment the girl fell to the ground without life or movement.

Her brothers found her lying dead. They wept and wailed and made her a bier and tied it on to their father's camel's back and said,

Carry her, O camel of our father,
Carry her back to her mother.
Stop not to rest on the way thither
Stop not for man, or woman either.
Kneel only for him who says "Shoo!"

The camel lifted itself up to do as they bid. Neither halting nor running, it walked along the road it had traveled before. When half the distance had been crossed, three men spied what looked like a riderless camel lost in the wild. 'Let us catch it for ourselves!' they said, and shouted to make it stop. But the camel continued on.

Suddenly one of the men called to his friends. 'Wait while I tie on my shoe!' As soon as the camel heard the word 'shoe' it began to lower itself on to its knees. Joyfully the men ran to seize its halter. But what did they find? A wooden bier and lying on it a lifeless girl! 'Her people are wealthy,' said one, 'look at the ring on her finger!' And swiftly as the thought entered his head he began to pull off the shining jewel for himself. But in moving the ring the robber dislodged the nail from the Ghoul's little finger which had pierced Wudei'a's skin as she swept. The girl sat up alive and breathing. 'Long life to him who brought me back from death,' she said. Then she turned the camel's head towards her brothers' castle.

Weeping and falling upon Wudei'a's neck, the youths welcomed their lost sister back. 'Let us go and kiss the hands of our father and mother before they die,' said the eldest. 'You have been a father to us,' said the others, 'and your word like a father's,' Mounting their horses, all seven, with their sister on her camel making the eighth, set out for home.

'O sons, what made you leave the world I live in?' said their father when he had kissed and welcomed them. 'What made you leave me and your mother weeping night and day in grief over you?' On the first day and the second and the third, the youths rested and said nothing. But on the fourth when they had eaten, the oldest brother told the story from the time when their aunt had so falsely sent them into the wilderness until they had all found each other again. And from that day, they all lived together and were happy.

So ends the story of Wudei'a Who Sent Away Subei'a.

The Market of the Dead
(West African: Dahomey)

HERE were two co-wives. The first wife gave birth to twins, but herself died in childbirth. So the second wife took care of them. The elder twin was called Hwese, the other Hwevi. When the stepmother pounded grain, she took away the fine flour on top, and gave them what was not fit to eat.

One day the stepmother gave them each a small gourd, and told them to go for water. They went to the stream, but on the way back Hwese slipped and broke his gourd. The other said, 'If we go home now, she will beat Hwese, and let me go free. So I'll break mine, too.' He threw it down and broke it.

When the stepmother saw what had happened, she got a whip and whipped them.

Hwevi said, 'I am going to buy a bead.' Hwese said, 'Yes, let us each buy a bead for Ku. We will go there and visit the one who watches Death's door. Perhaps he will let us see our mother.'

The grave is deep,
Deep, deep,
Stepmother bought some gourds,
But Hwese broke his gourd,
And Hwevi broke his, too.
When we told our stepmother,
She flogged us with a whip,
So Hwese bought a bead,
And Hwevi bought one, too.

Good. So they went to see the guardian of Death's door. He asked them, 'What do you want?'

Hwesi said, 'Yesterday, when we went to get water, my brother Hwese broke his gourd. So I broke mine, too. Our stepmother beat us, and did not give us anything to eat all day. So we have come to beg you to let us enter here. We want to see our mother.'

When the guardian heard this, he opened the door.

The grave is deep,

Deep, deep.
Stepmother bought some gourds,
But Hwese broke his gourd,
And Hwevi broke his, too.
When we told our stepmother,
She flogged us with a whip,
So Hwese bought a bead,
And Hwevi bought one, too.
We gave these to the door's guardian
And the door opened.

Inside there were two markets, the market of the living, and the market of the dead.

Good. Everybody asked them, 'Where do you come from, where do you come from?' The living asked this, and the dead asked it, too. The children said, 'This is what happened. Yesterday we broke the little gourds our stepmother gave us. She beat us and gave us nothing to eat. We begged the man who watches at the door to let us come in to see our mother, so she might buy two other gourds for us.'

Good. Then their mother came and bought some *acasa* in the market of the living for them. Then she turned her back, and gave money to a living man to buy two gourds in the market of the living for them, and gave these to her children. Then she herself went to the market of the dead, and bought palm nuts to send to her husband's other wife. For she knew that the other liked these nuts very much. Now, once the woman ate the palm nuts, she would surely die.

Good. Then the mother said to the children, 'All right. Go home now, and tell your stepmother good-day. Thank her for looking after you so well.'

The grave is deep,
Deep, deep.
Stepmother bought some gourds,
But Hwese broke his gourd,
And Hwevi broke his, too.
When we told our stepmother,
She flogged us with a whip,
So Hwese bought a bead,
And Hwevi bought one, too.
We gave these to the door's guardian

And the door opened.
Our mother, hearing our story,
Bought us two gourds,
For our stepmother.

The stepmother looked for the two boys. She looked for them everywhere, but she could not find out where they had gone. When they came back, she asked them, 'Where were you?'

They said, 'We went to see our mother.'

But their stepmother scolded them. She said, 'No, you lie. Nobody can visit the dead.'

Good. The children gave her the palm nuts. They said, 'Here, our mother sent these to you.'

The other woman laughed at them. 'So you found a dead one to send me palm nuts?'

But when the stepmother ate these palm nuts, she died.

The grave is deep,
Deep, deep.
Stepmother bought some gourds,
But Hwese broke his gourd,
And Hwevi broke his, too.
When we told our stepmother,
She flogged us with a whip,
So Hwese bought a bead,
And Hwevi bought one, too.
We gave these to the door's guardian
And the door opened.
Our mother, hearing our story,
Bought us two gourds,
For our stepmother.
At home our stepmother wanted to buy life,
But we gave her the fruit
In abundance, abundance.

In Dahomey, when a person dies, the family goes to a diviner and he makes the dead talk so that you hear his voice. So when they called the dead stepmother she said, 'Tell all the other women that my death came from the orphans. Tell them also that Mawu says that when there are several wives, and one dies and leaves children, the others must care for the children of the dead woman.'

This is why, if a man has two wives, and one dies leaving a

child, you give that child to the second wife, and the second wife must look after the dead woman's child better than after her own children. And this is why one never mistreats orphans. For once you mistreat them, you die. You die the same day. You are not even sick. I know that myself. I am an orphan. My father never lets me go out alone at night. Whenever I ask him for something, he gives it to me.

The Woman Who Married Her Son's Wife
(Eskimo)

NCE there lived an old woman who desired her son's pretty young wife. This son was a hunter who often would be gone for many days at a time. Once, while he was gone, the old woman sat down and made herself a penis out of sealbone and skins. She fastened this penis to her waist and showed it to her daughter-in-law, who exclaimed: 'How nice . . .' Then they slept together. Soon the old woman was going out to hunt in a big skin kayak, just like her son. And when she came back, she would take off her clothes and move her breasts up and down, saying: 'Sleep with me, my dear little wife. Sleep with me . . .'

It happened that the son returned from his hunting and saw his mother's seals lying in front of the house. 'Whose seals are these?' he asked of his wife.

'None of your business,' she replied.

Being suspicious of her, he dug a hole behind their house and hid there. He figured that some hunter was claiming his wife in his absence. Soon, however, he saw his mother paddling home in her kayak with a big hooded seal. Mother and son never caught anything but big hooded seals. The old woman reached land and took off her clothes, then moved her breasts up and down, saying: 'My sweet little wife, kindly delouse me . . .'

The son was not pleased by his mother's behaviour. He came out of hiding and struck the old woman so hard that he killed her. 'Now,' he said to his wife, 'you must come away with me because our home place has a curse on it.'

The wife began to quiver and shake all over. 'You've killed my dear husband,' she cried. And would not stop crying.

The Little Red Fish and the Clog of Gold

(Iraqi)

NEITHER here nor there lived a man, a fisherman. His wife had drowned in the great river and left him a pretty little girl not more than two years old. In a house nearby lived a widow and her daughter. The woman began to come to the fisherman's house to care for the girl and comb her hair, and every time she said to the child, 'Am I not like a mother to you?' She tried to please the fisherman, but he always said, 'I shall never marry. Stepmothers hate their husband's children even though their rivals are dead and buried.' When his daughter grew old enough to pity him when she saw him washing his own clothes, she began to say, 'Why don't you marry our neighbor, Father? There is no evil in her, and she loves me as much as her own daughter.'

They say water will wear away stone. In the end the fisherman married the widow, and she came to live in his house. The wedding week was not yet over when sure enough, she began to feel jealous of her husband's daughter. She saw how much her father loved the child and indulged her. And she could not help but see that the child was fair, and quick, while her own daughter was thin and sallow, and so clumsy she did not know how to sew the seam of her gown.

No sooner did the woman feel that she was mistress of the house then she began to leave all the work for the girl to do. She would not give her stepchild soap to wash her hair and feet, and she fed her nothing but crusts and crumbs. All this the girl bore patiently, saying not a word. For she did not wish to grieve her father, and she thought, 'I picked up the scorpion with my own hand; I'll save myself with my own mind.'

Besides her other errands, the fisherman's daughter had to go down to the river each day to bring home her father's catch, the fish they ate and sold. One day from beneath a basket load of three catfish, suddenly one little red fish spoke to her:

Child with such patience to endure,

I beg you now, my life secure.
Throw me back into the water,
And now and always be my daughter.

The girl stopped to listen, half in wonder and half in fear. Then retracing her steps, she flung the fish into the rver and said, 'Go! People say, "Do a good deed for, even if it is like throwing gold into the sea, in God's sight it is not lost."' And lifting itself on the face of the water, the little fish replied:

Your kindness is not in vain –
A new mother do you gain.
Come to me when you are sad,
And I shall help to make you glad.

The girl went back to the house and gave the three catfish to her stepmother. When the fisherman returned and asked about the fourth, she told him, 'Father, the red fish dropped from my basket. It may have fallen into the river, for I couldn't find it again.' 'Never mind,' he said, 'it was a very small fish.' But her stepmother began to scold, 'You never told me there were four fishes. You never said that you lost one. Go now and look for it, before I curse you!'

It was past sunset and the girl had to walk back to the river in the dark. Her eyes swollen with tears, she stood on the water's edge and called out,

Red fish, my mother and nurse,
Come quickly, and ward off a curse.

And there at her feet appeared the little red fish to comfort her and say, 'Though patience is bitter, its fruit is very sweet. Now bend down and take this gold piece from my mouth. Give it to your stepmother, and she will say nothing to you.' Which is exactly what happened.

The years came and the years went, and in the fisherman's house life continued as before. Nothing changed except that the two little girls were now young women.

One day a great man, the master of the merchants' guild, announced that his daughter was to be married. It was the custom for the women to gather at the bride's house on the 'day of the bride's henna' to celebrate and sing as they watched the girls' feet, palms, and arms beng decorated for the

172

wedding with red henna stain. Then every mother brought her unwed daughters to be seen by the mothers of sons. Many a girl's destiny was decided on such a day.

The fisherman's wife rubbed and scrubbed her daughter and dressed her in her finest gown and hurried her off to the master merchant's house with the rest. The fisherman's daughter was left at home to fill the water jar and sweep the floor while they were gone.

But as soon as the two women were out of sight, the fisherman's daughter gathered up her gown and ran down to the river to tell the little red fish her sorrow. 'You shall go to the bride's henna and sit on the cushions in the center of the hall,' said the little red fish. She gave the girl a small bundle and said, 'Here is everything you need to wear, with a comb of pearl for your hair and clogs of gold for your feet. But one thing you must remember: be sure to leave before your stepmother rises to go.'

When the girl loosened the cloth that was knotted round the clothes, out fell a gown of silk as green as clover. It was stitched with threads and sequins of gold, and from its folds rose a sweet smell like the essence of roses. Quickly she washed herself and decked herself and tucked the comb of pearl behind her braid and slipped the golden clogs on to her feet and went tripping off to the feast.

The women from every house in the town were there. They paused in their talk to admire her face and her grace, and they thought, 'This must be the governor's daughter!' They brought her sherbet and cakes made with almonds and honey and they sat her in the place of honor in the middle of them all. She looked for her stepmother with her daughter and saw them far off, near the door where the peasants were sitting, and the wives of weavers of peddlers.

Her stepmother stared at her and said to herself, 'O Allah Whom we praise, how much this lady resembles my husband's daughter! But then, don't they say, "Every seven men were made from one clod of clay"?' And the stepmother never knew that it was her very own husband's daughter and none other!

Not to spin out our tale, before the rest of the women stood up, the fisherman's daughter went to the mother of the bride to say, 'May it be with God's blessings and bounty, O my aunt!' and hurried out. The sun had set and darkness was falling. On her way the girl had to cross a bridge over the stream that flowed into the king's garden. And by fate and divine decree, it happened that as she ran over the bridge one of her golden clogs fell off her foot and into the river below. It was too far to climb down to the water and search in the dusk; what if her stepmother should return home before her? So the girl took off her other shoe, and pulling her cloak around her head, dashed on her way.

When she reached the house she shucked her fine clothes, rolled the pearly comb and golden clog inside them, and hid them under the woodpile. She rubbed her head and hands and feet with earth to make them dirty, and she was standing with her broom when her stepmother found her. The wife looked into her face and examined her hands and feet and said, 'Still sweeping after sunset? Or are you hoping to sweep our lives away?'

What of the golden clog? Well, the current carried it into the king's garden and rolled it and rolled it until it came to rest in the pool where the king's son led his stallion to drink. Next day the prince was watering the horse. He saw that every time it lowered its head to drink, something made it shy and step back. What could there be at the bottom of the pool to frighten his stallion? He called to the groom, and from the mud the man brought him the shining clog of gold.

When the prince held the beautiful little thing in his hand, he began to imagine the beautiful little foot that had worn it. He walked back to the palace with his heart busy and his mind full of the girl who owned so precious a shoe. The queen saw him lost in thought and said, 'May Allah send us good news; why so careworn, my son?' 'Yammah, Mother, I want you to find me a wife!' said the prince. 'So much thought over one wife and no more?' said the queen. 'I'll find you a thousand if you wish! I'll bring every girl in the kingdom to be your wife if you want! But tell me, my son, who is the girl who has stolen your reason?' 'I want to marry the girl who owns this clog,' replied the prince, and he told his mother how he had found it. 'You shall have her, my son,' said the queen. 'I shall begin my search tomorrow as soon as it is light, and I shall not stop till I find her.'

The very next day the prince's mother went to work, in at one house and out at the next with the golden clog tucked under her arm. Wherever she saw a young woman, she measured the shoe against the sole of the maiden's foot. Meanwhile the prince sat in the palace gate waiting for her return. 'What news, Mother?' he asked. And she said, 'Nothing yet, my son. Be patient, child, put snow on your breast and cool your passion. I'll find her yet.'

And so the search continued. Entering at one gate and leaving at the next, the queen visited the houses of the nobles and the merchants and the goldsmiths. She saw the daughters of the craftsmen and the tradesmen. She went into the huts of the water carriers and the weavers, and stopped at each house until only the fishermen's hovels in the bank of the river were left. Every evening when the prince asked for news, she said, 'I'll find her, I'll find her.'

When the fisherfolk were told that the queen was coming to visit their houses, that wily fisherman's wife got busy. She bathed her daughter and dressed her in her best, she rinsed her hair with henna and rimmed her eyes with *kohl* and rubbed her cheeks till they glowed red. But still when the girl stood beside the fisherman's daughter, it was like a candle in the sun. Much as the stepchild had been ill-treated and starved, through the will of Allah and with the help of the little red fish, she had grown in beauty from day to day. Now her stepmother dragged her out of the house and into the yard. She pushed her into the bakehouse and covered its mouth with the round clay tray on which she spread her dough. This she held down with the stone of her handmill. 'Don't dare move until I come for you!' said the stepmother. What could the poor girl do but crouch in the ashes and trust in Allah to save her?

When the queen arrived the stepmother pushed her daughter forward, saying, 'Kiss the hands of the prince's mother ignorant child!' As she had done in the other houses, the queen set the girl beside her and held up her foot and measured the golden clog against it. Just at that moment the neighbor's rooster flew into the yard and began to crow,

Ki-ki-ki-kow!
Let the king's wife know
They put the ugly one on show
And hid the beauty down below!
Ki-ki-ki-kow!

He began again with his piercing cry, and the stepmother raced out and flapped her arms to chase him away. But the queen had heard the words, and she sent her servants to search both high and low. When they pushed aside the cover off the mouth of the oven, they found the girl – fair as the moon in the midst of the ashes. They brought her to the queen, and the golden clog fit as if it had been the mold from which her foot was cast.

The queen was satisfied. She said, 'From this hour that daughter of yours is betrothed to my son. Make ready for the wedding. God willing, the procession shall come for her on Friday.' And she gave the stepmother a purse filled with gold.

When the woman realized that her plans had failed, that her husband's daughter was to marry the prince while her own remained in the house, she was filled with anger and rage. 'I'll see that he sends her back before the night is out,' she said.

She took the purse of gold, ran to the perfumer's bazaar, and asked for a purge so strong that it would shred the bowels to tatters. At the sight of the gold the perfumer began to mix the powders in his tray. Then she asked for arsenic and lime, which weaken hair and make it fall, and an ointment that smelled like carrion.

Now the stepmother prepared the bride for her wedding. She washed her hair with henna mixed wth arsenic and lime, and spread the foul ointment over her hair. Then she held the girl by the ear and poured the purge down her throat. Soon the wedding procession arrived, with horses and drums, fluttering bright clothes, and the sounds of jollity. They lifted the bride on to the litter and took her away. She came to the palace preceded by music and followed by singing and chanting and clapping of hands. She entered the chamber, the prince lifted the veil off her face and she shone like a fourteen-day moon. A scent of amber and roses made the prince press his face to her hair. He ran his fingers over her locks, and it was like a man playing with cloth of gold. Now the bride began to feel a heaviness in her belly, but from under the hem of her gown there fell gold pieces in thousands till the carpet and the cushions were covered with gold.

Meanwhile the stepmother waited in her doorway, saying, 'Now they'll bring her back in disgrace. Now she'll come home all filthy and bald.' But though she stood in the doorway till

dawn, from the palace no one came.

The news of the prince's fair wife began to fill the town, and the master merchant's son said to his mother, 'They say that the prince's bride has a sister, I want her for my bride.' Going to the fisherman's hut, his mother gave the fisherman's wife a purse full of gold and said, 'Prepare the bride, for we shall come for her on Friday if God wills.' And the fisherman's wife said to herself, 'If what I did for my husband's daughter turned her hair to threads of gold and her belly to a fountain of coins, shall I not do the same for my own child?' She hastened to the perfumer and asked for the same powders and drugs, but stronger than before. Then she prepared her child, and the wedding procession came. When the merchant's son lifted her veil, it was like lifting the cover off a grave. The stink was so strong that it choked him, and her hair came away in his hands. So they wrapped the poor bride in her own filth and carried her back to her mother.

As for the prince, he lived with the fisherman's daughter in great happiness and joy, and God blessed them with seven children like seven golden birds.

Mulberry, mulberry,
So ends my story.
If my house were not so far
I'd bring you figs and raisins in a jar.

The Wicked Stepmother
(West African: Togoland)

THERE was once a certain man who had two wives. The first one bore him a boy-child and the other had no children. Now it came to pass that the mother of the boy became sick, and when she knew that death was near she sent for the second wife and placed in her charge her son, saying: 'I am going away now and must leave my boy. Take him and care for him and feed him as if he were your own. The second wife agreed, and shortly after the woman died.

But the surviving wife forgot her promise and ill-treated the motherless boy. She gave him neither food nor clothing, and the wretched child had to seek what he could find for himself.

One day the woman called the child to her and said that he was to accompany her into the bush to get firewood. The boy obeyed and went with the woman. When they were a long way from the village the woman went into the bush for the sticks and the boy sat down in the shade of a big tree. Presently he noticed a lot of fruit had fallen from the tree and he began to eat it. He was very hungry and only when all the fallen fruit had been eaten was his hunger satisfied. He then fell asleep, and after a while when he awoke he found he was again hungry. But there was no fruit on the ground and he was far too small to reach up to the branches to gather some. So he began to sing, and as he sang a song in praise of the tree, lo! the branches of the tree bent down to him and enabled him to climb up. He then took all the food he could eat and collected some to take home in the rag which did service for a cloth. Then, still singing, he climbed down and waited for the woman. She soon came and they both went home.

Some days later the boy was seated outside the house eating the fruit he had gathered when the woman saw him and asked him what he had there. He told her, and the woman took some and said that it was good. She then told the boy to go with her to the tree so that they could get some more of this new and excellent fruit.

They went, and when they drew near the tree the boy began

to sing again, and the tree obediently bent down its branches, and the woman climbed up. Then the boy ceased his song and the branches sprang up, taking with them the woman. The woman called to the boy, but he answered that Nyame had now given him sense and had shown him how to procure food, and that as she had neglected him so he would now neglect her. He then went home to the village.

Now when he arrived all the people asked him where was the woman, and he replied that she had gone to the bush to get firewood. Evening came and still no woman. So the people assembled under the village tree and again asked the boy, but he replied as before.

On the following morning they again collected, and began to beg the boy to show them where he had left his stepmother. When they had begged him for a long time he at last consented and led then into the bush, where the people saw the woman at the top of the tree. They asked her how she had managed to get there and she told them. Then they all begged the boy to sing. For a long time he refused, but at last as they begged him so long he agreed and began to sing his praise of the tree. Immediately the branches bent down and the woman was freed.

Then everyone went back to the village and reported to the chief what they had seen. He at once called all the elders and sent for the woman. He told her that had the boy not consented to sing she would not have been rescued, and he ordered her to give an account of how she had treated the motherless child. She confessed she had done wrong, and then the chief said: 'Now let all men know from this that when a man has many wives the children shall be treated as the children of them all. To each woman her husband's son shall be a son, and each child shall call each of his father's wives mother.'

Tuglik and Her Granddaughter
(Eskimo)

ONCE there was a big narwhal hunt to which everyone went but an old woman named Tuglik and her granddaughter Qujapik. The two of them were getting rather hungry, but they hadn't any idea of how to hunt for their food. Yet old Tuglik knew a few magical words, which she uttered during a trance. All of a sudden she changed into a man. She had a seal-bone for a penis and chunk of *mataq* for testicles. Her vagina became a sledge. She said to her granddaughter:

'Now I can travel to the fjords and get some food for us.'

The girl replied: 'But what about dogs to pull your sledge?'

And so strong was the old woman's magic that she was able to create a team of dogs from her own lice. The dogs were barking and yelping and ready to go, so Tuglik cracked her whip and off she went with them to the fjords. Day after day she went off like this, and she would always return in the evening with some sort of game, even if it was only a ptarmigan or two. Once, while she was away hunting, a man

181

came to their hut. He looked around and said:

'Whose harpoon is this, little girl?'

'Oh,' said Qujapik, 'it is only my grandmother's.'

'And whose kayak is this?'

'Just my grandmother's.'

'You seem to be pregnant. Who is your husband?'

'My grandmother is my husband.'

'Well, I know someone who would make a better husband for you . . .'

Now the old woman returned home with a walrus thrown over her sledge. 'Qujapik!' she called out, 'Qujapik!' But there was no Qujapik at all. The girl had gathered up all her things and left the village with her new husband.

Tuglik saw no point in being a man any more – man or woman, it's all the same when a person is alone. So she uttered her magic words and once again she was a wrinkled old hag with a vagina instead of a sledge.

The Juniper Tree
(German)

LL this took place a long time ago, most likely some two thousand years ago. There was a rich man who had a beautiful and pious wife, and they loved each other very much. Though they did not have any children, they longed to have some. Day and night the wife prayed for a child, but still none came, and everything remained the same.

Now, in the front of the house there was yard, and in the yard stood a juniper tree. One day during winter the wife was under the tree peeling an apple, and as she was peeling it, she cut her finger, and her blood dripped on the snow.

'Oh,' said the wife, and she heaved a great sigh. While she looked at the blood before her, she became quite sad, 'If only I had a child as red as blood and as white as snow!' Upon saying that, her mood changed, and she became very cheerful, for she felt something might come of it. Then she went home.

After a month the snow vanished. After two months everything turned green. After three months the flowers sprouted from the ground. After four months all the trees in the woods grew more solid, and the green branches became intertwined. The birds began to sing, and their song resounded throughout the forest as the blossoms fell from the trees. Soon the fifth month passed, and when the wife stood under the juniper tree, it smelled so sweetly that her heart leapt for joy. Indeed, she was so overcome by joy that she fell down on her knees. When the sixth month had passed, the fruit was large and firm and she was quite still. In the seventh month she picked the juniper berries and ate them so avidly that she became sad and sick. After the eighth month passed, she called her husband to her and wept.

'If I die,' she said, 'bury me under the juniper tree.'

After that she was quite content and relieved until the ninth month had passed. Then she had a child as white as snow and as red as blood. When she saw the baby, she was so delighted that she died.

Her husband buried her under the juniper tree, and he

began weeping a great deal. After some time he felt much better, but he still wept every now and then. Eventually, he stopped, and after more time passed, he took another wife. With his second wife he had a daughter, while the child from the first wife was a little boy, who was as red as blood and as white as snow. Whenever the woman looked at her daughter, she felt great love for her, but whenever she looked at the little boy, her heart was cut to the quick. She could not forget that he would always stand in her way and prevent her daughter from inheriting everything, which was what the woman had in mind. Thus the devil took hold of her and influenced her feelings toward the boy until she became quite cruel toward him: she pushed him from one place to the next, slapped him here and cuffed him there, so that the poor child lived in constant fear. When he came home from school, he found no peace at all.

One time the woman went up to her room, and her little daughter followed her and said, 'Mother, give me an apple.'

'Yes, my child,' said the woman, and she gave her a beautiful apple from the chest that had a large heavy lid with a big, sharp iron lock.

'Mother,' said the little daughter,' shouldn't brother get one too?'

The woman was irritated by that remark, but she said, 'Yes, as soon as he comes home from school.' And, when she looked out of the window and saw he was coming, the devil seemed to take possession of her, and she snatched the apple away from her daughter.

'You shan't have one before your brother,' she said and threw the apple into the chest and shut it.

The little boy came through the door, and the devil compelled her to be friendly to him and say, 'Would you like to have an apple, my son?' Yet, she gave him a fierce look.

'Mother,' said the little boy, 'how ferocious you look! Yes, give me an apple.'

Then she felt compelled to coax him.

'Come over here,' she said as she lifted the lid, 'Take out an apple for yourself.'

And as the little boy leaned over the chest, the devil prompted her, and *crash!* she slammed the lid so hard that his head flew off and fell among the apples. Then she was struck by fear and thought, How am I going to get out of this? She went up to her room and straight to her dresser, where she took out a white kerchief from a drawer. She put the boy's head back on to his neck and tied the neckerchief around it so nothing could be seen. Then she set him on a chair in front of the door and put the apple in his hand.

Some time later little Marlene came into the kitchen and went up to her mother, who was standing by the fire in front of a pot of hot water, which she was constantly stirring.

'Mother,' said Marlene, 'brother's sitting by the door and looks very pale. He's got an apple in his hand, and I asked him to give me the apple, but he didn't answer, and I became very scared.'

'Go back to him,' said the mother, 'and if he doesn't answer you, give him a box on the ear.'

Little Marlene returned to him and said, 'Brother, give me the apple.'

But he would not respond. So she gave him a box on the ear, and his head fell off. The little girl was so frightened that she began to cry and howl. Then she ran to her mother and said, 'Oh, Mother, I've knocked my brother's head off!' And she wept and wept and could not be comforted.

'Marlene,' said the mother, 'what have you done! You're not to open your mouth about this. We don't want anyone to know, and besides there's nothing we can do about it now. So we'll make a stew out of him.'

The mother took the little boy and chopped him into pieces. Next she put them into a pot and let them stew. But Marlene stood nearby and wept until all her tears fell into the pot, so it did not need any salt.

When the father came home, he sat down at the table and asked, 'Where's my son?'

The mother served a huge portion of the stewed meat, and Marlene wept and could not stop.

'Where's my son?' the father asked again.

'Oh,' said the mother, 'he's gone off into the country to visit his mother's great uncle. He intends to stay there for a while.'

'What's he going to do there? He didn't even say goodbye to me.'

'Well, he wanted to go very badly and asked me if he could stay there six weeks. They'll take good care of him.'

'Oh, that makes me sad,' said the man. 'It's not right. He should have said goodbye to me.' Then he began to eat and said, 'Marlene, what are you crying for? Your brother will come back soon.' Without pausing he said, 'Oh, wife, the food tastes great! Give me some more!' The more he ate, the more he wanted. 'Give me some more,' he said, 'I'm not going to share this with you. Somehow I feel as if it were all mine.'

As he ate and ate he threw the bones under the table until he was all done. Meanwhile, Marlene went to her dresser and took out her best silk neckerchief from the bottom drawer, gathered all the bones from beneath the table, tied them up in her silk kerchief, and carried them outside the door. There she wept bitter tears and laid the bones beneath the juniper tree. As she put them there, she suddenly felt relieved and stopped crying. Now the juniper tree began to move. The branches separated and came together again as though they were clapping their hands in joy. At the same time smoke came out of the tree, and in the middle of the smoke there was a flame that seemed to be burning. Then a beautiful bird flew out of the fire and began singing magnificently. He soared high in the air, and after he vanished, the juniper tree was as it was before. Yet, the silk kerchief was gone. Marlene was very happy and gay. It was as if her brother were still alive, and she went merrily back into the house, sat down at the table, and ate.

Meanwhile, the bird flew away, landed on a goldsmith's house, and began to sing:

'My mother, she killed me.
My father, he ate me.
My sister, Marlene, she made sure to see
my bones were all gathered together,
bound nicely in silk, as neat as can be,
and laid beneath the juniper tree.
Tweet, tweet! *What a lovely bird I am!'*

The goldsmith was sitting in his workshop making a golden chain. When he heard the bird singing on his roof, he thought it was very beautiful. Then he stood up, and as he walked across the threshold, he lost a slipper. Still, he kept on going, right into the middle of the street with only one sock and a slipper on. He was also wearing his apron, and in one of his

186

hands he held the golden chain, in the other his tongs. The sun was shining brightly on the street as he walked, and then he stopped to get a look at the bird.

'Bird,' he said, 'how beautifully you sing! Sing me that song again.'

'No,' said the bird, 'I never sing twice for nothing. Give me the golden chain, and I'll sing it for you again.'

'All right,' said the goldsmith. 'Here's the golden chain. Now sing the song again.'

The bird swooped down, took the golden chain in his right claw, went up to the goldsmith, and began singing:

'My mother, she killed me.
My father, he ate me.
My sister, Marlene, she made sure to see
my bones were all gathered together,
bound nicely in silk, as neat as can be,
and laid beneath the juniper tree.
Tweet, tweet! *What a lovely bird I am!'*

Then the bird flew off to a shoemaker, landed on his roof, and sang:

'My mother, she killed me.
My father, he ate me.
My sister, Marlene, she made sure to see
my bones were all gathered together,
bound nicely in silk, as neat as can be,
and laid beneath the juniper tree.
Tweet, tweet! *What a lovely bird I am!'*

When the shoemaker heard the song, he ran to the door in his shirt sleeves and looked up at the roof, keeping his hand over his eyes to protect them from the bright sun.

'Bird,' he said. 'How beautifully you sing!' Then he called into the house, 'Wife, come out here for a second! There's a bird up there. Just look. How beautifully he sings!' Then he called his daughter and her children, and the journeyman, apprentices, and maid. They all came running out into the street and looked at the bird and saw how beautiful he was. He had bright red and green feathers, and his neck appeared to glisten like pure gold, while his eyes sparkled in his head like stars.

'Bird,' said the shoemaker, 'now sing me that song again.'

'No,' said the bird, 'I never sing twice for nothing. You'll have to give me a present.'

'Wife,' said the man, 'go into the shop. There's a pair of red shoes on the top shelf. Get them for me.'

His wife went and fetched the shoes.

'There,' said the man. 'Now sing the song again.'

The bird swooped down, took the shoes in his left claw, flew back up on the roof, and sang:

'My mother, she killed me.
My father, he ate me.
My sister, Marlene, she made sure to see
my bones were all gathered together,
bound nicely in silk, as neat as can be,
and laid beneath the juniper tree.
Tweet, tweet! *What a lovely bird I am!'*

When the bird finished the song, he flew away. He had the chain in his right claw and the shoes in his left, and he flew far away to a mill. The mill went *clickety-clack, clickety-clack, clickety-clack.* The miller had twenty men sitting in the mill, and they were hewing a stone. Their chisels went *click-clack, click-clack, click-clack.* And the mill kept going *clickety-clack, clickety-clack, clickety-clack.* The bird swooped down and landed on a linden tree outside the mill and sang:

'My mother, she killed me.'

Then one of the men stopped working.

'My father, he ate me.'

Then two more stopped and listened.

'My sister, Marlene, she made sure to see . . .'

Then four more stopped.

' . . . my bones were all gathered together,
bound nicely in silk, as neat as can be.'

Now only eight kept chiseling.

'And laid beneath . . .'

Now only five.

'. . . the juniper tree.'

Now only one.

Tweet, tweet! *What a lovely bird I am!'*

Then the last one also stopped and listened to the final words.
'Bird, how beautifully you sing! Let me hear that too. Sing
your song again for me.'

'No,' said the bird. 'I never sing twice for nothing. Give me
the millstone, and I'll sing the song again.'

'I would if I could,' he said. 'But the millstone doesn't belong
to me alone.'

'If he sings again,' said the others, 'he can have it.'

Then the bird swooped down, and all twenty of the miller's
men took beams to lift the stone. 'Heave-ho! Heave-ho!
Heave-ho!' Then the bird stuck his neck through the hole, put
the stone on like a collar, flew back to the tree, and sang:

> *'My mother, she killed me.*
> *My father, he ate me.*
> *My sister, Marlene, she made sure to see*
> *my bones were all gathered together,*
> *bound nicely in silk, as neat as can be,*
> *and laid beneath the juniper tree.*
> Tweet, tweet! *What a lovely bird I am!'*

When the bird finished his song, he spread his wings, and in
his right claw he had the chain, in his left the shoes, and
around his neck the millstone. Then he flew away to his
father's house.

The father, mother, and Marlene were sitting at the table in
the parlor, and the father said, 'Oh, how happy I am! I just feel
so wonderful!'

'Not me,' said the mother. 'I feel scared as if a storm were
about to erupt.'

Meanwhile, Marlene just sat there and kept weeping. Then
the bird flew up, and when he landed on the roof, the father
said, 'Oh, I'm in such good spirits. The sun's shining so
brightly outside, and I feel as though I were going to see an old
friend again.'

'Not me,' said his wife, 'I'm so frightened that my teeth are
chattering. I feel as if fire were running through my veins.'

She tore open her bodice, while Marlene sat in a corner and kept weeping. She had her handkerchief in front of her eyes and wept until it was completely soaked with her tears. The brid swooped down on the juniper tree, where he perched on a branch and began singing:

'*My mother, she killed me.*'

The mother stopped her ears, shut her eyes, and tried not to see or hear anything, but there was a roaring in her ears like a turbulent storm, and her eyes burned and flashed like lightning.

'*My father, he ate me.*'

'Oh, Mother,' said the man, 'listen to that beautiful bird singing so gloriously! The sun's so warm, and it smells like cinnamon.'

'*My sister, Marlene, she made sure to see . . .*'

Then Marlene laid her head on her knees and wept and wept, but the man said, 'I'm going outside. I must see the bird close up.'

'Oh, don't go!' said the wife. 'I feel as if the whole house were shaking and about to go up in flames!'

Nevertheless, the man went out and looked at the bird.

'*. . .my bones were all gathered together,*
bound nicely in silk, as neat as can be,
and laid beneath the juniper tree.
Tweet, tweet! *What a lovely bird I am!*'

After ending his song, the bird dropped the golden chain, and it fell around the man's neck just right, so that it fit him perfectly. Then he went inside and said, 'Just look how lovely that bird is! He gave me this beautiful golden chain, and he's as beautiful as well!'

But the woman was petrified and fell to the floor. Her cap slipped off her head, and the bird sang again:

'*My mother, she killed me.*'

'Oh, I wish I were a thousand feet beneath the earth so I wouldn't have to hear this!'

'My father, he ate me.'

Then the woman fell down again as if she were dead.

'My sister, Marlene, she made sure to see . . .'

'Oh,' said Marlene, 'I want to go outside too and see if the bird will give me something.' Then she went out.

' . . . my bones were all gathered together,
bound nicely in silk, as neat as can be.'

Then the bird threw her the shoes.

'And laid beneath the juniper tree.
Tweet, tweet! *What a lovely bird I am!'*

Marlene felt gay and happy. She put on the new red shoes and danced and skipped back into the house.

'Oh,' she said, 'I was so sad when I went out, and now I feel so cheerful. That certainly is a splendid bird. He gave me a pair of red shoes as a gift.'

'Not me,' said the wife, who jumped up, and her hair flared up like red-hot flames. 'I feel as if the world were coming to an end. Maybe I'd feel better if I went outside.'

As she went out the door, *crash!* the bird threw the millstone down on her head, and she was crushed to death. The father and Marlene heard the crash and went outside. Smoke, flames, and fire were rising from the spot, and when it was over, the little brother was standing there. He took his father and Marlene by the hand, and all three were very happy. Then they went into the house, sat down at the table, and ate.

Nourie Hadig
(Armenian)

HERE was once a rich man who had a very beautiful wife and a beautiful daughter known as Nourie Hadig [tiny piece of pomegranate]. Every month when the moon appeared in the sky, the wife asked: 'New moon, am I the most beautiful or are you?' And every month the moon replied, 'You are the most beautiful.'

But when Nourie Hadig came to be fourteen years of age, she was so much more beautiful than her mother that the moon was forced to change her answer. One day when the mother asked the moon her constant question, the moon answered: 'I am not the most beautiful, nor are you. The father's and mother's only child, Nourie Hadig, is the most beautiful of all.' Nourie Hadig was ideally named because her skin was perfectly white and she had rosy cheeks. And if you have ever seen a pomegranate, you know that it has red pulpy seeds with a red skin which has a pure white lining.

The mother was very jealous – so jealous in fact, that she fell sick and went to bed. When Nourie Hadig returned from school that day, her mother refused to see her or speak to her. 'My mother is very sick today,' Nourie Hadig said to herself. When her father returned home, she told him that her mother was sick and refused to speak to her. The father went to see his wife and asked kindly, 'What is the matter, wife? What ails you?'

'Something has happened which is so important that I must tell you immediately. Who is more necessary to you, your child or myself? You cannot have both of us.'

'How can you speak in this way?' he asked her. 'You are not a stepmother. How can you say such things about your own flesh and blood? How can I get rid of my own child?'

'I don't care what you do,' the woman said. 'You must get rid of her so that I will never see her again. Kill her and bring me her bloody shirt.'

'She is your child as much as she is mine. But if you say I must kill her, then she will be killed,' the father sadly answered. Then he went to his daughter and said, 'Come, Nourie Hadig, we are going for a visit. Take some of your clothes and come with me.'

The two of them went far away until finally it began to get dark. 'You wait here while I go down to the brook to get some water for us to drink with our lunch,' the father told his daughter.

Nourie Hadig waited and waited for her father to return, but he did not return. Not kowing what to do, she cried and walked through the woods trying to find a shelter. At last she saw a light in the distance, and approaching it, she came upon a large house. 'Perhaps these people will take me in tonight,' she said to herself. But as she put her hand on the door, it opened by itself, and as she passed inside, the door closed behind her immediately. She tried opening it again, but it would not open.

She walked through the house and saw many treasures. One room was full of gold; another was full of silver; one was full of fur; one was full of chicken feathers; one was full of pearls; and one was full of rugs. She opened the door to another room and found a handsome youth sleeping. She called out to him, but he did not answer.

Suddenly she heard a voice tell her that she must look after this boy and prepare his food. She must place the food by his bedside and then leave; when she returned, the food would be gone. She was to do this for seven years, for the youth was under a spell for that length of time. So, every day she cooked and took care of the boy. At the first new moon after Nourie Hadig had left home, her mother asked, 'New Moon, am I the most beautiful or are you?'

'I am not the most beautiful and neither are you,' the new moon replied. 'The father's and mother's only child, Nourie Hadig, is the most beautiful of all.'

'Oh, that means that my husband has not killed her after all,' the wicked woman said to herself. She was so angry that she went to bed again and pretended to be sick. 'What did you do to our beautiful child?' she asked her husband. 'Whatever did you do to her?'

'You told me to get rid of her. So I got rid of her. You asked me to bring you her bloody shirt, and I did,' her husband answered.

'When I told you that, I was ill. I didn't know what I was saying,' his wife said. 'Now I am sorry about it and plan to turn you over to the authorities as the murderer of your own child.'

'Wife, what are you saying? You were the one who told me what to do, and now you want to hand me over to the authorities?'

'You must tell me what you did with our child!' the wife cried. Although the husband did not want to tell his wife that he had not killed their daughter, he was compelled to do so to save himself. 'I did not kill her, wife. I killed a bird instead and dipped Nourie Hadig's shirt in its blood.'

'You must bring her back, or you know what will happen to you,' the wife threatened.

'I left her in the forest, but I don't know what happened to her after that.'

'Very well, then, I will find her,' the wife said. She traveled to distant places but could not find Nourie Hadig. Every new moon she asked her question and was assured that Nourie Hadig was the most beautiful of all. So on she went, searching for her daughter.

One day when Nourie Hadig had been at the bewitched house for four years, she looked out the window and saw a group of gypsies camping nearby. 'I am lonely up here. Can you send up a pretty girl of about my own age?' she called to them. When they agreed to do so, she ran to the golden room and took a handful of golden pieces. These she threw down to the gypsies who, in turn, threw up the end of a rope to her. Then a girl started climbing at the other end of the rope and quickly reached her new mistress.

Nourie Hadig and the gypsy soon became good friends and decided to share the burden of taking care of the sleeping boy. One day, one would serve him; and the next day, the other would serve him. They continued in this way for three years. One warm summer day the gypsy was fanning the youth when he suddenly awoke. As he thought that the gypsy had served him for the entire seven years, he said to her: 'I am a prince, and you are to be my princess for having cared for me such a long time.' The gypsy said, 'If you say it, so shall it be.'

Nourie Hadig, who had heard what was said by the two, felt very bitter. She had been in the house alone for four years before the gypsy came and had served three years with her friend, and yet the other girl was to marry the handsome prince. Neither girl told the prince the truth about the arrangement.

Everything was being prepared for the wedding, and the prince was making arrangements to go to town and buy the bridal dress. Before he left, however, he told Nourie Hadig: 'You must have served me a little while at least. Tell me what you would like me to bring back for you.'

'Being me a Stone of Patience,' Nourie Hadig answered.

'What else do you want?' he asked, surprised at the modest request.

'Your happiness.'

The prince went into town and purchased the bridal gown, then went to a stone cutter and asked for a Stone of Patience.

'Who is this for?' the stonecutter asked.

'For my servant,' the prince replied.

'This is a Stone of Patience,' the stonecutter said. 'If one has great troubles and tells it to the Stone of Patience, certain changes will occur. If one's troubles are great, so great that the Stone of Patience cannot bear the sorrow, it will swell and burst. If, on the other hand, one makes much of only slight grievances, the Stone of Patience will not swell, but the speaker will. And if there is no one there to save this person, he will burst. So listen outside your servant's door. Not everyone knows of the Stone of Patience, and your servant, who is a very unusual person, must have a valuable story to tell. Be ready to run in and save her from bursting if she is in danger of doing so.'

When the prince reached home, he gave his betrothed the dress and gave Nourie Hadig the Stone of Patience. That night the prince listened outside Nourie Hadig's door. The beautiful girl placed the Stone of Patience before her and started telling her story:

'Stone of Patience,' she said, 'I was the only child of a well-to-do family. My mother was very beautiful, but it was my misfortune to be even more beautiful than she. At every new moon my mother asked who was the most beautful one in the world. And the new moon always answered that my mother was the most beautiful. One day my mother asked again, and the moon told her that Nourie Hadig was the most beautiful one in the whole world. My mother became very jealous and told my father to take me somewhere, to kill me and bring her my bloody shirt. My father could not do this, so he permitted me to go free,' Nourie Hadig said. 'Tell me, Stone of Patience, am I more patient or are you?'

The Stone of Patience began to swell.

The girl continued, 'When my father left me, I walked until I saw this house in the distance. I walked toward it, and when I touched the door, it opened magically by itself. Once I was inside, the door closed behind me and never opened again until seven years later. Inside I found a handsome youth. A voice told me to prepare his food and take care of him. I did this for four years, day after day, night after night, living alone in a strange place, with no one to hear my voice. Stone of Patience tell me, am I more patient or are you?'

The Stone of Patience swelled a little more.

'One day a group of gypsies camped right beneath my window. As I had been lonely all these years, I bought a gypsy girl and pulled her up on a rope to the place where I was confined. Now, she and I took turns in serving the young boy who was under a magic spell. One day she cooked for him and the next day I cooked for him. One day, three years later, while the gypsy was fanning him, the youth awoke and saw her. He thought that she had served him through all those years and took her as his betrothed. And the gypsy, whom I had bought and considered my friend, did not say one word to him about me. Stone of Patience, tell me, am I more patient or are you?'

The Stone of Patience swelled and swelled and swelled. The prince, meanwhile, had heard this most unusual story and rushed in to keep the girl from bursting. But just as he stepped into the room, it was the Stone of Patience which burst.

'Nourie Hadig,' the prince said, 'it is not my fault that I chose the gypsy for my wife instead of you. I didn't know the whole story. You are to be my wife, and the gypsy will be our servant.'

'No, since you are betrothed to her and all the preparations for the wedding are made, you must marry the gypsy,' Nourie Hadig said.

'That will not do. You must be my wife and her mistress.' So Nourie Hadig and the prince were married.

Nourie Hadig's mother, in the meanwhile, had never stop-

ped searching for her daughter. One day she again asked the new moon, 'New moon, am I the most beautiful or are you?'

'I am not the most beautiful, nor are you. The princess of Adana is the most beautiful of all,' the new moon said. The mother knew immediately that Nourie Hadig was now married and lived in Adana. So she had a very beautiful ring made, so beautiful and brilliant that no one could resist it. But she put a potion in the ring that would make the wearer sleep. When she had finished her work, she called an old witch who traveled on a broomstick. 'Witch, if you will take this ring and give it to the princess of Adana as a gift from her devoted mother, I will grant you your heart's desire.'

So the mother gave the ring to the witch, who set out for Adana immediately. The prince was not home when the witch arrived, and she was able to talk to Nourie Hadig and the gypsy alone. Said the witch, 'Princess, this beautiful ring is a gift from your devoted mother. She was ill at the time you left home and said some angry words, but your father should not have paid attenton to her since she was suffering from such pain.' So she left the ring with Nourie Hadig and departed.

'My mother does not want me to be happy. Why should she send me me such a beautiful ring?' Nourie Hadig asked the gypsy.

'What harm can a ring do?' the gypsy asked.

So Nourie Hadig slipped the ring on her finger. No sooner was it on her finger than she became unconscious. The gypsy put her in bed but could do nothing further.

Soon the prince came home and found his wife in a deep sleep. No matter how much they shook her, she would not awaken; yet she had a pleasant smile on her face, and anyone who looked at her could not believe that she was in a trance. She was breathing, yet she did not open her eyes. No one was successful in awakening her.

'Nourie Hadig, you took care of me all those long years,' the prince said. 'Now I will look after you. I will not let them bury you. You are always to lie here, and the gypsy will guard you by night while I guard you by day,' he said. So the prince stayed with her by day, and the gypsy guarded her by night. Nourie Hadig did not open her eyes once in three years. Healer after healer came and went, but none could help the beautiful girl.

One day the prince brought another healer to see Nourie Hadig, and although he could not help her in the least, he did not want to say so. When he was alone with the enchanted girl, he noticed her beautiful ring. 'She is wearing so many rings and necklaces that no one will notice if I take this ring to my wife,' he said to himself. As he slipped the ring off her finger, she opened her eyes and sat up. The healer immediately returned the ring to her finger. 'Aha! I have discovered the secret!'

The next day he exacted many promises of wealth from the prince for his wife's cure. 'I will give you anything you want if you can cure my wife,' the prince said.

The healer, the prince and the gypsy went to the side of Nourie Hadig. 'What are all those necklaces and ornaments? Is it fitting that a sick woman should wear such finery? Quick,' he said to the gypsy, 'remove them!' The gypsy removed all the jewelry except the ring, 'Take that ring off, too,' the healer ordered.

'But that ring was sent to her by her mother, and it is a dear remembrance,' the gypsy said.

'What do you say? When did her mother send her a ring?' asked the prince. Before the gypsy could answer him, the healer took the ring off Nourie Hadig's finger. The princess immediately sat up and began to talk. They were all very happy: the healer, the prince, the princess and the gypsy, who was now a real friend of Nourie Hadig.

Meanwhile, during all these years, whenever the mother had asked the moon her eternal question, it had replied, 'You are the most beautiful!' But when Nourie Hadig was well again, the moon said, 'I am not the most beautiful, neither are you. The father's and mother's only daughter, Nourie Hadig, the princess of Adana, is the most beautiful of all.' The mother was so surprised and so angry that her daughter was alive that she died of rage there and then.

From the sky fell three apples: one to me, one to the storyteller and one to the person who has entertained you.

Beauty and Pock Face
(Chinese)

THERE were once two sisters; the eldest was very beautiful and everyone called her 'Beauty'; but the younger had a face covered with pock marks, and everyone called her 'Pock Face'. She was the daughter of the second wife, and was very spoilt, and had a bad character. Beauty's mother had died when her daughter was very small, and after her death she had turned into a yellow cow, which lived in the garden. Beauty adored the yellow cow, but it had a miserable existence, because the stepmother treated it so badly.

One day, the stepmother took the ugly daughter to the theatre and left the elder one at home. She wanted to accompany them, but her stepmother said: 'I will take you tomorrow, if you tidy the hemp in my room.'

Beauty went off and sat down in front of the stack of hemp, but after a long time she had only divided half. Bursting into tears, she took it off to the yellow cow, who swallowed the whole mass and then spat it out again all clearly arranged bit by bit. Beauty dried her tears, and gave the hemp to her mother on her return home: 'Mother, here is the hemp. I can go to the theatre tomorrow, can't I?'

But when the next day came, her stepmother again refused to take her, saying: 'You can go when you have separated the sesame seeds from the beans.' The poor girl had to divide them seed by seed, until the exhausting task made her eyes ache. Again she went to the yellow cow, who said to her: 'You stupid girl, you must separate them with a fan.' Now she understood, and the sesame and beans were soon divided. When she brought the seeds all nicely separated, her stepmother knew that she could no longer prevent her going to the theatre, but she asked her: 'How can a servant girl be so clever? Who helped you?' And Beauty had to admit that the yellow cow had advised her, which made the stepmother very angry. Without, therefore, saying a word, she killed and ate the cow, but Beauty had loved the cow so dearly that she could not eat its flesh. Instead, she put the bones in an earthenware pot and hid them in her bedroom.

Day after day, the stepmother did not take her to the theatre, and one evening, when she had gone there herself with Pock Face, Beauty was so cross that she smashed every-thing in the house including the earthenware pot. Whereupon there was a crack, and a white horse, a new dress, and a pair of embroidered shoes came out. The sudden appearance of these things gave her a terrible fright, but she soon saw that they were real objects and, quickly pulling on the new dress and the shoes, she jumped on to the horse and rode out of the gate.

While riding along, one of her shoes slipped off into the ditch. She wanted to dismount and fetch it, but could not do so; at the same time she did not want to leave it lying there. She was in a real quandary, when a fishmonger appeared. 'Brother fishmonger! Please pick up my shoe,' she said to him. He answered with a grin: 'With great pleasure, if you will marry me.' 'Who could marry you?' she said crossly. 'Fishmongers always stink.' And seeing that he had no chance, the fish-monger went on his way. Next, an assistant of a rice shop went by, and she said to him: 'Brother rice broker, please give me my shoe.' 'Certainly, if you will marry me,' said the young man. 'Marry a rice broker! Their bodies are all covered with dust.' The rice broker departed, and soon an oil merchant came by, whom she also asked to pick up her shoe. 'I will pick it up if you consent to marry me,' he replied. 'Who could want to marry you?' Beauty said with a sigh. 'Oil merchants are always so greasy.' Shortly after a scholar came by, whom she also asked to pick up her shoe. The scholar turned to look at her, and then said: 'I will do so at once if you promise to marry me.' The scholar was very handsome, so she nodded her head in agreement, and he picked up the shoe and put it on her foot. Then he took her back to his house and made her his wife.

Three days later, Beauty went with her husband to pay the necessary respects to her parents. Her stepmother and sister had quite changed their manner and treated them both in the most friendly and attentive fashion. In the evening, they wanted to keep Beauty at home, and she, thinking they meant it kindly, agreed to stay and to follow her husband in a few days. The next morning her sister took her by the hand and said to her with a laugh: 'Sister, come and look into the well. We will see which of us is the more beautiful.' Suspecting nothing, Beauty went to the well and leant over to look down, but at this moment her sister gave her a shove and pushed her into the well, which she quickly covered up with a basket. Poor Beauty lost consciousness and was drowned.

After ten days, the scholar began to wonder why his wife had still not returned. He sent a messenger to inquire, and the stepmother sent back a message that his wife was suffering from a bad attack of smallpox and was not well enough to return for the moment. The scholar believed this, and every day he sent over salted eggs and other sickbed delicacies, all of which found their way into the stomach of the ugly sister.

After two months, the stepmother was irritated by the continual messages from the scholar and made up her mind to practise a deception, and to send back her own daughter as his wife. The scholar was horrified when he saw her and said: 'Goodness! How changed you are! Surely you are not Beauty. My wife was never such a monster. Good Heavens!' Pock Face replied seriously: 'If I am not Beauty, whom do you think I am then? You know perfectly well I was very ill with smallpox, and now you want to disown me. I shall die! I shall die!' And she began to howl. The tender-hearted scholar could not bear to see her weeping, and although he still had some doubts, he begged her forgiveness and tried to console her, so that gradually she stopped weeping.

Beauty, however, had been transformed into a sparrow, and she used to come and call out when Pock Face was combing her hair: 'Comb once, peep; comb twice, peep; comb thrice, up to the spine of Pock Face.' And the wicked wife answered: 'Comb once, comb twice, comb thrice, to the spine of Beauty.' The scholar was very mystified by this conversation, and he said to the sparrow: 'Why do you sing like that? Are you by any chance my wife? If you are, call three times, and I will put you in a golden cage and keep you as a pet.' The sparrow called out three times, and the scholar bought a golden cage to keep it in, The ugly sister was very angry when she saw that her husband kept the sparrow in a cage, and she secretly killed it and threw it into the garden, where it was once more transformed into a bamboo with many shoots. When Pock Face ate them, an ulcer formed on her tongue, but the scholar found them excellent. The wicked woman became suspicious again and had the bamboo cut down and made into a bed, but when she lay on it, innumerable needles pricked her, while the scholar found it extremely comfortable. Again she became very cross and threw the bed away.

Next door to the scholar lived an old woman who sold money-bags. One day, on her way home, she saw the bed and thought to herself: 'No one has died here, why have they thrown the bed away? I shall take it,' and she took the bed into her house and passed a very comfortable night. The next day, she saw that the food in the kitchen was ready cooked. She ate it up, but naturally she felt a little nervous, not having any idea who could have prepared it. Thus for several days she found she could have dinner the moment she came home, but finally, being no longer able to contain her anxiety, she came back early one afternoon and went into the kitchen, where she saw a dark shadow washing rice. She ran up quickly and clasped the shadow round the waist. 'Who are you?' she asked, 'and why do you cook food for me?' The shadow replied: 'I will tell you everything. I am the wife of your neighbour the scholar and am called "Beauty". My sister threw me into the well and I was drowned, but my soul was not dispersed. Please give me a rice-pot as head, a stick as hand, a dish-cloth as entrails, firehooks as feet, and then I can assume my former shape again.' The old woman gave her what she asked for, and in a moment a beautiful girl appeared, and the old woman was so delighted at seeing such a charming girl, that she questioned her very closely. She told the old woman everything, and then said: 'Old woman, I have got a bag, which you must offer for sale outside the scholar's house. If he comes out, you must sell it to him.' And she gave her an embroidered bag.

The next day the old woman stood outside the scholar's house and shouted that she had a bag for sale. Maddened by the noise, he came out to ask what kind of bags she sold, and she showed him Beauty's embroidered bag. 'Where did you get this bag?' he asked. 'I gave it to my wife.' The old woman then told the whole story to the scholar, who was overjoyed to hear that his wife was still alive. He arranged everything with the old woman, laid down a red cloth on the ground, and brought Beauty back to his house.

When Pock Face saw her sister return, she gave her no peace. She began to grumble and say that the woman was only pretending to be Beauty, and that in point of fact she was a spirit. She wanted to have a trial to see which was the genuine wife. Beauty, also, would not admit herself in the wrong, and said: 'Good. We will have a test.' Pock Face suggested that they should walk on eggs, and whoever broke the shells would be the loser, but although she broke all the eggs, and Beauty none, she refused to admit her loss and insisted on another trial. This time they were to walk up a ladder made of knives. Beauty went up and down first without receiving the tiniest scratch, but before Pock Face had gone two steps her feet were cut to the bone. Although she had lost again, she insisted on another test, that of jumping into a cauldron of hot oil. She hoped that Beauty, who would have to jump in first, would be burnt. Beauty, however, was quite unharmed by the boiling oil, but the wicked sister fell into it and did not appear again.

Beauty put the roasted bones of the wicked sister into a box and sent them over to her stepmother by a stuttering old servant woman, who was told to say: 'Your daughter's flesh.' But the stepmother loved carp and understood 'carp flesh' instead of 'your daughter's flesh'. She thought her daughter had sent her over some carp and opened the box in a state of great excitement; but when she saw the charred bones of her daughter lying inside, she let out a piercing scream and fell down dead.

Old Age
(Eskimo)

HERE was woman who was old, blind and likewise unable to walk. Once she asked her daughter for a drink of water. The daughter was so bored with her old mother that she gave her a bowl of her own piss. The old woman drank it all up, then said: 'You're a nice one, daughter. Tell me – which would you prefer as a lover, a louse or a sea scorpion?'

'Oh, a sea scorpion,' laughed the daughter, 'because he would not be crushed so easily when I slept with him.'

Whereupon the old woman proceeded to pull sea scorpions out of her vagina, one after another, until she fell over dead.

Part Seven

MORAL TALES

Little Red Riding Hood
(French)

NCE upon a time, there lived a pretty little girl whose mother adored her, and her grandmother adored her even more. This good woman made her a red hood like the ones that fine ladies wear when they go riding. The hood suited the child so much that soon everybody was calling her Little Red Riding Hood.

One day, her mother baked some cakes on the griddle and said to Little Red Riding Hood:

'Your granny is sick; you must go and visit her. Take her one of these cakes and a little pot of butter.'

Little Red Riding Hood went off to the next village to visit her grandmother. As she walked through the wood, she met a wolf, who wanted to eat her but did not dare to because there were woodcutters working nearby. He asked her where she was going. The poor child did not know how dangerous it is to chatter away to wolves and replied innocently:

'I'm going to visit my grandmother to take her this cake and this little pot of butter from my mother.'

'Does your grandmother live far away?' asked the wolf.

'Oh yes,' said Little Red Riding Hood. 'She lives beyond the mill you can see over there, in the first house you come to in the village.'

'Well, I shall go and visit her, too,' said the wolf. 'I will take *this* road and you shall take *that* road and let's see who can get there first.'

The wolf ran off by the shortest path and Red Riding Hood went off the longest way and she made it still longer because she dawdled along, gathering nuts and chasing butterflies and picking bunches of wayside flowers.

The wolf soon arrived at Grandmother's house. He knocked on the door, rat tat tat.

'Who's there?'

'Your granddaughter, Little Red Riding Hood,' said the wolf, disguising his voice. 'I've brought you a cake baked on the griddle and a little pot of butter from my mother.'

Grandmother was lying in bed because she was poorly. She called out:

'Lift up the latch and walk in!'

The wolf lifted the latch and opened the door. He had not eaten for three days. He threw himself on the good woman and gobbled her up. Then he closed the door behind him and lay down in Grandmother's bed to wait for Little Red Riding Hood. At last she came knocking on the door, rat tat tat.

'Who's there?'

Little Red Riding Hood heard the hoarse voice of the wolf and thought that her grandmother must have caught a cold. She answered:

'It's your granddaughter, Little Red Riding Hood. I've brought you a cake baked on the griddle and a little pot of butter from my mother.'

The wolf disguised his voice and said:

'Lift up the latch and walk in.'

Little Red Riding Hood lifted the latch and opened the door.

When the wolf saw her come in, he hid himself under the bedclothes and said to her:

'Put the cake and the butter down on the bread-bin and come and lie down with me.'

Little Red Riding Hood took off her clothes and went to lie down in the bed. She was surprised to see how odd her grandmother looked. She said to her:

'Grandmother, what big arms you have!'

'All the better to hold you with, my dear.'

'Grandmother, what big legs you have!'

'All the better to run with, my dear.'

'Grandmother, what big ears you have!'

'All the better to hear you with, my dear.'

Grandmother, what big eyes you have!'

All the better to see you with, my dear!'

Grandmother, what big teeth you have!'

'All the better to eat you up!'

At that, the wicked wolf threw himself upon Little Red Riding Hood and gobbled her up, too.

Feet Water
(Irish)

I N every house in the country long ago the people of the house would wash their feet, the same as they do now, and when you had your feet washed you should always throw out the water, because dirty water should never be kept inside in the house during the night. The old people always said that a bad thing might come into the house if the feet water was kept inside and not thrown out, and they always said, too, that when you were throwing the water out you should say '*Seachain!*' for fear that any poor soul or spirit might be in the way. But that is not here nor there, and I must be getting on with my story.

There was a widow woman living a long time ago in the east of County Limerick in a lonely sort of a place, and one night when she and her daughter were going to bed, didn't they forget to throw out the feet water. They weren't long in bed when the knock came to the door, and the voice outside said: 'Key, let us in!'

Well, the widow woman said nothing, and the daughter held her tongue as well.

'Key, let us in,' came the call again, and, faith! this time the key spoke up: 'I can't let you in, and I here tied to the post of the old woman's bed.'

'Feet water, let us in!' says the voice, and with that, the tub of feet water split and the water flowed around the kitchen, and the door opened and in came three men with bags of wool and three women with spinning-wheels, and they sat down around the fire, and the men were taking tons of wool out of the bags, and the little women were spinning it into thread, and the men putting the thread back into the bags.

And this went on for a couple of hours and the widow woman and the girl were nearly out of their minds with the fright. But the girl kept a splink of sense about her, and she remembered that there was a wise woman living not too far away, and down with her from the room to the kitchen, and she catches up a bucket. 'Ye'll be having a sup of tea, after all the work,' says she, as bold as brass, and out the door with her.

They didn't help or hinder her.

Off with her to the wise woman, and out with her story. ''Tis a bad case, and 'tis lucky you came to me,' says the wise woman, 'for you might travel far before you'd find one that would save you from them. They are not of this world, but I know where they are from. And this is what you must do,' and she told her what to do.

Back with the girl and filled her bucket at the well, and back with her to the house. And just as she was coming over the stile, she flung down the bucket with a bang, and shouted out at the top of her voice: 'There is Sliabh na mBan all on fire!'

And the minute they heard it, out with the strange men and women running east in the direction of the mountain.

And in with the girl, and she made short work of throwing out the broken tub and putting the bolt and the bar on the door. And herself and her mother went back to bed for themselves.

It was not long until they heard the footsteps in the yard once more, and the voice outside calling out: 'Key, let us in!' And the key answered back: 'I can't let you in. Amn't I after telling you that I'm tied to the post of the old woman's bed?' 'Feet water, let us in!' says the voice.

'How can I?' says the feet water, 'and I here on the ground under your feet!'

They had every shout and every yell out of them with the dint of the rage, and they not able to get in to the house. But it was idle for them. They had no power to get in when the feet water was thrown out.

And I tell you it was a long time again before the widow woman or her daughter forgot to throw out the feet water and tidy the house properly before they went to bed for them-selves.

Wives Cure Boastfulness
(West African: Dahomey)

HIS happened long ago. When the family head let out his pigeons in the morning, he mixed beans and corn and threw this to them. When the pigeons finished eating, there was a jar of water for them.

No sooner were they satisfied, than the pigeons began to annoy the girls with their boasting. They kept saying, 'If I had someone, I would fight him. If I had someone, I would fight him.' The pigeons always said that.

The women got together and said, 'After they eat, our husbands always say, "If I had someone I would fight him. If I had someone I would fight him." Are they really so strong?'

The women went to see Aklasu, the vulture, and said to him that their husbands were always looking for a fight. They said, 'Tomorrow you come, and when they are finished eating, you fight them. But you must not kill them. You can give them a good scare, though.' They repeated, 'But you must not kill them.'

When vulture came, he settled on a tree nearby. The male pigeons knew nothing about his being there. But the women knew. Now, as usual, the master had them all come out to eat.

At sunrise, they had corn and beans thrown to them, and when they finished with that, they drank the water.

Each began again. 'If I had someone, I'd fight him. If I had someone I'd fight him.' When they said this, the vulture threw himself at them, tearing at them, pulling at their feathers.

Now, the women were at the side and watched.

The pigeons cried, 'Let us go. We do not want to fight. We said that only to frighten the women. Let us go.' Vulture plucked all their feather and then he flew away.

Now, the women came to their husbands. The pigeons were all without feathers. The women repeated mockingly, 'If our husbands saw something, they'd fight. If our husbands had someone, they'd fight him.'

The battered pigeons pushed their wives away and said, 'What are you saying? What are you saying?'

Today Pigeon keeps saying, 'I don't want to fight. I am not here for a fight.'

Tongue Meat
(Swahili)

A SULTAN lived with his wife in his palace, but the wife was unhappy. She grew leaner and more listless every day. In the same town there lived a poor man whose wife was healthy and fat and happy. When the sultan heard about this, he summoned the poor man to his court, and asked him what his secret was. The poor man said: 'Very simple. I feed her meat of the tongue.' The sultan at once called the butcher and ordered him to sell all the tongues of all the animals that were slaughtered in town, to him, the sultan, exclusively. The butcher bowed and went. Every day he sent the tongues of all the beasts in his shop to the palace. The sultan had his cook bake and fry, roast and salt these tongues in every known manner, and prepare every tongue dish in the book. This the queen had to eat, three or four times a day – but it did not work. She grew even more thin and poorly. The sultan now ordered the poor man to exchange wives – to which the poor man reluctantly agreed. He took the lean queen home with him and sent his own wife to the palace. Alas, there she grew thinner and thinner, in spite of the good food the sultan offered her. It was clear that she could not thrive in a palace.

The poor man, after coming home at night, would greet his new (royal) wife, tell her about the things he had seen, especially the funny things, and then told her stories which made her shriek with laughter. Next he would take his banjo and sing her songs, of which he new a great many. Until late at night he would play with her and amuse her. And lo! the queen grew fat in a few weeks, beautiful to look at, and her skin was shining and taut, like a young girl's skin. And she was smiling all day, remembering the many funny things her new husband had told her. When the sultan called her back she refused to come. So the sultan came to fetch her, and found her all changed and happy. He asked her what the poor man had done to her, and she told him. Then he understood the meaning of *meat of the tongue*.

The Woodcutter's Wealthy Sister
(Syrian)

THERE was a man with ten children who lived at the foot of a hill. Every day he climbed to the hilltop and collected firewood to sell in town. At sunset his hungry family would wait, watching for his return, and he would bring them a loaf of bread with perhaps an onion or an olive for flavouring. He was a poor man – but what was worse, he lacked not only gold but brains.

One day when the dead wood on the hilltop was almost gone, he decided to try another hill farther off which was covered with trees. As he was walking home in the evening, his load on his back, he met a finely dressed woman jingling with gold bangles and rustling with rich stuffs. 'Don't you recognize your own sister, O my brother?' she asked. 'I wait and wait in vain for you to visit me, but there, not every heart is tender.' 'I have no sister,' said the man. 'What! Will you deny me altogether now? But tell me, brother, what you are doing here?' 'I am heading home after my day's work,' sighed the woodcutter. 'You should give yourself a rest from drudgery and let me care for you,' said the woman. 'Why not come and share my good fortune? Bring your children and your wife to live with me in my big house. I have plenty of good things: enough to suit your every mood!' 'Is that so?' replied the man, not knowing what to say. 'Would I deceive my own brother?' said the woman. 'Come with me now and see for yourself; then you will know the way tomorrow.' And she pulled him by the hand.

And what a house she had! Sack upon sack of wheat and lentils and dried broad beans! Row upon row of jars filled with olive oil and butterfat! The woman invited the woodcutter to eat and cooked a suckling lamb just for him. 'Now doesn't that remind you of our days of long ago?' she asked him. The poor man pounced on the food like a beggar, because it had been many months since he had tasted meat. 'I have never seen her before, but who can she be except my sister?' he wondered. 'Who else would make me so welcome, who else show me such hospitality?' And he hurried back to tell his wife, running so fast that it's a wonder he didn't hurt himself.

But the woodcutter's wife was not convinced. 'Wouldn't I have heard of it if I had a sister-in-law?' she asked. 'And if she is not my sister-in-law, for what good purpose does she want us all to live with her?' She tried to reason with her husband; she tried persuasion; but in the end she had to gather her ten children and, leading their scrawny cow by a rope, follow him to his sister's house.

Feast upon feast awaited them. For a month they did nothing but eat and drink and lie in the shade to rest. The children's faces, which had been thin as knife blades, began to fill out. The woodcutter laughed and said, 'A curse on all toilsome work! May Allah never bring back those weary times, but let us live forever like this — fresh as the cool of the day.'

Then one night while the woodcutter's family slept in the lower room of the house, the sister crept down from her loft and tried the door, muttering,

All my fat and my flour eaten and gone,
But now they are plump; I need not wait long.

For this was a She-Ghoul of the kind that feeds on human flesh. Then the cow who was tethered to the doorpost turned on the monster and said:

My eyes can burn you like a flame,
My tail can whip you till you're lame,
My horns can tear and gore and maim.

And the She-Ghoul had to go back the way she had come.

The next night the monster crept down again, and the cow kept her out as before. But on the third night the cow, moving to fend off the Ghoul, kicked the wooden door with her hoof and woke the woodcutter's wife. So the woman heard her husband's sister when she said,

All my fat and my flour eaten and gone,
But now they are plump, I need not wait long.

And she heard the cow's reply:

My eyes can burn you like a flame,
My tail can whip you till you're lame,
My horns can tear and gore and maim.

She shook her husband to wake him, but he was sunk in sleep from too much eating and would not stir.

In the morning, when the woodcutter's wife told him all she had heard in the night, he said that it must have been a bad dream. Yet at noon his wealthy sister came to him and said, 'O my brother, I have a craving for cow's meat today. Surely you will not begrudge me that bony beast of yours.' How could a man refuse his sister? So he killed his cow and made his wife cook the meat. She set the tastiest portion on a plate, and sent her eldest daughter to take it to her aunt. When the girl looked into the sister's room, she saw not her aunt but a demon. Its hair was wild and its eyes blazed red and from the rafters men and women were hanging dead. Without a sound she tiptoed back, but in her hurry she stumbled on the stair and all the food slipped off the dish and on to the floor. Her mother came to scold her, and the girl reported what she had seen. The mother repeated the tale to their father, but still the woodcutter said, 'That is childish talk. How can you want to kick away such comfort, when you should be thanking God and saying prayers for our blessing?'

That night there was no cow to stop the She-Ghoul from entering. The woodcutter's wife watched as the demon, feeling each of the children in their beds, repeated to herself:

All my fat and my flour eaten and gone,
But now they are plump; I need not wait long.

'Sister-in-law, what do you want?' called the woodcutter's wife, who had not closed an eye. 'I was just covering my nieces and nephews to keep them from the cold,' said the She-Ghoul, and climbed back up the stairs to her own bed.

Next day the woodcutter's wife boiled a ground lentil soup to feed her children and watched them splatter and stain their clothes without a word. Then she went to her sister-in-law and said, 'I want to go to the stream to wash my children's clothes. Lend me your copper pot so that I can heat water and bathe the children too.' And down she went to the *wadi* and lit a fire and heaped green wood on it to give off smoke. She hung a couple of rags where the wind would catch them and called her children to her. The she prayed, 'Open for us, O spacious gate of Allah's protection!' And holding the hem of her long gown between her teeth and pulling her children along by the

hands, she ran and ran away from the She-Ghoul's home back
to her own home at the foot of the hill.

From time to time the She-Ghoul stepped out of her house
to cast a glance down into the valley. She saw the thick smoke
rising and the cloth playing in the wind and she said, 'There
she is, still busy at her washing!' But when the day waned and
the sun began to set and still her guests had not returned, she
hastened down to see what could delay them. There she found
the place abandoned and mother and children gone. She
howled so loud that the hills around her rang. And she cried,

Why did I fatten and fatten them
When by now I might have eaten them!

The woodcutter, who was dozing under the grape arbor
outside the door, heard her howl. Now he began to be

alarmed. He looked around for a place to hide. He could hear the She-Ghoul coming and he knew that her knife was hot and sharpened for him and no one else. In his fright he dived into a rubbish heap and buried himself completely. The She-Ghoul entered the yard like a storm, biting her fingers and snorting when she breathed. Inside and out, from the pigeon houses on the roof to the hen coop under the stairs, she searched for him.

At last the She-Ghoul climbed on to the hill of rubbish to gain a better view. As she shifted her weight to the place where the woodcutter was hiding, out of his mouth popped a loud belch. 'Was that you sighing, O my headcloth?' shouted the demon. And she pulled it off. She stood on her toes to look as far as she could, and the woodcutter's stomach rumbled again. 'Was that you complaining, O my robe?' she said. And she threw it off. And now she stood in her own hairy skin, a monstrous She-Ghoul for all to see and run from. She heard the woodcutter beneath her once again, and she said. 'It is the rubbish making a noise! Let me see why.' And she flung one half of the heap to the right and the other to the left and pulled the poor woodcutter out.

'Now,' she said, 'tell me, O my brother, where shall I sink my teeth in first?'

Start with my two ears,
So deaf to my wife's fears!

he wept. 'And then?' said the demon.

Then go on to both my arms
Which dragged her into such harm.

'And then?'

Then go on to my two legs
Which did not go where she begged.

And so on, until she had eaten him all and nothing of him was left to question or to give an answer. But so it is with lazy men: using their own hands they dig the hole into which they fall.

My story I have told it the best I can.
Now it is for you to tell one in return.

Escaping Slowly
(Jamaican)

A GOAT was walking along with her two kids looking for some nice sweet grass when it began to rain. It was really coming down, so she ran under a big rock ledge to get some shelter, not knowing that it was Lion's house. When Lion saw the three goats coming, he purred to himself in a voice like thunder.

This frightened the mother and her kids and she said, 'Good evening, Minister,' And the lion said, 'Good evening.' She said that she was looking for a minister to baptize these two kids, because she wanted to give them names. Lion said he'd be happy to do that: 'This one's name is Dinner and this one's name is Breakfast Tomorrow and your name is Dinner Tomorrow.'

So now after hearing this roared out by the Lion, the goats were really frightened, and the kids' hearts began to leap, *bup bup bup*. Lion asked the mother goat what was the matter with her two kids and she said, 'Well, they always get feeling this way when the room they are in gets so hot.' So she asked Lion that since they were feeling that way, could they go out and get a little cool air. Lion agreed that they could go out until dinner-time, but then they must come back in. So the mother whispered to the two kids to run as hard as they could until dark came.

So when the lion saw that evening was falling, and he didn't, see the kids coming back, he started to roar again. She said that she was wondering why they were staying out so long, so she asked Lion if she shouldn't go out and get them before it got too dark. The lion agreed. And as soon as the mother got out, she really took off running.

Women know more about life than men, especially when it comes to the children.

Nature's Ways
(Armenian)

THERE was once a king who had only one daughter. He wanted her never to marry so that he could take care of her and have her under his watchful eye. He wanted her to know nothing of the world, nothing of life, and never to love anyone but himself.

After much thought he called in his adviser and discussed this problem. Together they planned a beautiful palace on a lonely island in the middle of a lake. The girl, only seven at this time, was to live there with women servants only and a female teacher.

The king carried out his plan. He had a beautiful palace built for his daughter, and several female servants and a woman teacher were hired. There were no windows in the palace so that the girl could not see out. She had no visitors except her father who saw her for three or four hours on Sunday. All the doors of the building were locked, and only the king had a key to the outside door.

Years went by until this daughter became eighteen years old. She learned a great many things, but it seemed to her that the books she read were dull and said nothing. She began to think for herself. 'What kind of a life is this? All my servants are women; my teacher is a woman. If all the world is peopled only by girls, what is my father?' If she had had more courage, she would have asked her father about this, but as it was she only asked her teacher.

'I am going to ask you a question, but you must tell me the truth. I have no mother, no sister, no friend. You are everything to me. Answer me as a mother. Why am I on this island alone? All the people around me are women, but my father is different. How is this?'

The teacher had been told not even to whisper of such matters to her pupil. So she said, 'I am not to speak or think of such things, and neither are you. Never let your father hear you saying such things or our lives won't be worth even one *para* [Turkish coin].'

But the girl persisted in asking questions and wanted books which would explain life and the world. The teacher finally brought her such a book but asked the girl not to tell anyone about her reading.

The girl began thinking of her future. 'Am I going to spend all my days in this prison?' she asked herself over and over again. Now this girl had learned a good deal about magic. One day she asked her teacher to get her flour, eggs, butter and milk with which she was going to make some dough. After she had kneaded the dough, she modeled the form of a man with it. She drew the features and made the figure of human size.

She used all her magic in making the image and then began praying to God to give this image the soul of a human being. 'I made him with my hands, I drew him with my mind, and with my tears I pray that this image may become a human being,' she said. She repeated this prayer over and over again, always asking God to give this image a soul.

Finally, God heard her voice and granted her wish: the image was given a soul. The teacher managed to bring clothes for the man. The two young people fell in love, and the girl was careful to hide the boy so that no one saw him except the teacher who, of course, had helped them.

The girl knew the time of her father's weekly visits and was careful that he should not discover her secret. But one Sunday she overslept, and so did the man and so did the teacher. The father entered the palace, and what did he see but a man by his

daughter's side! He was enraged! He had gone through much trouble and expense to stop this very thing! The king took all of them – daughter, man, teacher and servants – to prison and ordered that the boy and the girl be killed immediately.

'Give us an opportunity to defend ourselves,' the girl pleaded with her father. Finally, because he loved his daughter dearly, the king consented to listen. A court was assembled and the guilty ones brought before the judge. The princess, as the chief wrong-doer, spoke first, telling the truth about the matter, from the very beginning to the very end.

'My father did not want me ever to get married, and so he built a prison and put me in it. All my servants and my teacher were women. Yet I could see that my father, who visited me each Sunday, was different. I wanted to live and to know what love was! With my knowledge of magic, I made the image of a man with flour, butter, eggs and milk. I made this image with my hands, drew it with my mind and, with my tears, prayed God to give it a human soul. God, through His kindness, heard my voice and granted my wish. This man standing beside me, I have made myself. He has no family, no ties. If you kill us, you will commit the greatest crime imaginable. I have had my wish: I have lived, I have loved and been loved. If you kill me, I have no regrets.'

'Is such a thing possible?' all were saying to one another.

'I will have an investigation made of this,' the king said. However, the investigation revealed that the princess was telling the truth, that the man had no family and there was no evidence that he had ever been born.

'My children, I have committed a great crime. I shall try to undo the harm and suffering that I have caused you. I am having a beautiful palace built and furnished for you. May you live in peace forever,' the king told his daughter and her mate.

The king fulfilled his promise. A beautiful palace was built for the young people, and they lived in happiness forever after.

From the sky fell three apples: one to me, one to the story-teller and one to her who has entertained you.

And so you see: Nature helps man understand God's laws, the way of life. No one can or should change these natural laws.

The Two Women Who Found Freedom
(Eskimo)

NCE there lived a man who had two wives. His name was Eqqorsuaq. And he was so jealous of these wives that he would keep them locked up in his hut. He would thrash them if they did not behave themselves. Or he would thrash anyone who happened to lay eyes on them. He killed a man named Angaguaq because rumour had it that Angaguaq had slept with one of the wives. Which he hadn't done. Eqqorsuaq was a somewhat mean-spirited person.

Finally the two women got a bit tired of their husband. They left him and fled along the coast until they were all worn out and hungry. When they could go no further, they saw the huge carcass of a whale washed up on a beach. They crawled in through the mouth and hid inside this carcass. The smell was foul, but better a foul smell than another thrashing.

Now Eqqorsuaq was in a furor. He searched high and low for his wives. He questioned everyone in the village and threatened not a few. But no one seemed to know about the missing women. At last the man paid a visit to the local witch doctor, who told him:

'You must look for the body of a big whale which is on the Skerry of the Heart-Shaped Mountain.'

And so Eqqorsuaq set out for the Skerry of the Heart-Shaped Mountain. He sang old drum-songs all along the way,

for he looked forward to the pleasure of thrashing his wives. At last he arrived at his destination and saw the dead whale. But the stench was so awful that he could get nowhere near it. He called out again and again for the women, yet there came no answer. Perhaps they were no longer here. Eqqorsuaq camped on the beach for three days and then went home, determined to thrash the witch doctor.

Meanwhile the two wives lived on inside the whale. They had grown so accustomed to the stench that it did not bother them. They had plenty of food to eat, however rotten, and a warm place to sleep. It is said that they were very happy in their new home.

How a Husband Weaned His Wife from Fairy Tales

(Russian)

HERE was once an innkeeper whose wife loved fairy tales above all else and accepted as lodgers only those who could tell stories. Of course the husband suffered loss because of this, and he wondered how he could wean his wife away from fairy tales. One night in winter, at a late hour, an old man shivering with cold asked him for shelter. The husband ran out and said: 'Can you tell stories? My wife does not allow me to let in anyone who cannot tell stories.' The old man saw that he had no choice; he was almost frozen to death. He said: 'I

can tell stories.' 'And will you tell them for a long time?' 'All night.'

So far, so good. They let the old man in. The husband said: 'Wife, this peasant has promised to tell stories all night long, but only on condition that you do not argue with him or interrupt him.' The old man said: 'Yes, there must be no interruptions, or I will not tell any stories.' They ate supper and went to bed. Then the old man began: 'An owl flew by a garden, sat on a tree trunk, and drank some water. An owl flew into a garden, sat on a tree trunk, and drank some water.' He kept on saying again and again: 'An owl flew into a garden, sat on a tree trunk, and drank some water.' The wife listened and listened and then said: 'What kind of story is this? He keeps repeating the same thing over and over!' 'Why do you interrupt me? I told you not to argue with me! That was only the beginning; it was going to change later.' The husband, upon hearing this – and it was exactly what he wanted to hear – jumped down from his bed and began to belabor his wife: 'You were told not to argue, and now you have not let him finish his story!' And he thrashed her and thrashed her, so that she began to hate stories and from that time on forswore listening to them.

The End

Notes

These notes are not so much scholarly as idiosyncratic. I have included my sources and what I could find out about the various sources; sometimes it wasn't much, sometimes a lot. Sometimes the stories were self-explanatory and didn't need any notes. Sometimes they opened up into other stories, sometimes they seemed complete in themselves.

1. Sermerssuaq
'Told as a joke at a birthday party, Eskimo Point, Northwest Territories.'
Arctic Canada. *A Kayak Full of Ghosts*, Eskimo tales 'gathered and retold' by Lawrence Millman (California, 1987), p. 140.

Part One: BRAVE, BOLD AND WILFUL

2. The Search for Luck

This text comes from Pontos, in eastern Greece, reprinted from *Modern Greek Folktales*, chosen and translated by R.M. Dawkins (Oxford, 1953), p. 459. 'The story is widely told throughout Greece and Bulgaria, says Dawkins, although usually it is a man who goes off to find his luck, or fate – or, rather, who goes off in search of the *reason* for his bad luck or miserable fate.

3. Mr Fox

> *'The wind blew high, my heart did ache*
> *To see the hole the fox did make,'*

says the girl in the version of 'Mr Fox' told to Vance Randolph in the Ozark mountains in Arkansas in the early forties.

'After that, poor Elsie wouldn't go with nobody, because she figured men were all son-of-a-bitches. And so she never did get married at all, but just stayed around with the kinfolks. They was glad to have her, of course.'

The Arkansas storytelling manner is relaxed, easy, confidential; this storyteller *is* attempting to massage you into the suspension of disbelief. The fairy tale is changing, almost imperceptibly, into the tall tale, the outrageous lie imparted with an utterly straight face for the pure pleasure of it.

But this story was already ancient when the first English settlers took their invisible cargo of stories and songs across the Atlantic in the sixteenth and seventeenth centuries; Benedick, in *Much Ado About Nothing*, refers to Mr Fox's hypocritical denial: 'Like the old tale, my Lord, 'it is not so, nor 'twas not so, but, indeed, God forbid it should be so' (Act. I, sc. i). This Mr Fox was originally contributed to Malone's variorum edition of Shakespeare in 1821 to elucidate that very speech, which probably accounts for the text's 'literary' flavour.

Cunning, greed and cowardice make the fox's name a universal byword in popular lore, although in China and Japan they believe that foxes can take the form of beautiful women (cf. current US slang use of 'fox' and 'vixen' to denote an attractive woman). The fox's incarnation as psychopathic murderer in this story and its relations gives an added *frisson* to veterans of British childhoods who recall the 'foxy gentleman' who wanted to eat Jemima Puddleduck. (Joseph Jacobs, *English Fairy Tales* [London, 1895].)

4. Kakuarshuk

Collected from Severin Lunge, Rittenback, West Greenland (Millman, p. 47).

5. The Promise

Reprinted from a manuscript collection of ancient stories illustrating the finer points of legal practice in old Burma: Maun Hbin Aung, *Burmese Law Tales*, (Oxford, 1962), p. 9.

6. Kate Crackernuts

Joseph Jacobs printed this in *English Fairy Tales*, taking it from an edition of *Folk-Lore*, September 1890, contributed by Andrew Lang, of *Red, Blue, Green, Violet*, etc., *Fairy Book* fame. 'It is very corrupt,' complained Jacobs, 'both girls being called Kate, and I have had largely to rewrite.'

This is an authentic fairy tale. Those interested in the origin of the fairies may look up the appropriate reference in Katharine Briggs's *A Dictionary of Fairies* (Allen Lane, 1976). Are they spirits of the dead or fallen angels – or, as J.F. Campbell (*Popular Tales of the West Highlands*, ed. and transl. J.F. Campbell [London, 1890]) thought, race memories of the Picts, the swarthy and diminutive Stone Age inhabitants of North Britain? Be that as it may, the fairy life cycle closely mimics the human one, with births (that fairy baby!), marriages and deaths. The poet William Blake claimed to have seen a fairy funeral. These fairies do not have spangled wings; traditionally, they ride through the air on ragwort stems, or twigs, astride like witches on broomsticks, levitating themselves by means of magic passwords. John Aubrey (*Miscellanies*) heard one, once: 'Horse and hattock.' These beings, of a brusque and unromantic nature, are, literally, earthy – they prefer to live *inside* hills, or earthen mounds, and are rarely benign.

7. The Fisher-Girl and the Crab

A story from Chitrakot, Bastar State, from the Kuruk, one of the tribal peoples of middle India: Verrier Elwin, *Folk-Tales of Mahakoshal* (Oxford, 1944), p. 134.

'The crab is generally regarded as monogamous and a model of domestic fidelity,' assures Elwin. 'The affection and care shown by the male crab when the female is moulting has been noted in the case of swimming crabs, as also the fact that among burrowing crabs a burrow is occupied by only one male and one female.'

Part Two: CLEVER WOMEN, RESOURCEFUL GIRLS AND DESPERATE STRATAGEMS

1. Maol a Chliobain

This is a collation, from Western Scotland – mainly from the Gaelic of Ann McGilbray, Islay – translated by J.F. Campbell, with additional passages interpolated from versions by Flora MacIntyre, of Islay, and by an unnamed young girl, 'nursemaid to Mr Robertson, Chamberlain of Argyll', at Inverary. This girl's version ended with the drowning of the giant. '"And what became of Maol a Chliobain?" asked Campbell. "Did she marry the farmer's youngest son?" "Oh, no; she did not marry at all."'

This is a variant of 'Hop O' My Thumb', with a full-sized heroine instead of a pint-sized hero (Campbell, Vol. 1, p. 259).

2. The Wise Little Girl

From the collection made by Aleksandr Nikolayevich Afanas'ev (1826–71), the Russian counterpart of the Grimms, who published his collection from 1866 onwards. Federal Russia was an extraordinarily rich source of oral literature at this time, owing to widespread illiteracy amongst the rural poor. As late as the close of the eighteenth century, Russian newspapers still carried advertisements from blind men applying for work in the homes of the gentry as tellers of tales, recalling how, two hundred years before, three blind ancients had followed one another in rotation at the bedside of Ivan the Terrible, telling the insomniac monarch fairy tales until at last he managed to sleep.

This story is a battle of wits in three rounds. There is something purely satisfactory about the spectacle of the child taking on the judge, and winning; the story is as satisfying as Hans Andersen's 'The Emperor's New Clothes, but better, because nobody is humiliated and everybody gets prizes. This is my favourite of all the stories in this book.

But there is more to it than meets the eye. The anthropologist Claude Lévi-Strauss says that a close relationship exists between riddles and incest because a riddle unites two irreconcilable terms and incest unites two irreconcilable people.

Robert Graves, in his half-crazed but well-annotated study of pagan anthropology *The White Goddess*, quotes the following story from Saxo Grammaticus's late-twelfth-century *History of Denmark*:

> Aslog, the last of the Volsungs, Brynhild's daughter by Sigurd, was living on a farm at Spangerejd in Norway, disguised as a sooty-faced kitchen-maid . . . Even so, her beauty made such an impression on the followers of the hero Ragnar Lodbrog that he thought of marrying her, and as a test of her worthiness told her to come to him neither on foot nor riding, neither dressed nor naked, neither fasting nor feasting, neither attended nor alone. She arrived on goatback, one foot trailing on the ground, clothed only in her hair and a fishing-net, holding an onion to her lips, a hound by her side.
>
> (*The White Goddess*, p. 401)

Graves also describes a miserere seat in Coventry Cathedral (presumably the building destroyed in World War II), which the guidebook he refers to calls 'a figure emblematic of lechery'; it is 'a long-haired woman wrapped in a net, riding sideways on a goat and preceded by a hare'.

Which reminds me that Louise Brooks, the great silent-movie actress, proposed to title her tell-all autobiography 'Naked on My Goat', a quotation from Goethe's *Faust*, the *Walpurgisnacht* scene, where the young witch says: 'Naked on my goat, I display my fine young body.' ('You'll rot,' the old witch tells her.)

The main function of riddles is to show us how a logical structure can be made up entirely of words.

3. Blubber Boy

Collected throughout the Arctic and Greenland. Compare with the Armenian story 'Nature's Way' (p. 00) (Millman, p. 100).

4. The Girl Who Stayed in the Fork of a Tree

This story comes from the Bena Mukini people, who inhabit what is now Zambia. (*African Folktales and Sculpture*, ed. Paul Radin [New York, 1952], p. 181.)

5. The Princess in the Suit of Leather

This Egyptian story comes from *Arab Folktales*, translated and edited from a variety of – mostly – written sources by Inea Bushnaq (New York, 1986), p. 193. Here is the 'She Stoops to Conquer' theme; princesses disguise themselves in all manner of ways – in donkey skins, in wooden barrels, even as boxes – and bedaub themselves with cinders, pitch, etc.

6. The Hare

Jan Knappert writes:

> The Swahili lived at the crossroads of two worlds. An unknown number
> of African peoples have settled along the east coast of Africa ... An
> equally unknown number of Oriental peoples, sailors and traders, with
> or without their families, have settled on the same coast, blown towards it
> from Arabia, Persia, India or Madagascar.

The result is a people combining African (Bantu) language with an Islamic
culture, spread out along a thousand miles of coast between Mogadishu
and Mozambique. Swahili storytellers believe that women are incorrigibly
wicked, diabolically cunning and sexually insatiable; I hope this is true, for
the sake of the women. (Jan Knappert, *Myths and Legend of the Swahili*,
[London, 1970], p. 142.)

7. Mossycoat

The gypsy Cinderella. Collected from the gypsy – Taimie Boswell – at
Oswaldwhistle, Northumberland, England, in 1915. Reprinted from *Folktales of England*, ed. Katharine M. Briggs and Ruth L. Tongue (London,
1965), p. 16.
  'It is the technique of gypsies and tinkers to go to the front door, and try
to see the mistress of the house,' say the editors of *Folktales of England*.
'They have a rooted distrust of servants and underlings. In many versions
of the tale, it is the young master who ill-treats the heroine and not the
servants.'

8. Vasilisa the Priest's Daughter

Afanas'ev, p. 131

9. The Pupil

Knappert, p. 142.

10. The Rich Farmer's Wife

In the nineteenth century Norway, like many other European countries
hitherto dominated by greater powers, began to seek a form of expression
uniquely its own. Peter Christen Asbjornsen and Jorgen Moe modelled
their procedures on those of the Brothers Grimm and were moved by the
same nationalistic impulse; their collection of tales was published in 1841.
This translation was made by Helen and John Gade for the American-
Scandinavian Foundation in 1924 (*Norwegian Fairy Tales*, p. 185).

11. Keep Your Secrets

From what is now Ghana, told by A.W. Cardinall, once district commissioner of the Gold Coast, in *Tales Told in Togoland* (Oxford, 1931), p. 213.

The witch duel, or duel of transformations, commemorated in the European children's game 'Scissors, paper, stone', is a recurring phenomenon amongst supernatural beings. Compare the contest between the afreet and the princess in the tale of the Second Calendar in the *Arabian Nights*; the pursuit of the pygmy, Gwion, by the goddess, Kerridgwen, in the Welsh mythological cycle the *Mabinogion*; the Scots ballad 'The Twa Magicians': 'Then she became a gay grey mare,/And stood in younder slack,/And he became a gilt saddle/And sat upon her back,' etc. (*English and Scottish Popular Ballads*, ed. F.J. Child [Boston, 1882], vol. 1, no. 44.)

At her trial in 1662, Isobel Gowdie of Auldearne, Scotland, gave the witch formula for turning oneself into a hare: 'I shall go into a hare/With sorrow and sighing and mickle care/And I shall go in the Devil's name/Aye, till I come home again.'

This is the best of all 'Mother knows best' stories.

12. The Three Measures of Salt

Dawkins, p. 292; from the island of Naxos. 'This story is a novel on a small scale,' says Dawkins, and indeed it is the pure stuff of soap opera, with its misunderstandings, its lost children, its deserted wives, and its casual wealth – 'in those days everyone was a king.'

13. The Resourceful Wife

Elwin, p. 314.

14. Aunt Kate's Goomer-Dust

Collected in the Ozark mountains in Arkansas, USA, by Vance Randolph; included in *The Devil's Pretty Daughter and Other Ozark Folk Tales*, collected by Vance Randolph with notes by Herbert Halpert (New York, 1955).

15. The Battle of the Birds

J.F. Campbell did not edit this story, so neither did I, although the interestingly self-mutilated heroine does not enter the picture until the second part of this discursive tale. It was told by John Mackenzie, in April 1859; Mackenzie lived near Inverary, on the estate of the Duke of Argyll. He had known the story from his youth, and 'has been in the habit of repeating it to his friends on winter nights, as a pastime'. He was about sixty at that time and could read English, play the bagpipes, and had 'a memory like Oliver and Boyd's Almanac'. (Campbell, vol. 1, p. 25.)

16. Parsley-girl

Collected by Daniela Almansi, aged six, from her babysitter, in Cortona, near Arezzo, Tuscany, Italy, and contributed to the editor by Daniela's mother, Claude Beguin. Claude Beguin adds the information that parsley is a popular abortifacient in Italy. *A Dictionary of Superstitions*, ed. Iona Opie and Moira Tatem (Oxford, 1989), contains two English recipes for this purpose, but also examples of the widespread belief that babies were found in the parsley bed.

17. Clever Gretel

Jacob Ludwig Grimm (1785–1863) and Wilhelm Carl Grimm (1786–1859) were instrumental in the creation of our idea of what a fairy tale is, transforming it from rustic entertainment to reading matter directed primarily, though not exclusively, at children, for both didactic and romantic reasons – to instruct them in the German genius, in morality and justice, certainly, but also in wonder, terror and magic. The Grimms were scholars, grammarians, lexicographers, philologists, antiquarians, but also poets. Indeed, the poet Brentano had first suggested they collect fairy tales from oral sources.

The Grimms' *Kinder und Hausmärchen* [Children and Household Tales], first published in 1812 and continually revised and, indeed, rewritten in an increasingly 'literary' manner until the final edition in 1857, is one of the key volumes to the sensibility of nineteenth-century Romanticism in Europe, and the stories remain indelibly marked on the imaginations of children who read them, helping to shape our consciousness of the world. But as well as the blood-spattered, mysterious, ferociously romantic, enigmatic stories that appealed to the poets in the souls of the Grimms, they could not forbear to publish such genial tales as this one, about sassy Gretel with her red-heeled shoes and her gourmandise, a direct reflection of middle-class fears of what the servants get up to down there in the kitchen.

From *The Complete Fairy Tales of the Brothers Grimm*, translated and with an introduction by Jack Zipes (New York, 1987), p. 75.

18. The Furburger

Those familiar with Chaucer or Boccaccio will recognize this story as a 'merry tale', or exercise in broad humour applied to human relations. The 'merry tale' is an area relatively unexplored by folklorists, although ancient in origin, ubiquitous in distribution, endless in variety, easy to remember, and flourishing today as bravely as ever, wherever two or three people of any gender are gathered in informal circumstances. The sexual joke is easily the most widespread form of folktale in advanced, industrialized societies, and even when told amongst women it is often marked by a profound misogyny; it is the reservoir for a vast amount of sexual anxiety and surmise.

The vindictiveness and anger in this story make its heroine's the most desperate stratagem of all. Note the intended rape of the husband.

From *Jokelore: Humorous Folktales from Indiana*, ed. Ronald L. Barker (Indiana, 1986), p. 73.

Part Three: SILLIES

1. A Pottle o' Brains

Joseph Jacobs, *More English Fairy Tales*, (London, 1894), p. 125. 'The noodle family is strongly represented in English folk-tales,' observes Jacobs. Not amongst the female members, though.

2. Young Man in the Morning

The story was told, with a reprehensible lack of sisterly feeling, by Mrs Mary Richardson – 'a wisp of a woman', says Richard Dorson, 'her nose squashed in by hoodoo evil.' Mrs Richardson, aged seventy when she talked to Dorson in the early 1950s, was born in North Carolina and later moved to Chicago, then to Calvin, in Southwestern Michigan, a black farming settlement founded by freedmen before the American Civil War. During the Depression in the 1930s, Southern-born Black men and women who fled poverty only to find it again on Chicago's South Side settled in Calvin and communities around it, bringing with them a fund of stories with roots in a complex fusion of Black African and European traditions. The musical legacy, Gospel and rhythm and blues, bore fruit later in the decade in the musicians who created the Detroit sound.

This story is also found in Russia, Estonia and Finland. Dorson's other informants told other versions; Georgia Slim Germany said that the old woman sang out: 'I'm shivering cold tonight, but I'm going to marry a young man in the morning, and I'm going to play rat-trap tomorrow night.' (*Negro Folktales in Michigan*, collected and edited by Richard M. Dorson [Cambridge, MA, 1956], p. 193.)

3. Now I Should Laugh, If I Were Not Dead

Please note that if a wedding is the ultimate destination of so many fairy tales, marriage itself and its conditions are universally depicted as a joke.

From *Icelandic Legends*, collected by Jon Arnason, translated by George Powell and Eirikr Magnusson (London, 1866), vol. 2, pp. 627–30.

4. The Three Sillies

Joseph Jacobs, *English Fairy Tales*, p. 9.

5. The Boy Who Had Never Seen Women

Told by a Mrs E.L. Smith. Dorson, p. 193.

6. The Old Woman Who Lived in a Vinegar Bottle

Heard around a camp fire in 1924 and published in Katharine M. Briggs, *A Sampler of British Folk Tales* (London, 1977), p. 40.

7. Tom Tit Tot

The people of Suffolk, whence this story, have long held a reputation for foolishness. When my maternal grandfather, from Lavenham, took the queen's shilling in the 1890s, he joined a regiment with the soubriquet the 'Silly Suffolks'. (Joseph Jacobs, *English Fairy Tales*, p. 1.)

8. The Husband Who Was to Mind the House

From Asjbornsen and Moe again, this time in a handsome Victorian translation by Sir George Webb Darsent (*Popular Tales From the Norse* [Edinburgh, 1903], p. 269.)

Part Four: GOOD GIRLS AND WHERE IT GETS THEM

1. East o' the Sun and West o' the Moon

Asjbornsen and Moe once more, again in the Darsent translation (Darsent, p. 22). This is one of the most lyrically beautiful and mysterious of all Northern European fairy tales, and one that has proved irresistible to 'literary' writers for two thousand years, with its relation to the classical Cupid and Psyche story as retold in *The Golden Ass* by Apuleius, as well as to the lovely literary fairy tale 'Beauty and the Beast', written by Madame Leprince de Beaumont in the eighteenth century.

But Madame Leprince de Beaumont's Beauty is a well-brought-up young lady, designed to conform in a bourgeois, virtuous fashion. Madame Leprince de Beaumont worked as a governess for twenty years; she wrote extensively on good behaviour. But *this* young woman does not hesitate to go to bed with a strange bear and is betrayed by her own desire when she first sees the young man under the bearskin: ' . . . she thought she couldn't live if she didn't give him a kiss there and then.' Then he disappears. But she get him in the end.

2. The Good Girl and the Ornery Girl

'Told by Miss Callista O'Neill, Day, Mo, September 1941,' to Vance Randolph. The story is called 'Mother Holle' in Grimm. (Vance Randolph, *The Devil's Pretty Daughter and Other Ozark Folk Tales* [New York, 1955].)

3. The Armless Maiden

This horrid story depicts the misfortunes of virtue with the glee of a Marquis de Sade – cf. the Grimms' 'Armless Maiden'. (Afanas'ev, p. 294.)

Part Five: WITCHES

1. The Chinese Princess

The French medieval fairy Mélusine changed into a snake from the waist down once a week. The English Romantic poet John Keats has a poem, 'Lamia', about a snake that turns into a beautiful woman. In Freudian terms, this is the return of the repressed with a vengeance.

From *Folk Tales of Pakistan*, compiled by Zainab Ghulam Abbas (Karachi, 1957).

2. The Cat-Witch

Mary Richardson again (Dorson, p. 146).

3. The Baba Yaga

Baba Yaga, the Russian witch, lives in the forest in a hut with chicken's legs that run around when she wants them to. Some say she is the devil's grandmother. She is bad, but stupid, and was characterized thus during the Stalinist period by the Soviet folklorist E.A. Tudorovskaya: 'Baba Yaga, the mistress of the forest and animals, is represented as a real exploiter, oppressing her animal servants.' (W.R. Ralston, *Russian Folk Tales* [London, 1873], pp. 139–42.)

4. Mrs Number Three

This comes from G. Willoughby-Meade, *Chinese Ghouls and Goblins* (London, 1928), a collection of popular lore (p. 191). Names and locations are given with unusual precision. Compare the fate of Mrs Number Three's guests with that of the hero of Apuleius's 'The Golden Ass', and compare Mrs Number Three herself with Circe, the enchantress in Homer's *Odyssey*, who transformed her clients into swine.

Part Six: UNHAPPY FAMILIES

1. The Girl Who Banished Seven Youths

Bushnaq, p. 119.

2. The Market of the Dead

Melville J. and Frances S. Herskovits, *Dahomean Narrative* (Northwestern University African Studies, Evanston, 1958), p. 290.

3. The Woman Who Married Her Son's Wife

Millman, p. 127. Told by Gustav Broberg, Kulusuk, East Greenland.

4. The Little Red Fish and the Clog of Gold

Bushnaq, p. 181.

5. The Wicked Stepmother

Cardinall, p. 87.

6. Tuglik and Her Granddaughter

Heard from Anarfik, Sermiligaq, East Greenland. (Millman, p. 191.)

7. The Juniper Tree

The definitive version of a tale of child abuse and sibling solidarity known all over the world, in very similar forms. Verrier Elwin prints one from Tribal India. In no other story does the happy ending have more of an ache of wish-fulfilment; it is obvious that this solution can only be imagined, not experienced in reality. (Grimm, p. 171.)

8. Nourie Hadig

This Armenian 'Snow White' was collected by Susie Hoogasian-Villa from Mrs Akabi Mooradian, in the Armenian community in the city of Detroit, Michigan, to which they both belonged. Mrs Mooradian settled in Detroit in 1929, after various wanderings imposed on her by the turbulent history of her homeland since her birth in 1904. (*100 Armenian Tales*, collected and edited by Susie Hoogasian-Villa [Detroit, 1966, p. 84].)

9. Beauty and Pock Face

Chinese Fairy Tales and Folk Tales, collected and translated by Wolfram Eberhard (London, 1937), p. 17.

10. Old Age

Millman, p. 192.

Part Seven: MORAL TALES

1. Little Red Riding Hood

From Charles Perrault's *Histoires ou Contes du Temps Passé* (Paris, 1697). I put it into English; my maternal grandmother used to say, 'Lift up the latch and walk in,' when she told it me when I was a child; and at the conclusion, when the wolf jumps on Little Red Riding Hood and gobbles her up, my grandmother used to pretend to eat me, which made me squeak and gibber with excited pleasure.

For an in-depth sociological, historical and psychological discussion of this story, plus thirty-one different literary versions including a feminist revision by the Merseyside Fairy Story Collective, see Jack Zipes, *The Trials and Tribulations of Little Red Riding Hood* (London, 1983). Jack Zipes thinks that 'The Story of Grandmother,' recorded in Nièvre, France, around 1885, is part of a 'Red Riding Hood' tradition of a thoroughly emancipated kind; this little girl, colour of clothing unknown, is not an awful warning but an example of quick thinking:

There was a woman who had some bread. She said to her daughter: 'Go carry this hot loaf and a bottle of milk to your granny.'

So the little girl departed. At the crossway she met *bzou*, the werewolf, who said to her:

'Where are you going?'

'I'm taking this hot loaf and a bottle of milk to my granny.'

'What path are you taking,' said the werewolf, 'the path of needles or the path of pins?'

'The path of needles,' the little girl said.

'All right, then I'll take the path of pins.'

The little girl entertained herself by gathering needles. Meanwhile the werewolf arrived at the grandmother's house, killed her, put some of her meat in the cupboard and a bottle of her blood on the shelf. The little girl arrived and knocked at the door.

'Push the door,' said the werewolf, 'it's barred by a piece of wet straw.'

'Good day, Granny. I've brought you a hot loaf of bread and a bottle of milk.'

'Put it in the cupboard, my child. Take some of the meat which is inside and the bottle of wine on the shelf.'

After she had eaten, there was a little cat which said: 'Phooey! ... A slut is she who eats the flesh and drinks the blood of her granny.'

'Undress yourself, my child,' the werewolf said, 'and come lie down beside me.'

'Where should I put my apron?'

'Throw it into the fire, my child, you won't be needing it any more.'

And each time she asked where she should put all her other clothes, the bodice, the dress, the petticoat, and the long stockings, the wolf responded:

'Throw them into the fire, my child, you won't be needing them any more.'

When she laid herself down in the bed, the little girl said:

'Oh, Granny, how hairy you are!'

'The better to keep myself warm, my child!'

'Oh, Granny, what big nails you have!'

'The better to scratch me with, my child!'

'Oh, Granny, what big shoulders you have!'

'The better to carry the firewood, my child!'

'Oh, Granny, what big ears you have!'

'The better to hear you with, my child!'

'Oh, Granny, what big nostrils you have!'

'The better to snuff my tobacco with, my child!'

'Oh, Granny, what a big mouth you have!'

'The better to eat you with, my child!'

'Oh, Granny, I've got to go badly. Let me go outside.'

'Do it in the bed, my child!'

'Oh, no, Granny, I want to go outside.'

'All right, but make it quick.'

The werewolf attached a woollen rope to her foot and let her go outside.

When the little girl was outside, she tied the end of the rope to a plum tree in the courtyard. The werewolf became impatient and said: 'Are you making a load out there? Are you making a load?'

When he realized that nobody was answering him, he jumped out of bed and saw that the little girl had escaped. He followed her but arrived at her house just at the moment she entered.

2. Feet Water

Kevin Danaher, *Folktales of the Irish Countryside* (Cork, 1967), pp. 127–9.

3. Wives Cure Boastfulness

Melville J. and Frances S. Herskovits, p. 400.

4. Tongue Meat

Knappert, p. 132.

5. The Woodcutter's Wealthy Sister

Bushnaq, p. 137.

6. Escaping Slowly

Afro-American Folktales, stories from Black traditions in the New World, edited and selected by Roger D. Abrahams (New York, 1985), p. 240.

7. Nature's Ways

Hoogasian-Villa, p. 338.

8. The Two Women Who Found Freedom

Millman, p. 112; from Akpaleeapik, Pond Inlet, Baffin Island.

9. How a Husband Weaned His Wife from Fairy Tales

Afanas'ev, p. 308.